T0333342

Litany of Lies

Litany of Lies

A Bradecote
and Catchpoll Mystery

SARAH HAWKSWOOD

Allison & Busby Limited
11 Wardour Mews
London W1F 8AN
allisonandbusby.com

First published in Great Britain by Allison & Busby in 2024.

Copyright © 2024 by Sarah Hawkswood

A CIP catalogue record for this book is available from
the British Library.

First Edition

ISBN 978-0-7490-3197-8

Typeset in 11/16 pt Adobe Garamond Pro by
Allison & Busby Ltd.

FSC
www.fsc.org
MIX
Paper | Supporting
responsible forestry
FSC® C171272

Printed and bound by
CPI Group (UK) Ltd, Croydon, CR0 4YY

For H. J. B.

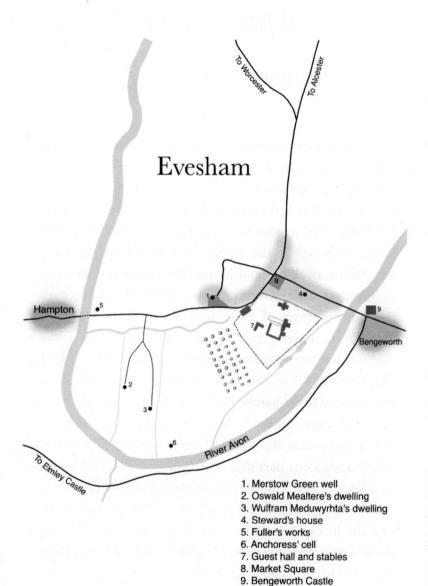

Evesham

To Worcester

To Alcester

Hampton

Bengeworth

To Elmley Castle

River Avon

1. Merstow Green well
2. Oswald Mealtere's dwelling
3. Wulfram Meduwyrhta's dwelling
4. Steward's house
5. Fuller's works
6. Anchoress' cell
7. Guest hall and stables
8. Market Square
9. Bengeworth Castle

Chapter One

Three days before Midsummer 1145

A baking hot day, one that had mellowed into an evening still too warm and airless for comfort, was drifting into an uncomfortable, sticky night. June had been a month of blazing sun that had seen the Avon's level drop, revealing her banks like a wanton flaunting her ankles, and flow lazily, as though it also found the heat exhausting. Only the visiting swallows and house martins seemed to be as energetic as always, busily raising their broods beneath the thatched eaves of the houses. Now, as the soft dark of a short, summer night descended, their screams and chirrups had been replaced by the faint flutterings of bats flitting about for moths, weaving between the houses and swooping over the parched grass of the Merstow green. At the north-west corner of the open ground a pair of posts and a crossbeam stood guard over a hole in the earth, where a well was part dug. The spoil bucket stood beside it, the rope coiled tidily within it like a sleeping adder, and off to one side was a neat pile of stone for the well lining, and the blocks from which the local mason was hewing them. Two men stood close by, barely a pace apart, glaring at each other, arguing in low voices.

'What sense is there to this?' the shorter man growled,

his features growing indistinct in the rapidly fading light. 'It would not be thought odd for us to be speaking together in passing. Think yourself fortunate I came, for I does not need to obey a summons from the likes of you at a foolish hour.'

'What I have to say will not be to your liking, though I care not, and you were never one to hide your thoughts. This is safer, and by neither's hearth, which seems fair.'

'Fair! Ha! When did you ever do "fair". So go on, say what you need and let me get to my wife and my bed.' The shorter man hunched his shoulders grumpily.

'I need more.'

'Need? What for? Is your position not high and mighty enough for you? Does you want the trappings of a lord?'

'Why I want it is not your concern. All you need to know is that when the rent falls due Midsummer Day, there is six shillings to pay on top of the rest.' The taller man folded his arms and looked obdurate.

'Six shillings?' The shorter man was taken aback and repeated the sum.

'Yes. Your business thrives. You can afford it.'

'No.' The refusal was blunt.

'You can afford it, I say.' The taller man persisted.

'No. I will not give you another six shillings. In fact, I will give *you* nothing at all.'

'What do you mean?' It was the taller man's turn to be surprised.

''Tis simple enough. You have had all you will get from me, even if you spouts your lies to turn folk against me. It don't scare me no more. You can accept that, or I will go to the lord Abbot with the truth of what has been going on.'

'He would not believe you.' The taller man snorted

derisively. 'Your word against mine? No contest. What is more, if you thought he would do so, you would have gone to him at the first.'

'Oh, do not be so sure. I now knows more than you think.' It was more guessing, but the man was not going to say so.

'But the lord Abbot would not believe a man who is ever late to pay his rent.' The taller man wished he could see the other man's reaction to that.

'I pays on time. You know that.' Outrage made the man's voice rise, and the taller man hissed at him to lower it.

'You pay me, but the abbey rent rolls show you have been short these last three quarters and only my good word has kept you from eviction.' The tone was triumphant, gloating, and he unfolded his arms to poke the shorter man in the chest with a long forefinger.

'Your good word! You bastard!' The shorter man launched himself towards the other and the pair tumbled to the dry earth, both half-winded by the fall. They rolled, like puppies at play, except this was in deadly earnest, each trying to inflict as much pain as possible upon the other. It was chance that they rolled towards the stone pile, but the hand that grabbed a worked piece of it moved with intent. There was a sharp crack, and one of the men slackened his hold and went limp. His opponent dragged the inert body to the well hole and cast it over the edge to drop the fifteen feet or so to the bottom of the workings. For good measure, he cast the lump of stone in after him. Breathing heavily, and with hands that shook a little, the victor went home to his bed, and disturbed slumbers.

* * *

Reginald Foliot, Abbot of Evesham, sighed, and rubbed his temples with the tips of his long, pale fingers. His relations with William de Beauchamp, lord Sheriff of Worcestershire, were not without complications, and de Beauchamp was a tetchy man who did not trust clerics, especially clerics with noble connections. Before Chapter he really must formulate how he was going to complain, yet again, about the theft of abbey property by the Bengeworth garrison, who had clearly crossed the bridge in the dark hours, scaled the wall, 'his' newly completed wall, built to protect the abbey in dangerous times, and stolen two casks of wine, quite good wine at that. The townsfolk of Evesham would not be so bold, and the garrison were a drunken lot, for the most part. The lord Sheriff would deny that it was his men, and say no proof could be brought, but it was always his men. The fact that the garrison changed regularly did not seem to make a difference. The abbot wondered if he ought to have stipulated the wall should be even higher, and sighed again, resolving to lead the brethren in a prayer after Chapter that God would put charity in the hearts of the sinful.

There came a knock upon the door, and at his bidding to enter, a youthful brother almost fell over the threshold in his haste to come in. Abbot Reginald frowned.

'Those things which we do in a rush, Brother Dominic, are not done with godliness of thought. Impetuosity should be constrained and—'

'Forgive me, Father, but . . .' The young man interrupted, his voice rather higher than usual in his excitement. 'Walter the Steward is dead.'

'That is assuredly unfortunate news, but death comes to us all, Brother, and is no cause for—'

'Dead by,' and the monk's voice now dropped, 'a terrible accident, Father. Prior Richard sent me to tell you immediately.'

'I see. Well, you have told me, and now you will compose yourself.' Abbot Reginald's voice was as calm as if he had been told that the weather was set fair for the day. It would not do, he thought, to show a poor example. 'We shall walk together to Prior Richard and hear exactly what has occurred.'

'Yes, Father.' Brother Dominic, gently chastised, coloured, and then folded his hands beneath his scapular, emulating his superior.

Prior Richard was in the courtyard by the western and primary gate of the abbey enclave, and with him were several men and a handcart bearing a covered body. The men were all trying to speak at once, and there was much gesticulating. The noise only ceased when Abbot Reginald himself was close enough to ask for calm.

'I am told our steward is dead. Who found him, and where?'

'I – we did, my lord Abbot, when we went to begin our labours for the day.' A short, broad-shouldered man, stepped forward and bowed.

'And you are?'

'Adam the Welldelver, my lord. And this is—'

'Hubert the Mason. Your face I know. So you found Walter the Steward on the green, where the well is being dug?'

'Not just on the green, but in my workings, though blind drunk 'e must have been to fall in when the soil hoist is all set up above it.'

'How deep have you dug thus far?'

'A good fifteen or sixteen feet, and a fall that far could kill a man.'

'Yes.' Abbot Reginald seemed to be only half attending, and a small frown gathered between his fine brows. 'Uncover the body.'

Hubert the Mason leant over the side of the cart, pulled back the cloth, and then crossed himself. Walter the Steward lay slightly contorted, facing to his left side, since nobody had wanted to move his death-stiff limbs, nor force the eyelids closed. The sightless stare unnerved Brother Dominic, who took an audible breath, and Abbot Reginald's frown deepened. Something jarred. One arm was clearly beneath the body and the other lay, almost casually, to the side. It would be odd for a man, even a drunken man, not to put his arms out if he tripped and fell. The side of the face that was visible bore little sign of injury, but there was a very distinct wound to the left temple, with congealed blood about it. The thin bone of the skull could be seen, like the broken shell of a goose egg.

'He was found just like this?' Abbot Reginald looked towards the well digger for confirmation.

'Aye, my lord Abbot.'

'I see. And there was nothing else in the well, no flagon or pot for ale?'

'Nothin' but a stone, one o'mine ready for the buildin' part.' This was Hubert the Mason. 'Odd, that.'

The mason might ponder, but the abbot had already reached an unwelcome conclusion.

'The death is not fully explained and may yet be the result not of an accident but foul design. I shall send to

12

the lord Sheriff. In the meantime, do not continue to dig, Master Welldelver.'

'Dig? Oh, I was not a-goin' to dig any deeper there. Tainted is that hole. A well that claims a life is never sweet, and this'n claimed it afore the water were even reached. No, we will start again elsewhere, and fill in the pit as soon as allowed.' The well digger was respectful but firm. Abbot Reginald might think it a little fanciful, bordering on superstitious, but he realised that if the man who dug wells thought it, then the folk of Evesham would think it also.

'So be it. The stone, other than the one that was in the well, can be used at the new location.' He sighed. 'Has anyone gone to inform the poor man's wife?'

There was silence. The brethren did not leave the enclave very often, but Father Prior was the man who had almost daily dealings with the abbey steward and knew his duty.

'I will go, Father.'

'Good. The body can lie in our own mortuary chapel until burial.' Abbot Reginald thought that showed respect for the man's service. He nodded to his subordinate, folded his hands, and retraced his steps to his lodging, already formulating a new letter to William de Beauchamp, and aware that adding his complaint about the theft of the wine at the end of it would sound almost petty. At least, he thought, the lord Undersheriff was easier to deal with, and not at all like the men in Bengeworth Castle.

William de Beauchamp made a sound that could best be described as a resigned snarl. He did not look happy, which made the lay brother from Evesham quake in his sandals.

'A violent death should be looked into, but the rest of

this,' he waved a hand towards the document held by the clerk who, long inured to both his lord's ill-temper and him not looking happy, had read it out in a monotone, 'is simply casting blame where it suits. All that Abbot Reginald's building of his much-vaunted wall about the enclave has done is cut him off even more from the townsfolk that put silver into his coffers. It is more than likely this theft of wine was by townsmen who had taken a little too much ale and saw the wall as a challenge and the wine as a prize. He thinks building that wall will protect Evesham from the fate of Ramsey, but it would not keep out an assault by troops, which it has proved by being scaled by ordinary men, and the tonsured within it would hide in their church and pray, not defend it.' That, thought de Beauchamp, would be reported back.

The taking of Ramsey Abbey and expulsion of its fraternity by the rebel Geoffrey de Mandeville, only two years earlier, had sent shock waves through the cloisters of England. Abbot Reginald had prided himself on his forethought, for he had already diverted masons from the construction of the nave of his abbey church to create a wall that was not merely a demarcation of the secular and claustral. De Beauchamp put this down to his ancestry, but then William de Beauchamp, who disliked clerics, disliked Reginald even more than most. The Foliots descended from one who had been at The Battle when Duke William had defeated Harold Godwinson and won England. De Beauchamp's maternal grandsire, Urse d'Abitôt, from whom the shrievalty, and William de Beauchamp's short temper, were inherited, had not been there, and came over from Normandy later. It ought not to matter, and yet it did, deep down. There was always that slight sense of superiority among those who could say their forebear hurled themselves at the shield wall on Senlac Ridge, and it showed, even when unspoken. William de Beauchamp had seen that in the face of Reginald Foliot. Monks were supposed to be humble, no longer interested in worldly things. Abbots and bishops, in his opinion, forgot that the moment they were offered power, and thereafter added the weight of the support of God to lord it over any secular authority who might challenge them. The Abbot of Evesham was nearly as powerful as a bishop, and this particular abbot had far too good aristocratic connections. Miles of Gloucester, the late Earl of Hereford, had been close kin, and a nephew, Gilbert, was the ambitious Abbot of Gloucester. He, like William de Beauchamp himself, had given his support to the Empress Maud after the Battle of Lincoln, and was still in communication with her.

What was more, Evesham, a wealthy house that flourished on the rents from the town about it as well as land well beyond, had been at odds with the Sheriffs of Worcester since Urse d'Abitôt had gained, or, as Evesham termed it, stolen, land that had previously been theirs. There had been no settling of that dispute in well over half a century, and William de Beauchamp had used the uncertainty of the times as a good reason to build the wooden palisades and barracks that constituted Bengeworth Castle, just across the bridge from Evesham Abbey and on land that the abbey still claimed. He had enjoyed that, and enjoyed even more the private knowledge that he had more recently given the garrison free rein to make depredations upon the abbey's lands, which he would obviously publicly deny. There had been a very lucrative theft of grain from one of the abbey granges on the shire border with Warwickshire, which he had put down to a band of outlaws known to be plaguing the sheriff of that shire. Climbing over Abbot Reginald's wall to steal a few wine barrels might be a smaller loss to the abbey, but it showed initiative and would most certainly mightily irritate Abbot Reginald, who would correctly deduce the culprits. It was a great pity that with news of this 'success' came also a plea for shrieval assistance over a killing. It tarnished the pleasure, but then again, Abbot Reginald was unlikely to have enjoyed making the request. This made William de Beauchamp feel better. He turned to a servant, who stood waiting upon his command.

'Find Serjeant Catchpoll.'

The man bowed and scurried away. It was some time before he returned, at least long enough for the lord Sheriff to be drumming his fingers upon the arm of his throne-like chair, and for the lay brother to wonder if he might just displace his own kneecap from his knees knocking in fear. He told himself that as he was his abbot's messenger, the lord Sheriff could not do anything terrible to him, but William de Beauchamp looking as if about to explode with frustrated anger gave him doubts. When the serjeant arrived, the lay brother just stared at him in disbelief, since he evinced no sign of concern at his superior's wrath.

'What took you so long?' De Beauchamp sounded as though Catchpoll had wilfully avoided coming on command.

'Well, my lord, I came as fast as these 'ere legs would carry me, but I was at the Sutheberi Gate explainin' to a man as how if he beat the poor, overloaded ass he were lashin' so as it gave up and died right there, there would be a charge for blockin' the lord King's road, and I might just make him drag the carcass to St Wulfstan's hospital and give it to the brothers to feed the sick and lame.'

'I doubt they would thank you for a scrawny donkey.'

'Indeed not, my lord, but the ass-beater only got as far as thinkin' of the weight of the beast, even when scrawny, and then cast away the stick.'

'Well, you can leave keeping the thoroughfares clear and get yourself to Evesham. The abbey steward is dead, and the abbot thinks it was not a natural death. He—' de Beauchamp stopped suddenly and looked at the lay brother, who was trying to be as near invisible as possible. 'You. Get out. Serjeant Catchpoll will come and find you when I have finished.'

The lay brother exited, giving thanks in prayer that he had been spared.

'The Abbot of Evesham thinks that the man did not fall, drunk, into a part-dug well, for the widow says he was sober when he left her late yesterday evening, and he said he would not be gone long. Also, there was a wound to the head and one large stone in the well, a stone from the pile made ready to build up the walls.'

'Looks like the Abbot of Evesham thinks like a serjeant, my lord.' Catchpoll grinned.

'He thinks like a grasping, "God is on my side" cleric, pox on him,' grumbled de Beauchamp.

'I doubts there is much chance of that visitin' upon 'im. Not the sort for the sins of the flesh, from what I judged.' Catchpoll took the lord Sheriff literally.

'Hmm, I forgot you have come in contact with him

before. Do not let him lord it over the Law, that is what I say, and you must pass that on to the lord Bradecote.' De Beauchamp thought highly of his undersheriff's abilities, but felt he was at times far too polite. In reality, it was just that Hugh Bradecote was not a man who kept a bad temper barely under control, nor was he one to take action first and think thereafter. He saw shades of grey where de Beauchamp saw but stark black and white.

'I thought as we would be takin' the lord Bradecote up on our way.' Catchpoll did not even ask whether Underserjeant Walkelin would complete the trio.

'It is barely off the Evesham road, so will not delay you. Tell him also to ignore any bleatings from the abbot about Bengeworth. You are not there to look into any complaint he might raise about my garrison there. Understood?'

'Aye, my lord.'

'Then be off, and find out what happened to this steward as quick as you can. I need you collecting the rents right after Quarter Day.'

Catchpoll correctly took this as his dismissal and went to tell his wife he would be away for some days. Within the hour he and Walkelin, with the lay brother upon his mule bringing up the rear, were heading out on the Evesham road, deviating only very slightly to the manor at Bradecote, though they found lady but not lord.

'I am sorry, Serjeant Catchpoll, but my lord is gone today to Himbleton. He holds a virgate of land there and likes to see how the crops are growing for himself.' Christina Bradecote smiled at Catchpoll.

'Then it looks as if Walkelin will be ridin' further today, my lady.'

'I take it you do not know how long he will be absent?' As the wife of the undersheriff she was used to her husband's sudden disappearances on duty.

'These things takes as long as they takes, my lady, but we is for Evesham Abbey, which is not so far.'

'Well, I will put together such things as I think my lord will need, and send them with Walkelin.' She looked directly at the young underserjeant. 'You are to tell him, Walkelin, that my usual commands apply. He is not to put himself at needless risk and he is to return to me with a whole skin.' The instruction was given with a smile, but her eyes did not echo it.

'You can be sure I will do so, my lady.' It was boldly said, but even as the words left his lips, Walkelin wondered how he would actually convey the message to his superior.

'Thank you.' She nodded and went to a chest, bringing out items of linen and putting them in the bedroll that her husband kept for his sudden calls away. 'There. I pray you have success.'

'We does, most of the time, but prayers are always welcome.' Catchpoll looked calm and confident. 'Now, I will ride steady, with the good brother of Evesham, and Walkelin can kick his heels into that horse of his and ride to Himbleton.' He turned to Walkelin. 'We meet on the Evesham road, and I reckon as you will catch us up before Pinvin.'

'I will be as swift as I can, Serjeant.' Walkelin bowed to Christina, then turned and hurried from the hall.

'Still eager.' Catchpoll grinned. 'Wait 'til his knees is as stiff as mine and then the pace will slow.'

'That may be true, Serjeant Catchpoll, but I refuse to

believe you are any less "eager". Admit it, being the lord Sheriff's Serjeant is what gets you from your bed in the morning.' This time Christina's eyes did light up with amusement.

'Now there you is wrong, my lady, for what gets me up of a mornin' is the need to—' He halted, aware he had fallen into an ease of speech that he had with lord, not lady, but Christina Bradecote, who knew Catchpoll well by now, blushed a little but laughed openly. Catchpoll still had the vestige of a smile on his face when he mounted his horse, and the lay brother wondered at a man who could smile when about to investigate a violent death.

It was in fact a mile beyond Pinvin that Hugh Bradecote and Walkelin caught up with Catchpoll and the mule-mounted lay brother, since Walkelin had needed directions in Himbleton to find the parcel of land that the lord Undersheriff held, and it was on the northern boundary of the manor. If Bradecote was not delighted to think he would not return to his own bed that night, he smiled at his love's wifely forethought, and at the message which Walkelin dutifully passed on, even if the youthful underserjeant looked uncomfortable, relaying the message in a very stilted manner.

'Afternoon, Catchpoll. So what exactly has us riding in the heat to Evesham Abbey?' Bradecote dropped his horse's pace to a trot. Walkelin, who had been given but the gist of the matter so that Catchpoll only had to tell the full tale once, had not been able to provide more than a suspicious death and a victim of importance to Evesham Abbey.

'The abbey's steward has been found dead, and the lord Abbot fears it was no accident.'

'And is this just a doubt in Abbot Reginald's mind or has he sound reasons? I hope the latter.'

'From what Brother Edwin here has told me, and before me the lord Sheriff, very sound reasons indeed, my lord. In fact, just the suspicions any of us three would have in the same place.'

'I cannot imagine myself as an abbot,' murmured Walkelin.

'Nor can your wife, I would vouch.' Catchpoll laughed lasciviously, and the lay brother blushed, remembering his own far from celibate past. 'The steward, Walter, was found early this morning in a hole, the diggings for a well, and there was a wound on the head that did not seem to be from the fall, and a single large stone also in the hole.'

'Could he not have fallen onto this stone?' Bradecote frowned.

'No, my lord, for the stone was a worked one from the pile the mason were makin' ready for the well linin', and that pile did not lie next to the pit.'

'So, someone hit the steward, pushed his body, dead or not, into the well working, and then threw in the stone for good measure. Abbot Reginald was right to be suspicious. Let us hope he can also provide us with a shortlist of those who might be responsible.'

Chapter Two

They entered Evesham on the road from the north, descending gently into the town, which lay bounded on three sides by the loop of the Avon in which it lay, and with the abbey, even though still incomplete, dominating it on a plateau before the ground dropped more steeply down to the eastern side and the bridge across to Bengeworth. The wooden palisades of the castle just beyond the bridge were visible, but looked inferior, subservient, beneath the clean stonework of the claustral buildings that shone in the sunlight with a creamy, golden glow. Men and animals alike were hot, and Walkelin wondered how Brother Edwin had managed in his woollen habit. The man had drawn up his cowl to protect his shaven tonsure from the sun's burning, but it must be hot beneath the folds of fabric, and he gave a sigh of relief as they walked on a loose rein in through the main gate of the abbey.

Hugh Bradecote felt not just the heat of the sun, but more importantly the tension in the atmosphere within the enclave wall when they entered. Everyone in the courtyard had stopped and turned at the sound of the horses' hooves as they passed under the arch of the abbey gate. This was an abbey not just of a large number of choir monks and lay brothers, but many folk who laboured within but lived outside, in the town that had grown about the monastic site. It was currently also the home to a team of masons working upon the nave of the abbey church and the claustral buildings, and it felt busy. The steward would have been the man to whom they all looked, regardless of whether they worked in kitchen, stable or orchard. Were they leaderless and lost, or were they glad he was gone, and had one of them seen to it being so? The thoughts buzzed inside his head as thickly as the flies about the ears of his steel grey horse. He dismounted and took the reins over its head as a youth came from the stables and took the animal to rub down and water. A thin, long-faced man that Bradecote recognised as the prior, came forward to greet him.

'My lord Bradecote, you are welcome, though the reason for your coming weighs heavily upon this House. Father Abbot would have you and your men attend him in his lodging, as soon as you have had the chance to take a little refreshment after your hot ride from Worcester.' He beckoned a novice and indicated that they should follow him to the guest hall. Then he turned to Brother Edwin, whose knees had nearly buckled when he dismounted, and who looked a little dazed and certainly spent. 'Good Brother, your efforts today are worthy of commendation. Let Brother Infirmarer ensure you have not taken harm from your exertions, and consider yourself excused all duties for the rest of today and tomorrow.'

Brother Edwin barely moved, aware of the praise in a slightly fuzzy way, but then roused at a thought.

'I must report first to Father Abbot.'

Prior Richard, smiled. 'If you think it important, I am

sure that he will come to the Infirmary and speak with you there.' The prior knew his superior well enough to feel confident that this would be the case.

Kind hands supported Brother Edwin's arm, and he was led away, unresisting.

After washing the sweat from their faces and taking a welcome draught of small beer, the shrieval trio were taken to the abbot's lodgings, and Abbot Reginald's parlour. The abbot was seated at a table, his elbows resting upon it and his hands clasped together. His face was solemn, and Bradecote thought the man looked more burdened than he had the year before. Of course, it might just be the reaction to losing his steward to violence.

'My lord Bradecote, I hope you and your men have been shown suitable hospitality. I am sorry to have had need of you, but . . .' He opened his hands in a gesture that mixed apology with what, welcome or defeat?

'Father Abbot, when you have need of us, the lord Sheriff sends us, gladly, to resolve the problem and establish the rule of law, which has been violated.' The words were diplomatic, but Bradecote was a little surprised to see a wry smile appear on the abbot's visage, and to hear Catchpoll cough to hide a guffaw. Abbot Reginald glanced at the serjeant.

'Yes, Serjeant, I too understand that the lord Bradecote's words are not ones put into his mouth by the lord Sheriff. I have already spoken briefly with Brother Edwin. However, I know that they reflect your own view, my lord, and I am grateful for it. I have great faith that through your efforts and the prayers of this community, the man who killed

Walter the Steward will be taken for justice, and we will have a name for he who must be prayed for when his soul is in great jeopardy.' Not only Bradecote could use gracious words.

Whilst aware of tensions between Evesham and William de Beauchamp, Hugh Bradecote had not been told of the lord Sheriff's reactions or instructions by Catchpoll, since that worthy had decided such things should not be spoken in front of one of the Benedictines.

'If you will tell us all you know, Father, and then if we could see the body and the place where it was discovered, we will be able to begin our active seeking of the truth in the morning.' Bradecote's tone and pace were as calm as the monk's.

'Of course, and please, do be seated – all three of you.' Abbot Reginald indicated a chair for the lord Undersheriff, and a bench against one wall for his companions. Walkelin had never sat in the presence of one so powerful, and was inclined to perch upon the edge, until the elm plank dug into the back of his legs and he had, perforce, to ease his position.

'The facts that I know are small in number, but I think them important. Our steward left his home yesterday evening, according to his wife, now widow, telling her he would return shortly. He told her to go to bed, which she did, and she slept heavily and did not waken until Father Richard came to her door and brought the awful news of her husband's death. He was not a man who drank to a point where his mind was befuddled, and there is no reason to assume that anything was different last night, although the first thought of the well digger was that a man must have been drunk to have fallen into the pit.'

'How deep is the pit, Father?' Bradecote knew they would see it soon enough, but it helped to get a mental picture in advance.

'Some fifteen or sixteen feet, I believe.'

'Enough of a fall to kill a man if he is unfortunate.' This was from Catchpoll.

'Yes. I am no physician, but our infirmarer, Brother Augustine, said that he thought the wound to the head would have killed him, even if other broken bones did not. I admit I saw the body only when it was brought into the abbey, but it had stiffened and was in much the same position as it had lain overnight. The head was turned to one side and the wound was clear upon the temple. It did not look as if it had come from hitting the earth and if it had, then Walter must have been conscious enough to lift and turn his head before he died. There was also a single large stone, one ready-worked for the building of the wall of the well, in the bottom of the pit.' Abbot Reginald closed his eyes for a moment, and then continued. 'To me it looked as if our steward had been pushed in, or rolled in. It did not look as if he had tried to save himself when falling, but just landed in a heap. One arm was beneath him and the other loosely flung to the side. I feared he was already dead, or out of his senses, when he landed, and that meant someone else was involved.'

'Thank you, Father. We would view the body ourselves, but we cannot learn as much when it is washed and shrouded as seeing it where the death happened. Your testimony adds much to our knowledge from the beginning.' Bradecote glanced at Catchpoll and saw him nod in agreement.

'You do not think I was mistaken.' It was not a question. Bradecote shook his head, and the abbot sighed.

'So what manner of man was Walter the Steward, Father? Would there be reason for any to have taken against him?'

'I would say he was a hard worker, thorough and conscientious. I never heard of him given up to drink, and he was always respectful, though perhaps a little proud of his position. I have not heard anyone speak against him, except his brother, and that was just a difference of opinion over how the town could grow. I think brothers argue out of the habit established in infancy, and William is most distressed at Walter's death. I have given him leave until after the burial before he takes up his new role.'

'Was he about to do so?'

'Oh, I am sorry. I should have said that the position of steward is inherited at Evesham, and has been since the time of Abbot Walter in the last century. He set aside the steward at the time, an Englishman of course, and replaced him with one of his own relatives from Normandy. I cannot say I am happy with the practice, but perhaps he felt that the stewardship was so important he had to have complete trust in the holder of the office. He was rebuilding and invigorating the abbey, building on the work, and legacy in silver, of Abbot Aethelwig. I am, in many ways, merely continuing those works. Several other posts became inherited, but gradually they are reverting to being filled by selection. In this instance there are no sons to follow on, and I am actually quite glad that William can step into his brother's shoes, for he knows the ways of the abbey very well, and has been working for us, marking out plans for the building of the new areas of the town, now so many wish to live and work here. He is very able.' This was said as though his ability did not quite compensate for a lack elsewhere in his character.

'"But", Father?' Bradecote raised an eyebrow, sensing there was perhaps more.

'He is not . . . flexible. Walter tried hard with those who were in arrears with their rents. He said that many things could affect an ability to pay at the due time, and this is true. Even with those who seem to be persistent underpaying tenants, he advocated waiting to see how they did in the future. I think that William will not be so generous, and will press for action. Walter's attitude sat well with our Christian duty, but every silver penny is needed in these days. Whilst this is a House of Benedictines who have left the secular world, it is also, in reality, an estate, with calls upon it for upkeep and for the works ongoing in the enclave. As you have seen, the wall to secure our perimeter has taken precedence even over the completion of the nave of our church, which is a matter for regret. Ensuring our income, increasing it, is not a matter of avarice, but enabling the growth of this community and its work and prayer. It is not an easy path to tread without a misstep.'

Bradecote wondered whether Abbot Reginald had made peace with his conscience by this justification. What he said was true enough, for the religious houses, those well-endowed by benefactors, held lands that matched the most puissant of lords, men like William de Beauchamp and Earl Waleran. They were rich, but needed much of those riches to sustain that power. He felt quite glad that his own holdings were on a far more modest scale and that his ambition was simply to leave all in order for his son

Gilbert when the time came, and for his manors to be well run. Then he realised that the abbot was looking at him, and that there was silence. He looked a little self-conscious.

'I, er, understand, Father. We should speak with William, Walter's widow and the well digger. We will intrude upon the daily life of the abbey as little as we can, but our presence will make a difference.'

'It is the death that makes the difference, my lord, and you being here keeps it in the forefront of thoughts, not just our prayers. You must do whatever is needful, and let us hope and pray you discover the truth of what happened.'

'Then we will leave you and go first to see the body and then where it was discovered.'

Bradecote rose, bowed his head, and, as Catchpoll and Walkelin followed suit, went to the door.

'My lord Bradecote, there is one more thing I should say.' Abbot Reginald spoke a little more hurriedly. 'Whilst there is no particular reason to link the occurrences, the day before yesterday the abbey cellarer reported the theft of two casks of wine, and there were marks in the earth on the inside of the wall of our graveyard that show someone came over the wall with a ladder. Tall ladders are rare, but would be found inside a castle. The garrison at Bengeworth make all manner of depredations upon us, from demanding a "toll" from those crossing the bridge to come to market, to stealing fruit from our orchards and now wine from our cellarage. Absolute proof has not been possible, but if Walter discovered something . . .' The abbot left the sentence hanging.

'We will speak with the garrison.' Bradecote did not want to say more.

As the trio walked to the church, Catchpoll passed on the lord Sheriff's instructions in an undervoice.

'The lord Sheriff has sent us to look into the killin' alone, my lord, and was clear we do not involve ourselves with any strife between abbey and castle. It is, after all, his castle and his garrison.'

'Yes, but if we ignore the fact that there could be a connection with the death, we are being remiss in our duty. There is a difference between getting "involved" in what sound to be aggravations rather than great crimes, and the possibility that those acts led to the killing of Walter the Steward. Only once any connection is dismissed can we ignore Bengeworth.'

'We should leave well alone, my lord, for all that. The lord Sheriff will not take it well if we disobeys his command.'

Bradecote halted and turned to look at the serjeant.

'And if it turned out later that someone from the castle killed a man of Evesham, and we did not discover them, what will the folk of Evesham think of the Law? Is it the King's Law, or the lord Sheriff of Worcestershire's Law?'

'The King's Law, my lord, but we has to live with the lord Sheriff as our lord, and we will never see the lord King.' Catchpoll was ever the pragmatist. 'I does not like it any more than you, but the warnin' has to be given.'

'You have given it and I have heard it. If the lord Sheriff is angered then let it be with me, not you or Walkelin.' Bradecote looked grim.

'Well, we has to live with you also, my lord, so mayhap 'tis best we just gets on with the task.' Walkelin felt both his superiors were right in their reasoning, and feared the lord Sheriff's displeasure greatly, but a killing was a killing.

'Good. So, before we see the body, we are agreed that the grieving brother, William, is not beyond suspicion?' The undersheriff reverted to investigating mode.

'A "Cain and Abel" killin' is none so rare, my lord, and the younger brother certainly had somethin' to gain.' Catchpoll looked thoughtful. 'I wonders whether Walter has young sons or none, and whether William be wed and a father. In the first case William's chance exists only while Walter's boys is too young to take up the position, too young even to be set aside now but trained to follow their uncle rather than father.'

'Yes, it might make a difference, but we must also discover how deep ran this argument about building in Evesham, and whether that was the extent of their antagonism.'

'That ought to be easy enough to discover, my lord.' Walkelin was hopeful. 'A rift in a family rarely lies hidden, and all Evesham would most-like know of it.'

'But Abbot Reginald does not,' Bradecote pointed out.

'My lord, he is the abbot. I doubts he hears the gossip of Evesham, and both brothers would not want to seem too uncharitable before 'im.' Walkelin had thought it through. 'And that might also mean that his view of the steward is not shared in the town, or even by those within the abbey who would not dare speak out. The lord Abbot spoke truthful, but 'tis but one view.'

'Very true, Walkelin.' They had now entered the church, whence they had been directed, and crossed to the north transept where a chapel was designated as the abbey mortuary chapel. From beyond the wooden 'wall' that divided chancel, crossing and transepts from the nave that was still under construction, came the muffled sounds of masons and carpenters about their toil, a different world beyond the consecrated. 'Let us first see if we read the death exactly as did Abbot Reginald and Brother Augustine.'

Whilst no longer in the attitude of death, and duly washed and made decent, Walter the Steward did not look peaceful when they uncovered his body. The bruising, combined with the settling of the blood to those parts that had contact with the earth, gave him a florid, blotchy purple-blueness that was almost inhuman. The left side of his face had but one small bruise by the lips and stood out like a pale half-mask, and at the temple the white bone, now cleaned of all blood, showed stark and cracked like the shards of a broken pot.

'That looks a blow that killed,' remarked Catchpoll, and gently lifted the head. Rigor mortis had waned enough for some movement. He felt the neck. 'Not broke. Mind you, some of them ribs shows damage and . . .' he paused and moved to handle the lower limbs, 'the right leg is broke mid-shin. If the ribs pierced heart or lungs then the fall would 'ave killed 'im, just taken a mite longer to do it. Either way, the wound makes intent likely.'

'Do you think he was surprised, or was there a struggle?' Bradecote was better at 'reading' the dead after nearly two years working with Catchpoll, but divorcing bruises from the blood-settling was not easy.

'Hard to say, my lord, and it might be the easier when we sees the place and the well pit. If they fought, then most bruises would be to the front anyways, but that little'n by the mouth could be a clashin' of heads, so I would say the blow to the temple did not come sudden, and besides, a man holdin' a stone that size would look threatenin' and you would keep back. My guess would be there was some struggle and the other man found the stone to hand and used it in the act of a moment, out of rage, or even fear. Walter the Steward was a tall man and not built like a willow-wand. The opponent might 'ave been losin' the fight.'

'There's no earth beneath the nails, which also says 'e lay still, dead or senseless, on the earth. A man alive, in pain, would claw with 'is fingers, mayhap?' Walkelin, once so squeamish in the face of cold death, had taken up a hand and peered close at it. 'Also, the knuckles of the right 'and is scuffed more than just from hittin' the ground. If Walter favoured that 'and, it could be a sign of a thrown punch that landed.'

'Very true, Young Walkelin, very true.' Catchpoll nodded approvingly. 'My lord, I think Walter 'as told us all 'e can.'

'So we will get directions to the well digging, and view the scene of the death. That will suffice for tonight, and we can plan who we speak with first on the morrow.' Bradecote was brisk.

Shortly afterwards they stood before the well pit, though not yet close enough to peer to the bottom. They stared at the rim of the pit.

'Trouble is, my lord, them as went down to bring up the body would disturb the ground so as to make it nigh on impossible to see if it were dragged to the edge and pushed over.' Catchpoll sounded regretful.

'If you met with a man, "by the well diggin'", you would not be right up to it, and since they would be the only ones in view, they might 'ave argued anywheres on this patch of green. Which means Walter the Steward might 'ave been dragged ten yards even, to get to it. That gives us a chance further from the pit.' Walkelin was the optimist, and leant forward, casting his eyes over the ground as a hound would seek a scent.

'Possible, but folk would come to stare once the news spread, and you can see as there is a fair amount of tramplin'.'

'I think we take it that any fight took place near, but not right next to, the pit, unless the killer always intended to end the steward and cast his body into the well digging. You would wonder at that, though, since it would be far better to kill a man down by the river and push the corpse into the water. If it got far enough into the current it would be a good way away by morning. This is far more likely to be seen.' Bradecote looked along the line of dwellings that marked the westward extent of the greensward, and the few upon the north side, clearly newer from the colour of daubed wall and more golden thatch. Part way along, a gap marked the beginning of a street, though it extended for only a couple of houses on either side.

'The brother, William, argued with Walter over the growth of Evesham town. The buildings on the north side are clearly of recent date, so perhaps this spot was chosen because of that significance?' Bradecote did not sound quite convinced, because he felt it worked if there was always the plan to kill, but it was still a very risky place to carry it out.

'In my bones, my lord, I feels this was an argument as got out of 'and, and a fight that got desperate.' Catchpoll was also clearly doubtful.

'I wonder if the metal strap end is missin' from Walter's belt?' wondered Walkelin. The question was random enough for his superiors to look at him in surprise, but he straightened up with something held between finger and thumb. 'It might 'ave got lost from anyone, and anytime, but if it is Walter's, we knows the fight was on this spot, at least for a part of it.'

'Or it 'as lain there lost some time and means nothin'.' Catchpoll was not instantly delighted by the discovery.

'If that were so, Serjeant, it would be dulled and with earth trampled in the decoration of it, but it looks fresh. Mayhap another man lost it in the last few days, but surely 'tis more likely to 'ave come away in a struggle.' Walkelin stood his ground, and Catchpoll nodded slowly, accepting the argument.

'And there is also the chance it came from his opponent, though it could be denied easily enough. A good find, Walkelin, and we will show it to the widow tomorrow.' Bradecote paused. 'The position of the mason's neat pile of worked stone fits with the fight coming close enough for one man to make a grab and strike a single blow. Do you think it likely that the body was thrown in, and Walter was already dead or at least out of his senses, and the stone aimed at his head where he lay? I think the chances of success small, and it was more an afterthought.'

'Makes no real sense unless it were that, a sort of "it might make sure the man's dead" idea.' Catchpoll sucked his teeth. 'Or a real end to it all. Very final.'

'Which means there was a fight, not a single blow, and at some point the other man grabbed the stone and hit Walter on the side of the head, knocking him at least senseless.'

Bradecote was getting a clearer picture in his head. 'He drags the limp body to the pit and rolls it in, or drops it if he had Walter thrown over his shoulder. He sees him lying at the bottom and . . . wait a minute. On a summer's evening there are people still out in the streets, talking with neighbours, returning from the alehouse. The meeting and the fight must have happened when it was dark or near dark, so the killer could not have seen into the pit and been able to aim his throw. It must have been the thought of a moment, just tossing it in. It all makes sense other than why it took place here.'

'My lord, need it be important, to the pair of 'em, that is?' Walkelin saw no problem. 'If there was a tree on the green, they might 'ave said "We meet at the tree". The well pit is just a clear place to meet.'

'You may be right, and I am thinking too deeply about it, Walkelin. Let us sleep on it all and begin after the monks go to Prime in the morning. We will speak with those close to Walter, then the well digger, and I think you will be knocking on the doors that face this green, Walkelin, in case anything was heard or even seen. On a hot night, shutters might be left open, or at least ajar.' Bradecote yawned, and the trio returned to the abbey and their quarters in the guest hall.

Chapter Three

Bradecote rose with the bell for Prime and went out into a morning that, whilst the air smelt fresh, held warmth even at the early hour. It would be another oppressively hot day, and he wished there might be a little break in the weather to give some rain and swell the grain in his manor's fields. He looked up. Men were all at the mercy of Heaven, but also the visible heavens and weather. He eased his shoulders, sighed, and went to shake Catchpoll and Walkelin, if they were not already awake.

In fact, he found them talking quietly about Bengeworth. Walkelin had not visited the castle before, and Catchpoll was describing it, not that it made Walkelin eager to go there.

'. . . and there is this damp smell, like cabbage four days old, and all who garrison it want nothing more than to end their time of duty and leave. It breeds discontent and misery, and the lord Sheriff makes sure 'e never actually stays there. He would rather ride home to his castle at Elmley in the moonless dark.'

'It is that bad?'

'It is, Walkelin, and what Serjeant Catchpoll says is true. I did service there once, and it was one of the worst months of my life. It would turn even a cheery fellow like you into a sag-shouldered gloom-sayer.' Bradecote, entering, joined the conversation, and he was clearly not speaking in jest. 'It is one of the benefits of being Undersheriff. I am spared Bengeworth.'

'That and the fact that you have the joy of our company, my lord.' Catchpoll's face remained impassive, but his eyes twinkled.

'And that, of course. Now, I think we divide. You and I, Catchpoll, will visit the grieving widow, and Walkelin, I want you to learn all about well digging. A man who feels confident and superior, because he has knowledge and another has not, will talk the more. Find out if anyone had been nosing around as it was being dug and shown more interest than most, and speak with the mason as well. Then knock upon the doors that face the green and ask if anything was heard or seen the night before last.'

'Would they not 'ave come forward by now, my lord? This must be the biggest news in Evesham in months, and we knows how folk like to touch upon the edges of a killin', whilst bein' safe themselves, to make tales for the hearthside come winter.' Walkelin had learnt a lot about his fellow man, the ones who did not think as he did.

'Probably, but then they may have dismissed what they heard as nothing, or have some fear that whoever did it might mete out the same fate to them. Fear shuts mouths as money opens them.'

'The both of you is soundin' more 'n more like me,' mused Catchpoll, with a small smile 'and all to the good, says I.'

'As long as I do not inherit your bad knees, Serjeant, I agrees.' It was Walkelin's turn to smile. 'I will be off, my lord, and if the well delver and mason are not yet at work,

I will knock on a door or two first.' With which Walkelin departed, privately hoping that if his superiors were swift in their interview with Walter the Steward's widow, they might visit Bengeworth Castle without him having to feel its depressing influence for himself.

Walter the Steward's house backed onto the newly erected perimeter wall of the abbey, and its good-sized plot faced onto the street that rose up the hill from the bridge, beyond which Bengeworth Castle squatted defiantly. Bradecote had guessed the steward's age to be about two score years, and when a woman who looked scarcely half that opened the door to them, he wondered if he might even be looking at a daughter. Abbot Reginald had said there were no sons, not no children. Catchpoll introduced them both, and the young woman stepped back and opened the door, dipping as she did so. When she looked up again her expression was worried, bordering on fearful.

'Does the lord Abbot want me out of 'ere afore the burial?' Her voice was very nervous, and breathy, and showed her to be the widow. She was comely, slim of figure, with a slightly upturned nose, a generous mouth, and hazel eyes in which Bradecote could not detect any hint of grief, but definitely ingrained fear.

'We is not 'ere to pass on commands from the lord Abbot. The death of your husband is the lord Sheriff's business, the lord King's business, and we are seekin' whoever caused it.' Catchpoll spoke calmly as they entered, but her cheeks, already a little pale, whitened.

'But 'twas not me. I slept from the time Walter left me, right until morn.'

39

'We are not suggesting that you did, Mistress Steward.' Bradecote sought to calm her. 'We want to know if anything unusual happened in the days before he was killed, whether he mentioned any argument, and whether you knew of anyone who bore some grudge against him.'

She shook her head vehemently, too vehemently for Catchpoll.

'What, or who, is you afraid of?'

'Nothin', nobody,' she averred, and though it was boldly said, there was a lie within the truth.

'Then who are you afraid *for*?' Bradecote altered the question, and her eyes opened wider for a moment. Her mouth, by contrast, closed so tightly her lips almost disappeared.

'We can wait.' Catchpoll sounded bored, and folded his arms. 'Not,' he then added, 'that it means you should leave the lord Undersheriff standin' before your hearth.'

'Would you care to sit, my lord?' she offered, instantly.

'How old are you?' Bradecote asked, ignoring her offer.

'Seventeen' – there was a short pause – 'September comin'.' It was half apology, half defiance.

'And how long have you been married?'

'Since Michaelmas last, my lord.' The colour now returned, in two patches on her cheeks. 'A good match. Everyone said so.'

'And did you think so?'

'I-I did, my lord.' The lie showed in voice as well as face. 'A girl may 'ave dreams but a woman must show sense.' It sounded something she had learnt by rote, and never come to believe.

'So who shared the dream with you?' Bradecote was guessing.

40

'We was not promised, not even secret-like, one to the other, and 'e would not do this, could not.' Her face crumpled, and she covered it with her hands and sobbed.

'Then there be no need to fear.' Catchpoll, unmoved by the tears, was practical. 'Give us the lad's name and we will speak with 'im. That will be the end of it, if'n he be innocent.'

Bradecote, who thought her assertion was as much to convince herself as them, doubted she would give the name.

'We will discover who it is, but it uses time we do not wish to spend. If you and a youth were often together, others will have noticed. We only have to ask about the town. You merely delay matters.' Bradecote sounded suitably lordly and displeased.

'Simon, son of Hubert the Mason.' The name was whispered.

'Thank you. Now other than possibly the mason's son, did anyone else dislike your husband?'

'Bein' the steward did not mean Walter were always popular, but that were the office. Nobody likes to pay their due rent, and many grumbles, but they would grumble at any who knocked upon their door for it.'

'Oh aye, and I gets the grumbles in Worcester, collectin' for the lord Sheriff.' Catchpoll nodded, and the young woman relaxed a little.

'You understands, then. Besides, who would complain to me, the man's wife? I kept the home and I were a dutiful wife in all things.' She made no pretence of having loved her husband, but that was not part of 'duty'.

'Then we have but one last question for you. Do you recognise this?' Bradecote took from his small scrip the strap end that Walkelin had found near the well pit. The design upon the copper-coloured metal was a stylised leaf.

'No, my lord. They sent Walter's clothes back to me, and I can prove 'is belt still has its strap end.'

'There is no need for proof. His clothes, are they as they came to you?'

'Yes, my lord. It seemed fittin' I still keep to the house, not be out washin' with Walter not yet buried.'

'We would look at them, in case we can learn anything from them.' Bradecote sounded less the voice of authority now she was being helpful. He also noticed the 'still'.

'I will fetch them, but what you might see I knows not, otherwise than they was dusty and dirty.' She went away, slightly puzzled.

'You never know, Catchpoll, there might just be something that advances us, and if we waited then the chance would be lost,' he murmured to Catchpoll.

'As you says, my lord.' The serjeant's lips barely moved, 'and we can make a step already.'

Walter's widow had disappeared behind a wooden screen that divided the single chamber, giving it a hint of 'hall and solar', no doubt to show Walter the Steward's elevated position in the town. She returned in short order with an armful of garments and a pair of shoes in her left hand and gave them to Catchpoll.

'Dusty and dirty, no more, and as they came back to me.'

They took Walter's clothing into the courtyard behind the house, where the north-facing length of the abbey's defensive wall stood at the end, looming almost menacingly. Time might mellow it, but its new stonework, as yet without the softening of fern or flower finding a home in its crevices, made it uncompromising. The cotte, belt and braies were laid upon the earth, and undersheriff and serjeant squatted on their haunches and peered closely at the front that would have been lain upon the earth, but might also show evidence of the fight that preceded the tumble into the pit.

'There's blood, but not much of it. If the blow came when Walter was upright, and 'e staggered, say, you would think there would be more blood around the neck edge and shoulder.' Catchpoll was talking to himself more than his superior, seeing what had happened in his mind, and progressing logically. 'If they was wrestlin' on the ground, that is where most blood would be. I think. My lord, this tells us they did not face each other with fists and batter each other, but struggled and rolled about, and 'twere a moonless night, so I doubts it were deep dark when they met. They end up near the worked stones, and the killer grabs one and hits Walter a good, 'ard blow. I doubts whether the man knew it were fatal or not at that moment, just that the fight went out of 'im. The man touches the wound and guesses Walter be either dead or dyin', gets up, drags the body to the well pit, thinkin' that the fall will make sure of it, and rolls 'im in. A real strong man might carry 'im, but Walter were a good height, and his opponent would likely be tired by the struggle. And', the serjeant took up the shoes that had been placed to one side, 'there's a lot of dust and scuff marks on the heel and back of the shoes, which fits with dragged not carried.'

'And casting the stone into the pit is an act of the moment, a marking, perhaps, that whatever brought them to this point is over and done with.' Bradecote was also imagining. 'Yes, Catchpoll, I think we see all the "how", though it helps us not at all with the "who".'

'It would scarce be a woman, and with the blow to the left side, most like the killer favours 'is right.'

'But that does not narrow it much, Catchpoll.'

'No, my lord, but every little narrowin' brings us closer to the answer.'

'And the answer may already be known, or guessed, by others who will not want to speak up. Unless the man lives alone, he would have had to return to family, and someone would waken.' Bradecote tried to move forward.

'And their clothes would be like these, dirty and even with blood on 'em. I knows my wife would word-beat me, come the morn, for the work it would give 'er, and ask questions.' Catchpoll smiled, wryly. 'The woman of the home knows, or fears she knows.'

'And so far, we have two homes to visit – that of his brother, William, and Simon, son of Hubert the Mason, since he and Walter's wife had been close. Could they have been lovers still and Walter found out? No, wait. If that were the case, Simon would not agree to meet at nightfall by the well pit and Walter would have been seeking him out direct.'

'I doubts Walter the Steward did the agreein', not unless the other man knew somethin' that would ruin Walter if spread. Most-like Walter told the other man where and when.' Catchpoll remembered Abbot Reginald saying Walter was proud of his position.

'I think we delay our visit to Bengeworth, Catchpoll, and go to the well pit, where we can find out what Walkelin has discovered, and speak with Hubert the Mason about his son. Let us give these things back to Walter's widow.' Bradecote took up the shoes, and Catchpoll bundled up the clothes. Bradecote did not offer condolences as they departed, for none seemed needed. The young woman might regret the loss of status as 'the abbey steward's wife', but the chances were another man would take her to wife and be a better husband. A thought occurred to him, and he voiced it as they walked across the green.

'Walter's widow said nothing about him being a caring man or thoughtful husband, yet Abbot Reginald stressed how he spoke up for those who were late or deficient in their dues to the abbey. Does that strike you as odd?'

'Now you mentions it, my lord, yes, though it might be that Walter wanted to be seen as charitable to all but acted the tyrant within 'is own four walls. Not common, but I remembers one such in Worcester, a good dozen years back, where a woman were strangled, and though it seemed none other than the 'usband might be the killer, all Worcester wanted to swear oaths for 'im, not just his own tithing. Only one soul spoke a bad word, an old woman next door. She said the wife never spoke to 'er or were seen gossipin' with others, only left the house with 'er 'usband for church or to do washin' or buyin' food, and looked like the mouse cornered by the cat. The rest called the old crone a mischief-maker and the wife just the quiet sort. The man came before the Justices, denyin' all, and the outcry was such you would think it were me as committed a crime, not 'im. Found innocent without even a trial, and I still thinks 'e did it, not some "stranger off the street" as was put out.' Catchpoll shook his head. 'Most men likes to make the big decisions. They wants a wife as is faithful, puts food on the table and keeps the home not like the hog pen it would be if the man alone 'ad the cleanin' of it, but 'tis not the same as a man keepin' 'is wife like a dog on a chain.'

'No, Catchpoll, it is not.' Bradecote looked grim. What Catchpoll said made sense. 'And I think that Walter kept his young wife on just such a "chain". When she said "still" stay at home, I got the impression that was how she had lived for some time. We might do well to send Walkelin to find out, quietly, if she lived as the murdered woman in Worcester had done. It would give an added reason for young Simon to want Walter dead, but we come back to there being no reason why he and Walter would meet on the green, and there would surely have to be some particular incident that sparked him acting now.' He halted, for Walkelin had seen them and was walking towards them. It would mean they could exchange information without others hearing.

Walkelin had been doing what he was best at, which was appearing as unthreatening and friendly, which skill was now honed and improved by learning the craft of asking questions without seeming to be interested at all. He had begun by knocking upon doors, though he had learnt but little of use. The householders were civil enough, but most shook their heads and denied having heard or seen anything two nights past. One woman admitted the shutters were open, but said her husband snored so loud she had been more worried the lord Abbot might send a brother to say it was disturbing the monks during the Night Offices.

'I suppose we will have William the Steward now.' She

sighed. 'Closed ears will 'e also possess, no doubt.'

Walkelin thought it best not to respond to this. The woman also offered the advice that knocking next door would be a waste of time, because the man who lived there was a grumpy old misery, who kept to himself and barely more than grunted at folk when he went to buy food. If he was in, he would not answer his door. Walkelin wondered how he earned his pennies.

'Oh, Cuthbert works, right enough, as a walker at Martin Fuller's. Starts early, finishes late, and smells of stale piss. Not surprisin' 'e is miserable and solitary, when you thinks on it.'

The process of fulling cloth included treading it in troughs of urine, and fullers tended to keep to the company of those whose trades needed a nose inured to the stinks.

Walkelin thanked her, and found her words were true. Either Cuthbert had already gone to his work or was not answering his door. After two more without a response, Walkelin abandoned a fruitless task to speak with the well digger, a bandy-legged man who was now in the noisy process of dismantling his soil hoist from above the well pit. Walkelin bade him a cheery good morning.

'Pity all that diggin' will go to waste, and in this summer sun too.'

'Better that than a sour well, I says. Does no good to a well delver's reputation, if one starts sour. 'Tis as bad as one that runs dry in May. One good thing – the abbey pays whether I takes the soil out or puts it back in this case.' The cross-beam was knocked up from its slot, and Walkelin stepped forward to help support the end as the well digger went to the other and repeated his actions with the mallet.

'Will it be hard to find another spot?' Walkelin's voice showed the strain as they lifted the beam and set in on the ground, but his eyes were alert, and noted the well delver's belt had a simple copper strap end.

'Thank you, for the help. I will not dig on the green again. I intends to try up aways.' Adam the Welldelver pointed to where the gap lay between the houses along the north side of the green. 'The abbey plans to build more houses and make a street there, and a turn where another road runs back to the street that descends in from the north and Worcester. I reckon as it might even be better. Leastways I 'as less than the stonemason, Master Hubert, to move.'

'Had the steward come and inspected your works? I cannot think as 'e would know much about the craft.' Walkelin thought using 'craft' showed he respected the well digger's skill, though it looked to him like digging a deep hole until it was wet and then making a tower of stone and backfilling round it.

'Ha, you is right there. No idea, but it did not stop 'im tellin' me what to do. I think 'e liked tellin' folk what to do. Not sure 'e was a man who could do much for hisself, mind. You know the sort.'

'Aye, that I does. Was 'e pokin' his nose in every day?'

'Pretty much. Said as a report must be made each day to the lord Abbot, but I asks you, would the Abbot of Evesham be interested in whether I 'ad gone down another three feet or four?'

'Mayhap the first thing the lord Abbot did every mornin' after Chapter, havin' dreamed all night of a fine, deep well, was send the steward to check progress.' Walkelin grinned, and Adam Welldelver laughed out loud until his eyes watered.

'Bless me, that be a picture in my mind as will linger.'

'Anyone else who liked to watch another man labour in the sun?' Walkelin made sure this sounded very casual.

'Plenty of the women. Mind you, 'tis mostly them as gets to fetch water so they will be keen for it to be in use. Also, this looks a good place to come and gossip, I reckons. Oh, and the maltster would come and complain that it would take the water from the channel as runs through the monks' orchards and has a run-off down to 'is maltin' house. Just shows that most folk does not understand water at all. Master Meduwyrhta only asked the once, and accepted what I said, as a fellow craftsman ought.' The well digger paused and a small frown appeared on his brow. 'Yes, I am sure he accepted my word and it were not that the steward shouted at 'im and fair ordered 'im to go away and stay away. Said it were none of 'is business, but if you needs good water for your livelihood, well 'tis fair enough to ask the once, surely?'

'I would say so. Mayhap there lay some old grievance betwixt the two and Walter the Steward liked to play high and mighty over the man.'

'That fits, fits well. Always sayin' how the stewardship ran in 'is family from a kinsman of Abbot Walter, way back, and that was why he 'ad been named Walter. Not sure why a man would brag about old kin as were Foreign, but there, and this Abbot Walter might 'ave been a simple monk afore 'e were raised up. If we goes back far enough we is all the children of Adam. I did say that I bear the name for that reason, just to annoy 'im, though in truth it came from my mother's brother as went off on the Crusade to Jerusalem and never returned.' The well digger chortled, and Walkelin grinned.

'Don't see as there is much to laugh about.'

They turned, and saw a man, whom Walkelin deduced must be Hubert the Mason, leading a donkey that pulled a small, low-sided cart.

'How far up aways does you want me to move the stone, Master Welldelver?' The mason spoke with the respect of one artisan to another, though Walkelin suspected it was so that he received as much respect in return.

'One hundred paces, by my guess, Master Mason,' responded the well digger.

Walkelin smiled to himself, since he was right.

'Leastways none of your labour is wasted, Master Mason.' He decided he would keep up the polite tone.

'Not as such, but I has to put it on the cart and lug it all to the spot for the new pit, and set it all down again too, on my own.' The mason wiped his brow with the back of an already dust-pale hand.

'And with the aid of that donkey.' Walkelin, seeing the donkey's sorrowful expression, felt it was unfair to ignore the fact that most of the lugging would be done by the beast. Its ears moved as if to listen to the praise, but turned back at its master's grumble.

'It just pulls. What makes the muscles ache is the liftin'.'

'Then get that lad o'yours. Big strong arms on 'im,' the well digger suggested, but Hubert the Mason just scowled and shook his head.

'Have you no journeyman, Master Welldelver?' Walkelin wondered at the man, for he was past looking 'young'.

'I do, but 'e twisted 'is knee the week afore last and can barely put weight upon it. So I left 'im back in Stratford, where I comes from, in the care of 'is mother and a good healer. I can still get by alone, though it takes a while longer.'

'And did Walter the Steward tell you your craft also, Master Mason? Master Welldelver told me 'e did with him.' Walkelin wanted to know how another regarded the man.

'I ignored 'im as I always does – did. Been tellin' folk what to do and where since the stewardship first fell to 'im, when Walter could 'ave owned to no more 'n a score and five years. Never saw 'im do anythin' for hisself, mind. All mouth and pride, that one.'

'Does not sound as though you liked the man much,' observed Walkelin, but without any sense of accusation.

'Not much, but then ask any in Evesham and you will get the same answer.' The mason swatted away a wasp, and he did not look the underserjeant in the eye.

Walkelin hid his surprise. How could this be the man whom Abbot Reginald had spoken of in almost glowing terms?

'The lord Abbot seems to 'ave valued the man.'

'The lord Abbot is a godly man, but also a powerful one, and Walter the Steward answered to 'im. He would not act "I am much more important than you" before Abbot Reginald. Oh no, it would be all meekness and mildness, though not the face that were shown to us outside, or to the abbey servants, in private.'

'So Evesham disliked the abbey steward.' Walkelin made it general.

'You could say that. What folk said in the alehouse and

beside the hearth . . . Let us say "disliked" would do for some.'

'But not all?' Walkelin looked mildly curious, no more, but Hubert the Mason tensed, his eyes narrowing and making the crows' feet at their outer aspect more prominent. His lips compressed. Walkelin raised a hand as though admitting defeat. 'No matter. It is enough to know that Walter the Steward was a man as might give cause for a fight, might even 'ave been the one as started it, and the other man defended hisself with what came to 'and, which was your stone.'

'Which passes no guilt to me. I could not know . . .' The mason was swift to respond, fearing some blame attaching to him.

'No, no, you could not know, not unless you was stood close by, watchin', and offered the stone.' Walkelin smiled, and unlike Catchpoll's smile, it relieved tension. 'And by the sounds of it, in that case you would be in queue to do so.'

'Pity it is that they picked my well pit to meet by. That is what I says.' Adam Welldelver spat on his palms, took up his spade, and cast the first dusty earth into the pit. The sound as it landed was like that of filling in a grave.

'But each day is a day paid, and Evesham will still get another well in the end.' Walkelin nodded to the pair and turned away. He saw his superiors approaching, and went to make his report. He made sure he did not look too urgent.

Walkelin's casual manner earned commendation from Catchpoll.

'We hope you has interesting information, but glad I am you did not come hastily and show the fact.'

'No, Serjeant, I thought of that. What I learnt will be useful, but does not give us a single man to seek. 'Tis clear Walter the Steward showed one face to the lord Abbot and another to his fellow townsmen. From what the mason said, "disliked" was the milder end of feelin' against the man.'

'We wondered about that from speaking with his widow. She said nothing that fitted with the thoughtful and charitable soul described by Abbot Reginald.' Bradecote was pleased that there was corroboration.

'Hubert the Mason said the steward felt better and more important than everyone else, acted lordly – when no right did 'e have to do so.' Walkelin added the last part in case it sounded as though acting lordly was of itself wrong.

'It would set up backs, but not be reason to kill the man. What we did discover, Walkelin, is that before she was married to Walter, his wife, who is young and pretty, seems to have been fond of a youth nearer her own age, and it was mutual. Did Hubert the Mason mention his son, Simon?'

'No, my lord, not of his own will, and never by name. The well delver suggested 'e used his son's strong arms to help lift the stone for movin' to the new diggin' site, and I thought as the mason did not look pleased.' Walkelin frowned. 'And 'twere a sensible thought, so why did it get that reaction?'

'It might well be that the mason wants to keep the lad lyin' low, out of our sight. Now, that might be from simple fear of us, or else the mason knows somethin' connects this Simon to the death.' Catchpoll knew some folk were simply afraid of anything involving the Law.

'Then let us find out which.'

'My lord, we might do better to wait until the donkey takes the first load of stone to the site for the new diggin',' Walkelin suggested. 'We can ask our questions without the well delver listenin', and the mason wore an apron tied about 'is waist, over 'is cotte, so I could not see 'is belt or any strap end.'

'Understood, Walkelin, and yours is a good idea. In the meantime, was anything learnt from those who live next to the green?'

'No, my lord, though a few did not answer. They might be already gone to their labours. A woman bemoaned that the new steward would 'ave "closed ears", and the impression I got was that this would not be new, but a continuation. That also fits with what we is learnin' of Walter the Steward.'

'Looks like the cart is on the move, my lord.' Catchpoll was the one facing towards the corner of the green and could see over Walkelin's shoulder.

'If we goes up the north street and cuts left at the top end of the marketplace, we should meet where the new well pit is to be, and do so without "followin'" the cart.' Walkelin had learnt the 'map' of Worcester's streets, and Evesham was a lot simpler.

Catchpoll was still smiling at his protégé's 'serjeant-craft' as the trio traversed the marketplace.

Chapter Four

If Hubert the Mason had looked suspiciously at Walkelin, he regarded the lord Undersheriff and Sheriff's Serjeant with blatant fear, and the donkey sensed it and began to back up in the shafts of the cart. Walkelin went to its head and tried to calm it. The mason, with four worked stones cradled in his arms, could do nothing but stand his ground and try to look less panicked.

'Best you sets them stones down afore you drops 'em on your foot,' advised Catchpoll, calmly.

Hubert obeyed. He still looked trapped.

'We would have you show us your belt.' Bradecote made it a command, and confusion was added to the man's worry.

'My belt, my lord? Well, 'tis naught but my apron strings this day. Not as thin as I once were, and all the bendin' to lift the stones would dig the buckle into the result of the wife's good pottage.' He patted his apron-covered belly, but his smile was nervous. He was trying too hard.

'Where is Simon, your son?' Bradecote was direct.

'Gone over to Hampton, my lord, to aid my brother, for the pease be ready early this year.'

'He is a labourer? I had thought you would have him follow your trade.' Bradecote's eyebrows rose, questioning.

'Oh, he will follow me, my lord, b-but just now I can

manage alone and my brother cannot.' It sounded a poor reason, and Hubert coloured slightly.

'And when did he go?'

'Oh, must 'ave been a week since, my lord. At the least. Ought to be back in a day or so.' This was said airily, but Hubert was tense. The lord Sheriff's men could tell he was lying.

'And was 'e sweet on Walter the Steward's wife after she wed the steward?' Catchpoll did not sound as if it made much difference to him.

'O'course not, not once she wed. Would not be right.' Outrage sped the words from the mason's lips, even as he realised he had confirmed the relationship had existed. 'Lads go cow-eyed over a girl very easy, but such things does not last. One girl one month, and a new one the next.' He laughed, though it rang false.

'Just a passin' fancy, eh?'

'Aye, and now forgotten.'

'Strange that Walter's widow 'as not forgotten, and assured us otherwise so strong it rang as much as a lie as the one you just spoke.'

'Women linger on such things. Men move on.' Hubert shrugged, ignoring the accusation of a lie.

'And it must be annoying that he is gone to your brother just when there is this commission for the well stones.' Bradecote kept up the pressure.

'Never short of work, a good mason, and I am that. This be a simple task. I does not need aid.'

'But if it is simple, then your journeyman, your son, could have done it alone and you could be working on something needing more skill.' The undersheriff was very reasonable.

'And we will go and find out just when he arrived in Hampton, if at all,' added Catchpoll, smiling his most unnerving smile.

'It might 'ave been just under a week. I did not count the days,' admitted Hubert, in a rush.

'Just long enough ago that he could not possibly have been the man to kill Walter the Steward. We understand.' Bradecote was almost soothing.

'Though of course it does not mean *you* could not 'ave done it.' Walkelin, who had remained silent, spoke up. 'Nobody liked 'im, as you said afore, and could well be you are one as loathed the man. It would give a reason for the meetin' bein' by the well pit.'

'No. I slept sound all night. The wife will swear to it.'

'Loyal wives always does,' murmured Catchpoll.

'And you knows nothin' of Walter the Steward if you thinks as 'e would agree to meet where another said. It must 'ave been at 'is own command.'

This, at least, gave a new line of thought.

'Do not take up an offer of work outside Evesham, Master Mason. We will see how true your words are about your son, and may need to speak further with you.' Bradecote sounded commanding. The man just nodded, and the shrieval trio left him to his stones.

'We will cross to Hampton and check the tale of the son and the pease. Walkelin, we want to know if Walter's widow was seen out and about freely, and alone, or is there gossip that he kept her close and "caged". Since they wed last Michaelmas, if she is the reason for his death, something must have happened recently, or come to light.'

'My lord, might Simon 'ave got close again, without 'is father's knowin'? 'Tis not somethin' a son would want to admit, committin' adultery.' Walkelin thought Hubert's rebuttal of the suggestion had rung true, but might be incorrect.

'That is a possibility. Take your whittling, or help some old woman with her bundle of washing, and play the helpful stranger. You are good at it.' Bradecote smiled. 'We will meet at the guest hall later, though we cannot tell when.' He gave directions to the steward's house.

'Yes, my lord. And what does the widow look like and what is her name?'

'She is not yet seventeen, good figure, turned up nose, shy. We do not have her name, but you will discover it, no doubt.' Bradecote nodded a dismissal and Walkelin strode away purposefully. 'And we are for Hampton, Catchpoll.'

'Indeed, my lord, and with luck, Kenelm the Ferryman will give us much of what we needs.'

Bradecote and Catchpoll headed south to the green and then west along the northern boundary of the abbey demesne, marked by a hawthorn hedge as it descended gently to the western side of the promontory and the Hampton ferry. At one point there was a gap in the hedge where a blackcap was singing, and a gate, with a track that went southward, bridged over what must be a brook or deep ditch, and led to a cluster of buildings. Perhaps they were the abbey's stores for the produce of the demesne gardens and orchards, for neat lines of trees were also just visible beyond the hedge.

The ferry was midstream, and bearing a man with a pig. When it arrived, and the pig had been 'encouraged' to disembark, the ferryman acknowledged them.

'Do you charge more for a pig?' Bradecote wrinkled his nose.

'I ought, and that be a fact. Mind you, that'n crossed none so bad. You needed in Hampton as well as Evesham, my lord? I would think one death enough for you to look into.'

Kenelm the Ferryman knew all the news that came from Evesham, and that which came in from the westward. It was Catchpoll who answered as they climbed onboard.

'Just castin' about to make sure what is told is true, friend.'

'And rare that be as fair-smellin' swine.' Kenelm often sifted hearsay from wishful thinking and downright malice.

'We heard as some from Evesham had come over to help kin with the pease harvest this last week.' Catchpoll was 'just making conversation'.

'It took several trips to get the lay brothers from the abbey across, that is for sure, and they returned but yesterday. The abbey 'as tended a vineyard in Hampton since Abbot Walter's time, but they gets a good pease yield also most years.'

'Anyone else?' Bradecote tried not to sound very interested but was not as good as Catchpoll.

'There was young Simon, the mason's son, but 'e only crossed yestermorn, so that would be too late to gather much, and 'e said as 'e were goin' to Aelfric, an uncle, for a few days since 'is father was on 'is back over the quality of 'is work. I said as we all makes mistakes, and time be a great teacher, but 'e did not look cheered.'

'Lads takes things to heart too easy.' Catchpoll sounded the voice of aged wisdom.

'That they does. That they does.' Silence fell, letting the

Avon whisper beneath the planking of the ferryboat. Kenelm might have been thinking about his youth, but the shrieval pair were wondering about Simon the mason's son. As the ferryman tied up on the western bank, Catchpoll asked directions to the pease field, and Bradecote dropped a silver penny into the ferryman's calloused palm.

'I doubt we will be long before we return.'

'I will be 'ere, my lord, or else on t'other side.' Kenelm touched his cap and grinned.

The pease field was not empty, but it was clear that the majority of the crop was in, and the haulms were being cut and left to dry for fodder. They asked for Aelfric, who was rather in awe of being spoken to by a lord, and who volunteered that his nephew was the lad with the wide-brimmed straw hat 'over yonder'. Bradecote and Catchpoll got within about five yards of him, approaching from behind, and then Catchpoll sneezed and the youth turned around, saw two men he did not know but who looked intent on knowing him, and ran. Catchpoll groaned. Bradecote, unconcerned about how it looked that a lord should run, gave chase, and if his legs were older, they were also longer, and although a stone mason would have strong muscles, they were not in his legs. It gave the undersheriff, who rode nearly every day, another advantage. At the same time Simon jinked about like a chased hare, and the others working in the field watched in a mixture of curiosity and some amusement. However, after a few minutes the journeyman mason tired, and tripped over a willow root. He went sprawling, and Bradecote was spared the possible indignity of launching himself to grab about his legs. He folded his arms and waited, just beyond arm's length, breathing fast but not desperate for air. Catchpoll, having gauged the direction and taken the shortest route at a dog trot, arrived, wheezing a little.

'Landed a fish, my lord? Looks like one.'

Simon was certainly trying to get as much air into his lungs as possible. He had rolled over and lay looking up at them, very frightened. They noted that his cotte was girdled by a narrow belt with a curved strap end, one that had a heart shape crudely etched into it.

'Mornin'.' Catchpoll grinned at him, and the youth's bowels nearly opened. 'You are Simon, son of Hubert the Mason. This is the lord Bradecote, Undersheriff of the Shire, and I am Serjeant Catchpoll. We doesn't look like outlaws, so why did you run from us?' Catchpoll sounded curious.

'It were not me,' blurted out Simon.

'That's good, then.' Catchpoll's grin widened, and grew more awful. 'So now you tells us what you did not do.'

'I did not kill 'im, on my oath, I did not.'

Catchpoll did not tease further and ask whom Simon meant.

'In which case, why run from Evesham yesterday morning, and why run from us now?' Bradecote did not raise his voice, but it held steel.

'Father told me to. Said I would be blamed for it, since everyone knew I loved Mærwynn.'

The youth, who could be no more than four or five years older than Walter's wife, sounded as if the noose was already about his throat, and his voice was a trembling gasp.

'Do you love her still, or was this all in the past?' Bradecote did not question the passionate verb.

'Still – not that we—I scarce spoke to 'er since she wed. She sort of disappeared, and Father said I must not give Walter the Steward reason to demand more.'

'Demand more?' Bradecote and Catchpoll spoke almost in unison, genuinely surprised.

'Somethin' about Quarter Day. I knows no more, but Father said as it risked our business, our 'ome. I did not see Mærwynn, I swears it, not 'til a week past. She looked so frightened, like a mouse in a trap, and she begged me not to even look at 'er.' Simon's voice strengthened. 'What sort of man frightens a wife like that?'

'Did you say anything to her?' Bradecote wanted to know the source of her fearing he had killed her husband.

'I said it were not right.' This was mumbled and Simon did not look at them.

'Tell us the words, exactly.' It was a command.

'I-I said a man like that did not deserve to live.' There was a pause. 'But I did not kill 'im, even though I rejoices that someone did. When the widow-time is past, I will ask again to wed 'er. We thought it would be agreed afore. Father and Mærwynn's father spoke of it, and it were part agreed, then she wed the steward, sudden-like, and without a reason to me. I tried to ask 'er father, but 'e just shook 'is head and said some things could not be.' He sighed. 'My lord, it looks bad, I knows that, but what I said to Mærwynn was just words, words sprung from shock. I meant 'em, in a way, but could not 'ave done the deed. When Father came and told me about the body in the well pit, I tried to imagine doin' it, throwin' the stone down onto the steward's head,' he mimed the action, but halted as if the stone did not leave his hand, 'but I could not.'

'Fair enough.' Bradecote glanced at Catchpoll. Simon had 'lifted' the stone with his left hand and thought that it was a lobbed stone that killed Walter the Steward. 'But between you and your father, and Mærwynn also, there have been lies and a fleeing that has taken us from the real path to who killed Walter the Steward.'

'But whoever did it did Evesham a favour.' Simon sounded sulky.

'It does not make it lawful, and the Law lies there to stop folk doin' what they wants out of spite, greed, vengeance or "doin' a favour" for themselves or others.' Catchpoll spoke almost magisterially, and it was one of those times when Bradecote was well aware that Catchpoll also meant he was the physical embodiment of the Law.

'If your uncle still has use for you here, then remain for a few days. It may mean, if we are fortunate, that whoever killed Walter the Steward will be taken by then, and even if not, you are better out of Evesham while this is on all lips and in all minds.' It was the best advice Bradecote could give.

'Yes, my lord. Will you tell Father? I think a bit of 'im feared I did it, even when I swore I did not.'

'We will tell 'im,' Catchpoll assured the young man, and as he and Bradecote made their way back to the ferry, he added that he would personally tell Hubert the Mason that all he had done was make things look worse than they were.

'I thinks some folk mishear the word "Law" for "wolf" and acts brainless, my lord.'

'Or the name "Catchpoll".'

Catchpoll was still laughing as Kenelm took them across the Avon.

* * *

Walkelin, left to tackle his task his own way, chose not to loiter and whittle some child's toy, as was his usual ploy, but sauntered past the house where Walter the Steward had lived, and apparently found a stone in his boot. He leant against the wall of the house next door, removed the boot and wobbled a little, tipping out the invisible stone and rubbing the ball of his foot with an expression of discomfort. He had caught the sound of voices within the neighbour's house, and hoped someone, preferably female, might emerge. He was in luck. A woman younger than his mother but much older than his Eluned, and with the same sing-song Welsh voice, propelled a lad of about tithing age into the street, with the injunction to 'go back to your father and tell him not to send you next time when he wants to make an excuse for bein' late. I knows it is the alehouse as calls him'. She glanced sideways to see who was leaning on 'her' wall, and Walkelin, exuding 'innocent man with painful foot', smiled and grimaced in one expression.

'Apologies, mistress. So sharp a pain it was I thought a nail was gone through the sole and into my foot.'

'A nail? There's bad.'

'No, Heaven be praised. 'Twere but a stone, though it hurt like a sharp nail.'

'A bruise can be very painful.'

'Indeed. I will hobble back to the abbey's guest hall, for sure.'

Her ears pricked at this. Evesham town was full of Walter the Steward's death, but all were convinced that what was known within the enclave far exceeded what was known outside.

'You are stayin' in the abbey? What is said there about,'

she dropped her voice conspiratorially, 'Walter the Steward, as is done to death, and lived next door?' She jerked her head to her left. This, thought Walkelin, was just the woman he needed. He decided to be bold.

'My lord, the lord Undersheriff, knows now that Walter the Steward was not liked in Evesham and . . .' he paused a moment, 'I ought not to speak of this openly.'

'Come inside, you poor soul, and I will find a pad for that foot of yours,' announced the woman, rather more loudly than needed. She almost grabbed his hand and he hopped into the darkness of her home. She dragged a stool for him to sit upon, shooed three small children out into the backyard, and came to sit opposite him. The pad seemed forgotten.

'I said as Walter would end bad. Told his wife as much, years ago.'

'Years ago? From what I heard, the man was recent married.' Walkelin continued to rub his foot and grimace, to a least keep up the illusion of injury.

'Oh, that is the second wife. No, I told the first, after the babe came too soon, see. Only time I ever stepped over the threshold, mind. Would never let anyone in, Steward Walter, never speak neighbour to neighbour, nor even laugh with the other men over a beaker of ale. Only let me in since she needed a woman there. When I told her she must rest in bed for a few days after she lost the child, she said she dare not, for he would not like it and would make her sleep on the floor again. What man makes a wife sleep on the floor? And if he did so when she was carrying his child, well no wonder she lost it. That is when I said 'e would come to a bad end if there was justice in the world. She whispered there was no justice, 'cept in Heaven.' The neighbour crossed herself.

'Mind you, this new one would have gone the same way as the first if the steward had lived. She looks the same, see.'

'Men often choose a wife who reminds them of the first.' Walkelin thought this unlikely, but it might get a response.

'Bless you, no. She looks the same way, not has the same face. Rarely gets beyond the front door, just the same. Nearest she gets to fresh air is feeding the chickens in the yard. She whispers, even to them. Last one whispered too. I hears, or heard, him often enough, orderin' this, demandin' that. They went to church together, but the way 'e took her arm was not husbandly . . .' she paused to think of the right word, 'more like a carpenter's vice.'

'What happened to the first wife?'

'Died, she did, winter afore last, coughing so loud I could hear it through the thick walls. But she did not want to live, mark you. Wore the woman down, he did, with misery and nothing being right. And another thing – dressed in fine clothes is the new one when they go to church, but I looks through a crack in the yard wall sometimes and see her in a thin gown even in winter. Something very odd and wrong there.' She sighed. 'Mind you, she is free of him now. If she possessed any spirit still, I would say she went after him the other night, quiet as the mouse she is, and pushed him into that well pit and cast the stone after, and small blame to the woman. But she would not have dared.' The woman smiled. 'Now, what is it you could not say outside?'

Walkelin had been thinking even as he had listened.

'Keep it close mistress, but it looks like whoever killed Walter the Steward was bein' threatened by him.'

'How?'

'W—The lord Undersheriff is not yet sure, but this is only

the first day he is huntin' the man who did it.'

'Definitely a man?'

'Oh yes.' He rubbed his foot and pushed it back into his boot. 'The foot feels much better now, mistress. One thing, though.'

'Yes?'

'What is the name of Walter's wife – widow?'

'Mærwynn. Pretty name. The daughter of Wulfram Meduwyrhta, she is, and I would have thought better of the man, giving his daughter to the steward none would speak a good word about, when there was an honest soul all ready and eager to take her to wife.'

'There was?' Walkelin sounded suitably surprised.

'Ooh yes. A well set-up *llencyn*, as you would expect in one who uses mallet and chisel each day. Must have been much more to the girl's taste.' The woman paused and frowned. 'Saw him this last week, I did, come to knock upon the door. Must have been some message from his *tad*, Hubert the Mason, who is working on the well, not that Steward Walter was at home. Knocked three times he did, and only then did the door open and that poor mouse just squeaked at him to go away or else she would pay for it, afore he spoke a single word. Sad, very sad.' She sighed.

'And did he go away without passing on the message?'

'He said something, but quickly, and I was not listening, mark you, so what he had been sent to say I know not, and she was so upset she would have forgotten all of it by the time the door was shut.'

'And if her words was true, passin' it on would mean only trouble, so mayhap 'twas for the best.' Walkelin gave no hint that anything other than a message for Walter the

Steward could have been the reason for the visit. 'Well, I had best get back to the abbey afore my lord returns from his askin' questions. Thank you, mistress.'

Walkelin left, hobbling slightly, and only then did the woman realise she had told him far more than he had told her.

Walkelin was back within the enclave some time before his superiors and decided that he might use the time to good purpose. Buoyed by his success with 'the woman next door', he thought he might see what could be learnt from those within the walls. He was also trying to work out in his head whether there was any significance in the fact that Walter the Steward had been dismissive and antagonistic to his wife's father, the mead maker, when the man had gone to look at the well pit and been reassured over his own source of water. If the steward was already a man disliked in Evesham, and he did not sound as if he had had some sudden change of character, why did the mead maker agree to the match, and why were relations between the two men poor afterwards?

In the newly built guest hall, he found a man sweeping the passage outside the few chambers reserved for the most high-status guests. The lord Bradecote had been allocated one and had said the three of them should use it to discuss things without other ears overhearing. Walkelin knocked upon the door, though he could hear no voices from within, and then addressed the sweeper.

'Never ends, sweepin'. My wife says 'tis the thing she hates most, and the dust gets in your nose too often.'

'That it does.'

'And no thanks does it earn.' Walkelin sounded sympathetic.

'Agreed. All we gets is complaints when things is not perfect, not praise when there is no fault.'

'And you will be hopin' the new steward is like the last, eh?'

'You never met the last one, then, and have not yet met the new one. Not peas in a pod, I grant, and barely spoke a word to each other, let alone a good 'un, but cut from the same cloth. Their father – ah, a hard man, and they took that from 'im. Our lives will be no better, just a mite different.'

'In what ways?' It just needed a nudge.

'The last one wanted to watch every little thing you did, and tell you to do it better. Then the silver pennies you earned was docked for the "mistakes". The new one will want you to do more, even if you work 'til you drop, and soon enough will dock them for "laziness". The stewardship be inherited, and it makes them proud and nasty.'

'Or they were proud and nasty from the start.'

'Ha, and gave pain to everyone as they gave pain to their mother as they came into the world.' The servant, seeing the guest master approaching, brushed more assiduously, and stopped talking. Walkelin, who felt that entering the lord Bradecote's chamber and waiting there felt wrong, went to find the shadiest spot from which he might still see the western gate and all who entered.

It was late morning, and the hint of a breeze, that had provided relief when he had gone to see the well pit, was barely a memory. Instead, the heat seemed to sear the skin and then entered the body with each breath. Fortunately for Walkelin, there was an aged walnut tree between the guest hall and the more lowly almonry, which was still a thatched, daub and wattle building. The tree looked very much as though it had been there as long as there had been monks in Evesham, and Walkelin wondered if it had been planted by a long dead herbalist for its nuts and medicinal properties. Certainly, nobody had sought to fell it to 'tidy' the enclave, and it now stood, the trunk etched with deep-gouged, vertical furrows like a wrinkled and venerable oldmother sat quietly in the corner, saying nothing, and observing through rheumy eyes. The shade was very welcome, and he sat down between the roots and leant back against its girth, brushing away a beetle that had seen his neck as a continuation of its path. The tree exuded a restfulness that was beguiling, soporific, and its message was that man was fleeting, like the beetle, and many had come to a violent end during its life, yet here it still stood. He should strive but not worry. Succumbing to the walnut's benevolent shade, Walkelin's breathing eased and his eyelids drooped.

He awoke with a start when a boot kicked him, without malice but enough force to pierce his slumber.

'Been a tirin' forenoon, has it? Glad you could get a little rest, then.' Catchpoll was sarcastic, in part from jealousy. A nap under a tree sounded a wonderful idea, and the walk back from the ferry, though barely a half mile, had been undertaken in glaring sun. The sweat had been running down the back of his neck and wiped from his brow, and right now, a cool drink and a shady tree sounded like Heaven upon earth.

'I only sat down a bit ago – I think.' Walkelin, getting up and dusting off his backside, was honest, and for all he knew he had dozed for an hour. 'I discovered what you wanted about—' he stopped as a Benedictine walked past, and dropped his voice a little, 'the widow, and how she were treated, though much came from the neighbour takin' a little thing and imaginin' more, and the widow's name is Mærwynn. What is more, she is the daughter of the mead maker, and we knows he went to ask about whether the well would change his supply of water, and that Walter the Steward shouted at 'im to go away, which is a bit of a surprise, given the link of daughter and wife.'

''Tis not uncommon for a man not to get on with 'is wife's family, but mostly the mother. Odd then, I grant.' Catchpoll pulled a thinking face.

'And what is more, my lord, the neighbour said the steward's first wife died, and was like this one, barely ever seen, quiet as a mouse and afraid to do what Walter did not like.'

'Let us discuss this inside.' Bradecote led the way to his chamber, which was cool enough, and shut the door. He sat upon the edge of the cot, and Catchpoll took the stool. Walkelin stood close to the wall and leant against its cool stone.

'Tell us everything.' Bradecote leant forward, resting his elbows on his knees, and looked at the underserjeant.

'Slowly,' added Catchpoll.

Walkelin gave them all he had learnt, with the addition of the opinion of the sweeper on the dead steward and his successor.

'So we have discounted the mason's son who was sweet on Mærwynn, have interest in her father, the mead maker, and still need to meet William, the new steward. Oh, and there is a possibility that Walter was taking more than just the Evesham Abbey rents from the tenants.'

'What discounted Simon, my lord?'

'Firstly, his belt did not lack a strap end. Also, he admitted he had made a bold and threatening comment to Mærwynn, not long before the killing, but it was clearly passionate words, not a sign of real intent.'

'And when the lad talked about the deed, imaginin' the actions as went with it, 'e went to "throw" the imagined stone with 'is left hand and assumed the death-blow came from the stone cast into the well pit.' Catchpoll gave the rest of the story. 'Mind you, it did me good to see the lord Bradecote run like a stag after the lad. Them long legs covers the ground well.'

'And that was more than enough running for today. Let us hope neither the mead maker nor Walter's brother William take to their heels at the sight of us.' Bradecote sat up and eased his shoulders.

'Who do we speak with first, my lord?'

'I think perhaps the brother, and then, if we are fortunate, he too can be discounted. Not being in charity with close kin is not the same as being prepared to kill them. We need to judge both how much he disliked Walter, and how much he wanted the stewardship.'

'And we needs to consider, my lord, that with Walter now with a new young wife, there was more "risk" of 'im fatherin' sons to inherit.' Catchpoll was less confident that William would be easily removed from those under suspicion.

'And the lord Abbot said William showed 'imself upset by his brother's death, which does not fit if they did not like each other.' Walkelin added his mite.

'Very true. I get the feeling that Abbot Reginald did not see the true side of either of them. Let us find William.'

Chapter Five

They went first to find the prior, who could direct them to William, brother of Walter. It seemed odd to call him 'the Steward' before his brother had even been laid in the earth or he had taken up his duties. Bradecote also wanted to see if the prior, with perhaps more frequent contact with both men, had a differing view of them to that of his abbot. Prior Richard was happy to tell them where William might most likely be found, though less eager to speak about his character, or that of his dead brother.

'Walter the Steward succeeded his father when he was about two and twenty, a good many years before I became prior. He was always very aware that his bloodline went back to Abbot Walter, or more precisely, his kindred, and I think he felt a little superior to those of purely English blood, though to me it was foolishness. God cares not about lineage, but about the quality of a soul.' Prior Richard sounded mildly disappointed in his fellow man. 'He worked hard, and was never late, nor absent without a very good cause. He was respectful to me and to Father Abbot, and he was devoted to the improvement of this House, in wealth and size.'

'Forgive me, Father, but that does not really tell us much about what you thought of him.'

'I am not sure it is relevant, my lord Bradecote.' The

mildest of reproofs could be detected in his voice.

'Father Prior, I can only be open with you. Father Abbot spoke highly of the steward, indeed commended his charity towards those who were remiss in paying their rents, but this is entirely at odds with what we have heard of him in the town.' Bradecote was not put off.

'As steward he would not always be popular. Those who collect the dues rarely are.'

'But nothing has been said in his favour, no "despite that, he was . . ." From a variety of people we have heard he was bullying, controlling, proud, and might even have been extorting more than just the due rents from some townsfolk.'

'Surely not.' The prior looked genuinely shocked.

'We have yet to discover the truth of it, or its extent, but yes, it has been suggested. It is almost beyond doubt that his wife, and the one who preceded her, have been kept, cowed and almost prisoners, in his house.'

'I was aware he had married again after his wife died, but we, within these walls, do not think about women. I would never have thought to ask about Walter's wife.'

'I am not suggesting blame, Father, merely that your steward was not the man he made himself out to be, and that means there may be more men who might have a reason, in their own mind, to end his life.'

'But such a mortal sin!' Prior Richard looked genuinely distressed.

'Father Abbot said that prayers would be said for our success in finding who killed Walter, not least so that their soul might be prayed for. Anything you can tell us, helps that being achieved.' Bradecote did not want the prior to withdraw into the shell of the tonsured who shut out the evils perpetrated beyond their enclosed world.

'Yes, I understand.' The prior clasped his hands together, and looked as if he was forcing himself to face the unpleasant realities of the world. He sighed, heavily. 'I suppose I chose to think the best, and ignore any signs of failings. Our House has thrived under his stewardship, so perhaps I am guilty of looking at the end and not at the means, but it is true, what Father Abbot told you. Steward Walter advocated that further time be given to those who were late, or fell short, in their rents come Quarter Day. He did seem most charitable in that, and yet,' the sigh was repeated, 'there were times when I felt the abbey servants looked . . . browbeaten, though I never heard him actually berating one. None of us go out into the town, into the world, unless for a very important reason, other than our lay brothers who return from a grange for a time, and then are sent out again. We would not hear what is said there, but it grieves me if Walter's actions brought this House into disrepute, and raised sinful thoughts and deeds among those who look to us as a beacon of godliness.'

Catchpoll kept to himself the thought that the prior was under an illusion if he thought that was how all the tonsured were regarded by the wider population.

'Now tell us what you think of the new steward, William.' Bradecote did not think he would get much more detail on Walter. 'Not the words that come easily, but, knowing how Walter was not all he seemed, look at how he truly appears to you, Father.'

'He is not tolerant as Walter wa—seemed to be, and seems very . . . driven. He is, I think, guilty of believing only he is right.'

'And was that the cause of disagreement with his brother over the expansion of the town, and the building of more houses?'

'Yes.' The word was drawn out a little. 'Though when one looks at it honestly, there was no fraternal love between them that shone. They kept mostly out of each other's way, and if they heard the other one had advocated something, they would say it was wrong, or should be done differently. But,' the prior cheered up a little, 'William was definitely much affected when he saw his brother's body. He wept, for all to see, which shows that deep down, there was brotherly love.'

Catchpoll had to cough to hide the growl that indicated it meant no such thing, and that it could as well be a way to deflect any suspicion.

'Was William jealous of his brother being steward?' Bradecote did not expect a definite answer and was surprised, though it came after a pause.

'I had not considered it, really, but yes. Or rather he resented his brother holding the office that he felt he would fill better, which is not quite the same thing, but similar.'

'Who "won" the argument over the town?'

'William. He made a very good case, not only before Father Abbot, but all at Chapter, since Father Abbot thought it was a decision which all the brethren should decide upon together. The works began in April and the digging of the well was part of that.'

'Thank you, Father Prior.' Bradecote acknowledged that the Benedictine had been forced to confront things he would have chosen to ignore.

'No, thank *you*, my lord Bradecote. You have made me consider what I would have avoided doing. It behoves me to make sure that William does not fall into the sins of his brother, nor become tyrannical now he has the name of "Steward". I shall be watchful. God has used you, and this terrible event, to some good purpose. I give thanks for it.' Prior Robert held up his hands and gazed upwards.

The sheriff's men left him to his prayers.

William the Steward, as he was practising calling himself, lived on the westward side of the market square, fewer than a hundred paces from his brother's house. It was a little smaller, and held more life within it, not least because William was the father of three sons below tithing age, who could be heard in the yard behind the burgage plot. There was also a daughter, a little older, assisting her mother in the house. William himself looked enough like his brother to be recognised as kin, even though the shrieval trio had only seen Walter in death. There was the same dark hair with a hint of a wave to it, heavy brows and a square chin, though the mouth was surprisingly delicate. He wore a longer cotte than most, and his belt boasted a large, ornate buckle, and an equally decorated end. He looked squarely at Bradecote when Catchpoll had introduced him, and, when the undersheriff said he wished to speak about his brother, he sent wife and daughter out 'to quiet the boys' but under instruction to remain outside.

'I do not want them upset.'

'Very thoughtful of you . . .' Bradecote felt the absence of a name beyond the Christian name, and his voice trailed off quite obviously.

'Since the duty falls upon me, I am not ashamed to answer

to William the Steward.' The man spoke ponderously, but with no sign that he disliked the 'duty'. He also spoke more like the clerics for whom he worked. No doubt it was part and parcel of being 'stewards by descent'.

'Though the lord Abbot 'as given you leave until your brother lies buried.' Catchpoll's tone hinted it might seem a little precipitate.

'He has, but it makes no difference. There is always a steward. When my father died, my brother took up the duty the moment the priest stopped intoning prayers at the bedside.'

'You seem very composed . . . Master Steward,' observed Bradecote, giving the title.

'No good would wailing do, and I cannot change what has happened.'

'Though you "wailed" when you first saw your brother's corpse brought into the abbey yard.' Bradecote was swift.

'And no good did it do, my lord. Shocked I was, I admit that, it being a sudden dying, and what came into my head was how my mother, on her deathbed, said as it gladdened her failing heart that after she was gone, we would have each other to lean upon. Not that I think it true, but I was thinking of her, and that made the tears fall. However, our fate is in God's hands,' he crossed himself piously, 'and we must accept it and move on.'

'And in the end of it, it favours you and yours.' Catchpoll made sure there was not time to prepare answers. He wanted the man a little rattled.

'The abbey will do better with me as steward, but even if it did not come to me, a son of mine would follow, and my line continue, not Walter and his feeble loins.' This was said with some disdain, and a hint of gloating.

'He got 'is first wife with child, so there would be no cause to think he could not do so with this new wife,' commented Walkelin, not quite sure whether he was meant to join in the barrage of questioning, and eyeing his superiors as much as William.

'Just the once, and the little I saw of the second in church, she was as pale as her coif and weak-looking too. If he picked her to give sons, he made another misjudgement.'

'Another?' Bradecote raised an eyebrow. 'Had he made others?'

'Others? Oh, most of his decisions were the wrong ones.' The brother sneered.

'Give me examples.'

'Well, my lord, he said the abbey should build up to the north only on the eastern side, toward Green Hill, but that is limited more by the steeper descent towards the river. On this side, the western one, the ground is flatter for much further and there is greater scope for better and larger burgage plots that will attract wealthy tradesmen and make Evesham more prosperous.'

It had to be said that this sounded logical.

'And will you be movin' into one of them, or takin' Walter's house?' enquired Walkelin, innocently, 'a bigger one befitting "the Steward of Evesham Abbey".'

'It would be sensible, and give more room for my family.'

'And rent free, no doubt?'

'The Abbey Steward has always been given his house without rent. There is nothing to that.'

'Other than your new one would otherwise be bringin'

in a good sum of silver each Quarter,' murmured Catchpoll, and got an angry look.

'What else did Walter do wrong?' Bradecote wanted more.

'Kept letting the laggards and the underpayers sit tight, for one thing. "They may do better" he would say, and did they? No. It was not even as though they were the widows and poke-hole plot holders. He always got the dues from them. It was the men whose trades prospered. They could pay, but they chose to hold back, and he let them.' William's lip curled. 'They will not do it next Quarter Day, or if they try, they will find themselves out of Evesham.'

'Where were you the night before last, at nightfall?' Bradecote took the questions on another tack.

'Here, in bed with my wife.'

It was the easy answer, and one that could not be disproved, unless a witness had seen him abroad and not spoken. William permitted himself the smallest of smiles, for he knew it as well as did the sheriff's men. It was also the smile of a man confident he was always right, always the winner. It annoyed Bradecote as it annoyed his subordinates, but there was not much more that could be asked at this point.

'But since any wife will support her husband, that assurance does not mean very much, Master Steward. We still know that of all Evesham, you had the most to gain from your brother's death. That means far more.' With which Bradecote turned on his heel and walked out, followed by serjeant and underserjeant.

'Not sayin' it wiped the smile from 'is face, but it soured it.' Catchpoll approved.

'And it is true.'

'Yes, my lord, it is.'

'What I wants to know is why the wealthiest was the worst rent payers. That makes no sense to me.' Walkelin was clearly niggled by the thought.

'Sometimes it is payin' late, or not at all, that keeps men wealthy. Look at Robert Mercet.'

Mercet was the man Catchpoll liked least in all Worcester, and the feeling was mutual.

'It might be that, but you are right to question it, Walkelin. We will go and see the mead maker, but then we will ask Father Prior to give us the list of those in Evesham who are behind with their dues to the monks.'

They had been given directions to the mead maker by the porter at the abbey gate, and so Bradecote and Catchpoll now knew at least one person who lived down the track onto the abbey demesne land. They went back along the well-worn trackway to the Hampton ferry, but then turned left onto the track that ran southwards from it, crossing the little bridge that spanned a deep ditch or conduit, which still had some water in it, even during this dry spell. The bridge looked both new and well-constructed. Two smaller ditches, with sluice gates set before them, ran from the water course, each supplying a cluster of buildings. A few yards after the bridge the track bifurcated, and from that point a line of posts stood in the ground between the run-offs, about a chain apart, not a fence but a very clear demarcation of who held which patch of earth.

'We were not told there were two paths,' complained Bradecote. 'And both has a run-off of water from the brook or conduit, so that helps us not at all.'

'Well, my lord, if we is wrong, then we can ask whoever lives next to the mead maker what sort of neighbour he is.' Walkelin was positive again.

Catchpoll shook his head at the optimism of youth.

They picked the more western path, which was a little rutted from cartwheels, and knocked upon the sturdy door of a house which had a stone-built building at right angles to it, with a taller portion at one end. Catchpoll knocked upon the door, but the smell already told them that this was not the mead maker's. They thought there was nobody within, and turned away, but then it creaked open and an old man challenged them.

'What do you want?' He was not welcoming.

'We seek the mead maker.' Catchpoll was blunt.

'Should 'ave taken the other path, then.' The response was equally terse. The old man's back was bent, and his head jutted forward. He was white-haired and with eyes milky white and near sightless. He looked angry, not so much at them as at the world as a whole, the sort who railed against his life as it had become, but resolutely held the door shut to death. He made to shut them out also, but Catchpoll stuck his foot in the way.

'Who else lives 'ere?' He guessed the old man was unlikely to live alone.

'What need 'as you to know?'

'I am the lord Sheriff's Serjeant, and this,' Catchpoll pointed to Hugh Bradecote, 'is the lord Undersheriff.' Walkelin, as often happened, was not introduced.

'Where be 'is horse, then?'

It was an unexpected question, and for a moment it

remained unanswered. Then Walkelin spoke up.

'The lord Bradecote's horse is stabled at the abbey.'

'Lords does not walk places.'

'I do, but then, I have long legs.' Bradecote decided this old man would neither be impressed by rank, nor scared by it. The old man looked him up and down and clearly decided this was a proper introduction.

'Aye, a real longshanks, but lords speak Foreign.'

'The most powerful ones like the King do, all the time, but English is as good for me, since it means I do not need another man to pass on my words.'

'And what words would you say to me – my lord?' The old man thawed just a little.

'I would ask you what Serjeant Catchpoll just asked you, and also what you can tell me about Wulfram Meduwyrhta?'

'Well then, my son lives with me, and 'is wife and my grandson, but she is gone to buy cherries in the town, and Oswald and the lad is in the *mealthus* next door.'

'So, you are a maltster.' It was logical that the craft was being passed from father to son.

'Was until the eyes and the bones failed me.' He sounded bitter. 'Now I just sits – and eats cherries if they comes to me. Little more use than a babe in arms.' He then shook off the melancholy and glowered. 'Wulfram Meduwyhtra is a thief, a thief I tell you.'

'He is?' Bradecote was so taken aback he let it show.

'Aye. Steals the water, 'e does, just when we needs it most. Keeps the sluice open on 'is channel so it all goes to 'im, longer than needful, and says as it is mischance that it is always flowin' 'is way when we needs it.'

Bradecote relaxed. This was a private dispute over water rights, not a matter for the Justices.

'So you think he does it to spite you?'

'I does not think it, I knows it. 'Is father were just as bad, and Wulfram makes more mead now the abbey 'as more bees. We both pays rent in kind, and then some silver. Wulfram thrives, since the honey be sold cheap to 'im by the monks, and saves 'im spendin' so much time seekin' the wild stuff. Then the sweetest mead, the best, goes in vessels to the abbey as part of 'is dues, and the other makes bee-piss for the rest of Evesham.' He spat into the rushes on the floor. ''Tis a foul drink.'

'Thank you. We will go and speak with your son, and trouble you no further.' Bradecote saw no need to linger, since the old man could not possibly have walked to the well pit without assistance and could not have survived any physical encounter with Walter the Steward.

Outside, the malt smell was now even stronger. A voice was raised within the stone building, and another answered it. They entered by one of a pair of doors, which would be wide enough for a cart to pass through. In front of them were three large tubs in which barley was soaking. Beyond the third one a lad of about seventeen, still gangly of limb, was scooping out grain with a slotted shovel, and piling it into a heap on the floor to allow it to sprout. The air was heavy with the smell of the damp barley, and the richer smell of the dried malt. At the far end of the chamber was a door, some three feet from the ground, and a man was raking out the dried grains from the malt kiln, ready to be winnowed and ground. The warm air from a small oven was drawn into the bowl of the kiln and rose through a mat of close-woven lathes and rods upon which the sprouting grains were laid out to dry.

'Oswald Mealtere.' Catchpoll raised his voice without thinking, and both men turned suddenly.

'Yes.' The man by the kiln door sounded suspicious, but not antagonistic.

'We wants to speak with you about Walter the Steward.'

The maltster set aside his rake, shut the door and came towards them without haste. He looked at the lad. 'You carry on 'til that be empty, and then finish the rake out.' He returned his gaze to Catchpoll. 'Now, we can speak outside.' He seemed calm and assured, and not at all on edge.

When he had shut the *mealthus* door he bowed, or rather bent, a little grudgingly, to Bradecote, being well dressed and so most likely important, but spoke to Catchpoll.

'I doesn't know how I can help you, if 'tis about 'is death, which it surely must be.'

'It is. And this is the lord Undersheriff.' Catchpoll always liked to make much of Bradecote's rank.

'You was worried about the new well that was being dug on the green.' Walkelin thought that a good thing to start the conversation, since it showed they already knew quite a lot.

'Yes, and what man would not be, as needs water from the southward? 'Tis bad enough that that *hnescehand* Wulfram Meduwyrhta cuts me off when 'e knows we is busy.'

'The man as lives over yonder?' Catchpoll pointed beyond the narrow channel. 'Why a "softhand"?'

'All 'e does is pours. Water goes in, they wait, drain off,

drain off again, mayhap again, and let the mead just mature. You see how we labour. This be proper work. What is more, there lies a grudge betwixt us. Wulfram could make good, but 'e will not. There were a fallin' out betwixt his father and mine, years ago, and you would think a shakin' of hands now would see all in the past, as long as I did not tell my father of it. He be too old to forgive.'

'What caused the breach?' It was probably not relevant, but all knowledge might become useful.

'You needs yeast, not just for ales but for mead also, though once you has it, you can keep it goin' year on year. My father sold some to Wulfram's father after their yeast was lost through a mistake. But the mead maker said it were a gift and refused to pay.'

'It cannot 'ave cost much. An odd thing to start a feud.' Walkelin looked puzzled.

'If you really needs a thing, it costs more.' Oswald's mouth lengthened into a small smile.

Bradecote saw this only as something that would make each man disparaging of the other and returned to the present.

'So, you were worried about having enough water. Worried enough to keep going back and asking the well delver.' Bradecote was wondering if those visits had ended in a similar way to the mead maker's, with Walter the Steward losing his temper. 'How did Walter the Steward take that, since the well is being dug upon the abbey's instruction?'

'I knows not, since I were spared 'is loud voice and proud manner. So full of "Walter the Steward, of the line of stewards" all the time, and that will mean nothing in the place 'e finds 'isself now.'

'You did not like him.' Bradecote did not make it a question.

'If you find a man in Evesham who says they did, then I will show you a liar, and that be fact – my lord.' Oswald realised he had not sounded very deferential.

'And where were you the night before last, as it got full dark?'

'Right 'ere, my lord. I came out to check the fire in the oven, to make sure it would keep goin' gentle overnight.' He pointed to a small, round-topped stone oven with an iron door.

'And nobody saw you?'

'The wife will vouch for me, and I saw Wulfram come down the track, and 'e staggered a bit so mayhap he abandoned mead for ale, eh?' He gave a short bark of a laugh. 'But 'e would not vouch for me. Pity of it is, we is in the same tithing, so we both knows one as would not swear oath for the other.'

'And this was when dark fell, you are sure?' Bradecote was not going to believe the maltster without corroboration, but by the same token was not going to dismiss what he said.

'Aye, since 'tis when you asked about, my lord. No moon shone, but our feet always knows the way home, down across the bridge, right enough. I saw to the fire, checked the hen coop was shut good and proper, since I heard a fox too near to like, then went in to the wife and my bed, and glad I was of both after a long day's labour.' He sounded the virtuous worker. 'First I heard of the steward's death, 'twere the wife bringin' the news from the market next forenoon.'

'Thank you. We will let you get back to your malt.' Bradecote thus dismissed the maltster, who nodded, and went back to shout more instructions at his son.

'So was the mead maker drinking with his friends, or was he meeting with Walter?' Bradecote voiced the obvious question.

'If he was ale drinkin' there should be plenty to confirm the story, my lord. I think there is but one alehouse in Evesham, and otherwise 'tis just sold by alewives at their door.' Walkelin expected to be the one sent to discover that truth.

'And if 'twas meetin' with Walter there will be no admission of it.' Catchpoll sniffed. 'Pity Oswald Mealtere hates the meduwyrhta's guts. If they was best friends there would be no cause to try and muddy the waters.'

'But then again, if that were so they might swear falsely to support the other, so would be equally useless to us.' Bradecote shrugged.

'The maltster wears a very new-lookin' belt, my lord.' Walkelin was observant.

'Yes. I wonder if that is chance.'

'And it might be worth speakin' with Brother Beekeeper, to find out 'is view of Wulfram, and see if it tallies in any way.' The underserjeant was thinking beyond the next interview.

'Indeed, but after we have come to our own view of the man.'

They moved on to the second cluster of buildings.

Chapter Six

The mead maker's house was much like any other, but it was abutted by one with greater height to the eaves. Another, much smaller, round building stood further towards the south, on the orchard side of the water channel and near the river, but it looked unused and very dilapidated.

Bradecote wondered if they should ignore the house and knock upon what would be the mead maker's place of labour, but as they drew near, the door opened and a woman with a besom stepped out and then stared at them. At the sight of Bradecote, she gasped and made a hasty obeisance.

'We seek your husband, Wulfram Meduwyrhta.' Bradecote thought it a reasonable assumption that this was his wife.

'Wulfram is with Brother Petrus, the beekeeper, in the orchard, my lord.' The woman, whose quite ordinary face was made attractive by limpid blue eyes, also made an assumption, this time of rank. 'But it should not be long afore 'e returns. If you would step inside, I will send our Edwin to speed 'is steps.' She stood back and beckoned them within. It felt churlish to refuse. The chamber was tidy and orderly, and a little girl of about five was playing with a tabby kitten.

'Thank you, mistress.' Catchpoll held up a hand, 'but we can as easily send Underserjeant Walkelin here.' He made it sound kindly, rather than ensuring Master Meduwyrhta did not disappear without trace, which would be damning, but embarrassing.

'As you choose. Edwin works but next door, so it would be no problem.'

'I will go, mistress.' Walkelin exuded eagerness as though haring off to meet a friend. He went out before the little girl had even turned to stare at the strangers.

'We met your daughter, Mærwynn. Will she return to you, now she is widowed?' Bradecote did not mention Walter the Steward's name.

'I hopes so, my lord.' The woman's face clouded. 'She is young and will get over it.'

This was somewhat cryptic, since it could mean the loss of her husband, but equally it could mean getting over having to live with him for nearly a year.

'Was she always a quiet one?' Catchpoll enquired, and the mother's expression became grim.

'No. A laughin', happy girl was our Mærwynn.' Her eyes suddenly flashed anger, but then she gulped and sniffed. 'I cannot but be glad she is free.'

'You make it sound as if she was chained, mistress.' Bradecote spoke gently.

'As good as, my lord. As good as. My poor girl! Not been close enough to say a single word since the day that man took 'er to wife. 'Twas wicked. I saw 'er in church, or rather what 'e left of 'er. It fair broke my heart to see the life fade from 'er. I begged Wulfram not to agree to the match, for all the man were the most powerful in the town, outside the abbey, and I kept telling 'im it would be the death of 'er, sooner rather than later. You could see it, week by week. I give thanks to Heaven she is released.' The woman's words were heartfelt, and she clearly had no idea that she was also giving a very sound reason why her husband might have killed Walter the Steward. 'It sounds unchristian, I know, but what mother would feel different?'

It was not a question they could answer without it sounding as though the representatives of the Law agreed with the killing, though both Bradecote and Catchpoll knew their wives would feel the same way as the mead maker's wife. The little girl with the kitten had abandoned play and came to hug her mother about the legs, as much comforting as seeking comfort. She looked at Bradecote, accusingly, and it made him feel guilty, though his questions had not been meant to cause upset.

Footsteps sounded outside, and a man entered, followed by Walkelin, who looked hot and a little out of breath, having run in the heat. Wulfram Meduwyrhta was a man of curves. He was not enormously fat, but he was far from skinny; his head and face were round and his nose slightly Roman; even his legs were not straight, but a little bowed. The bizarre thought hit Bradecote that if a bumblebee turned into a man, it would look like the mead maker.

'I am Wulfram Meduwyrhta. What need you from me, my lord Undersheriff?' He did not sound belligerent, but nor was he cowed and nervous.

'You went to speak with the well delver, when he commenced digging, and Walter the Steward, kindred by marriage to your daughter, sent you away angrily. Why was that?'

'He shouted at me, yes, and I left, but I did so 'cos Master Welldelver told me there was no cause to worry, and I believed the man. Walter the Steward liked the sound of 'is own voice.'

'Yet you agreed to his marrying your daughter, even against the wishes of your wife here.' Bradecote indicated her with his hand.

'I did not do so from choice, my lord.' Wulfram was defensive.

'He threatened you? How?'

'Said 'e would recommend the rent on this place rose, and make sure the honey from the abbey bees would no longer come to me. A new man has taken up one of the abbey holdings over the river in Bengeworth. He comes from Stow, which the abbey holds, and 'e made mead there. The man is a rival, and no mistake, though I doubts he could make it better, from the same honey. Mead 'as been in my family since afore Walter's line was stewards. I will not be rivalled on the quality of my mead, but the abbey bees takes from the orchards of apple and the black pear, and their honey,' the man almost licked his lips, ''tis of the finest flavour. Neither sendin' my lad out to seek wild honey over the river, nor payin' silver pennies to those who brings news of nests, could make up the difference in weight, nor ensure the taste. Only the lesser meads is made with those and they vary. For the sake of my livelihood, and my family as a whole,' he glanced at his wife, 'there was no choice.'

'You did not say, Wulf,' whispered the woman.

'There were enough worries, with little Win bein' ill. I did not want to add losin' the roof over our heads and the wherewithal to live.'

'You still should 'ave said.' His wife heaved a heavy sigh.

'Your neighbour says the monks sells you their honey

cheap.' Walkelin broke the spell between husband and wife. 'So you could 'ave offered to pay more—'

'And been refused. No, Walter would not 'ave accepted all I could find, just out of spite.'

'Could you not go directly to Father Prior or even to Abbot Reginald?' Bradecote frowned.

'No rightful access is there to either but through the steward, and Walter thought of that as well.' The mead maker stuck his thumbs into his belt, which had a strap end, though it looked askew and as if hammered hard to grip the leather. 'Said 'e would warn them I might use "honey words", and laughed, and said as I should not be believed. They trusted the man, and never has I thought the monks so blind. They must be so good they cannot see bad in others.'

'And then you saw what the marriage did to your daughter. It all gives you a very good reason to want Walter the Steward dead.'

'And glad I am he is, but I did not do it, my lord. I will swear my good oath upon it, and there's enough oathswearers in my tithing as would support me.'

'All of 'em?' Catchpoll wanted to know if he would admit to the breach with Oswald Mealtere.

'All but one, and 'e would deny me though the truth shone like the sun above today. The other eleven would swear to my bein' of good character and law abidin'. My neighbour,' he pointed across the ditches, 'and me we does not get on, to the point where 'e would see me drown before 'is eyes and laugh as I went under.'

'And you would do the same?' Bradecote's face showed no surprise, just mild interest.

'Well, I would not go so far as to laugh, my lord, but yes.

Nasty 'e is, and like the old stick of a father that lives still. Long ago, when I were but the age of my little Win indoors, my father lost the yeast one bitter winter. Now, next door, they is maltsters, so yeast is easy. Not sure why theirs did not get killed off too, but anyways, yeast the old man possessed, and Father asked for a little. Does not take much, since it grows and has a life to it. So some came to us, and then the bastard said as it would cost thirty silver pennies. Thirty! It were only worth tuppence at most, and a neighbour would give it for free, which is what Father assumed.'

'Where were you two nights past, when it got dark?'

'Why, settlin' into my bed as any man as works 'ard would be.'

'You did not go up into the town that evening?'

'No, my lord. Why would I do that?'

'To sit over a beaker of ale with friends?' Bradecote made it sound merely a suggestion.

'Not done that since Whitsun. Not an ale man, me, but then I makes mead so . . .' He spread his hands, and looked the picture of innocence, but saw that the sheriff's men did not let their expressions soften. His voice took on a desperate note. 'I am glad Walter is dead, and my Mærwynn is free, but as God sees me, I did not kill the man, and will try and pray for 'is soul when they lowers 'im into the ground this afternoon.'

Bradecote realised that they had not even asked at the abbey when the funeral would take place. Being present was important, so that they might see the reactions of those who came to see Walter the Steward interred.

'That is all we need to ask at present, but you will not leave Evesham.'

'I rarely does anyways, my lord, unless a good bees' nest is found close enough. I will be 'ere, should you need me.'

'Good.' Bradecote nodded, indicating the mead maker might be about his business, and Wulfram, both relieved and worried, returned to his labours, and helping his son with a second racking.

'So now we has to decide whether Wulfram Meduwyrhta is an honest man who does not drink much ale and keeps to 'is hearth, or is a man so full of guilt for marryin' off a well-loved daughter to Walter the Steward, a man he knew to be a bad 'un, that 'e confronted and killed 'im.' Catchpoll did not say which he favoured.

'And also whether Oswald Mealtere just wants to get 'is neighbour into as much trouble as 'e can, even as much as goin' before the Justices for murder.' Walkelin knew he ought not to be biased towards the mead maker just because his home looked happy and his little girl played with a kitten, but he did. A man whose life was contented did not strike Walkelin as one likely to jeopardise it without great cause, though the situation and condition of Mærwynn might have been just that. Walkelin was a contented man, though he wished his mother did not scowl every time he used a Welsh endearment to his Eluned, and that Eluned herself had not, of recent weeks, seemed a little quiet and preoccupied. He was sure he was being a good husband.

'One or other has to be lying, and we have to consider that even if it is the mead maker, it might just be that he thinks saying he was anywhere near the green that night risks a noose about his neck.' Bradecote was also trying to be even-handed.

'True enough, my lord. It complicates things when honest

men lies for fear the honest answer will condemn 'em. Mind you, most lies badly. This, if a lie, was well done.'

'He still remains of interest to us, as does the brother, but I fear we are going to find there were many more in Evesham who could join them.' Bradecote sighed and wiped sweat from his forehead. 'Let us go and find out how long a list it is.'

Father Prior was a little surprised to be asked for a list of the abbey tenants who had a poor record of payment, especially since the lord Undersheriff asked that it go back for at least two years. He had to call a clerk to bring the rolls from the muniment chamber, where all deeds, titles and financial documents resided, rather than the scriptural ones in the library.

'You think Steward Walter was killed because he was threatening someone who could not pay?' His long face looked even more burdened than normal. 'It is so hard to believe that this was a man who advocated leniency and compassion.'

'We do not know, Father, but a man who fears for the roof over his family's head may do things that he would not normally consider,' replied Bradecote.

There was a silence, with which the Benedictine was far more comfortable than the sheriff's men. The clerk returned with a bundle of Quarter rolls, and pored over one at a time, writing down the names and amounts paid late or not at all. Bradecote viewed it with misgiving. He thought he would be able to decipher names, but his Latin was only sufficient to obey simple instructions that his superior did not trust to verbal conveyance, and he was not at all sure he would understand words for many of the crafts. He hoped not many debtors shared the same Christian name, and realised the safest way was to risk embarrassment, and stumble through them before the clerk and prior so that they could correct, or translate, those beyond him. He was sure that in a community where the obedientiaries were literate, it would not occur to them to think of the majority of people to whom the written word was either useless or a struggle.

'Here, my lord, are all those remiss since Lady Day 1143.' The clerk handed him a piece of vellum, and Bradecote's heart sank as his eyes ran down the list.

'Aelred *vestiarius*, Baldwin *tinctor*. Father, I am sorry, but my Latin is only that of prayers and the Offices, and some basic commands. What is a "vestiarius", and for that matter a "tinctor",' he looked further down, and stumbled through several more words he had no hope of understanding.

'Ah, I am sorry, my lord.' The clerk, a precise, little man with ink-stained fingers, smiled apologetically. 'Aelred the Tailor, Baldwin the Dyer, Robert the Miller, Martin Fuller, Oswald Maltster, Grim the Thatcher, Wulfram Meadmaker, Walter Horsekeeper, though his brother William took over the lease when he, er, died . . .'

Bradecote remembered Walter Horsweard, though visually only as a sodden corpse, from the previous year, and also his hobbling brother Will.

'He did not just "die", Brother. He was killed by intent.'

'Indeed so, my lord. Now, there is also Alcuin the Ropemaker, Hubert the Mason and the Widow Potter.'

At least the widow could be crossed off the list as the killer, thought Bradecote.

'Thank you, Brother.' The undersheriff turned to Prior

Richard. 'We will speak with all these people, and find out if pressure was put upon them. It might be that the steward agreed to advocate on their behalf if they later paid not just the debt, but a "fee" to him, and—' He stopped as there came an urgent knock upon the door. The prior apologised, but called for the person to enter. A flustered monk entered.

'I am sorry, Father, but there is a . . . woman' – he said it as though it was a dangerous beast – 'at the gatehouse, making a great deal of noise and complaint, and demanding to see you or Father Abbot.'

'Why?'

'Because she was coming to market, over the bridge from Bengeworth, and two men-at-arms from the castle stopped her and demanded a quarter of her produce as toll. When she refused, they threw it all in the river. She is weeping and shouting and making things very unpleasant.' The Benedictine was evidently made nervous by all women, and especially agitated ones.

'I see. Bring her here, Brother Julian, and we will speak with her.'

Brother Julian eyed his prior with increased respect for this brave act, and left, to return swiftly with a woman of middle years, her rosy cheeks streaked with tears, her eyes red as the cherries she had been bringing to sell, and trying to catch her breath. She dipped to Father Prior, and, on seeing Bradecote, to him also, since he looked important.

'Now, my daughter, Brother Julian tells us you were . . . waylaid, on the way to market.'

'Just so, Father, oh just so, and what shall I do without the silver for my fruit and vegetables I does not know.' She wrung her hands together. 'A whole basket of cherries in my arms,

I 'ad, and a basket of the sweetest peas on my back, and all gone, gone.'

'Tell the lord Undersheriff exactly what happened. He will help you.' In one short sentence, Father Prior had cast all responsibility upon the Law. Bradecote's glance at him was not one of gratitude.

'I walked from Badsey, my lord, with my peas and cherries, to sell as I does this time every year, and afore I set foot upon the bridge two men, big men with sticks, stepped in front of me and barred my way. They said as there were a toll to pay to the castle, which is next to the bridge, and it would cost me a quarter of both baskets. Well, I said no, and then they said the toll just went up to 'alf, and I kicked one of 'em in the shin, right under the knee, and the other one grabbed the basket from my arms and threw both basket and cherries into the river. Then 'e cut the straps of the one on my back and did the same with that. Bless 'em, two lads down by the river's edge saw the baskets bob up and down and pulled 'em in with a stick, but nothin' is there for me to sell now. 'Tis not right, my lord, not right.' She sniffed and managed to look belligerent and vulnerable in one.

'It is not right, mistress, and I will go to the castle and speak with the commander of the garrison.' Bradecote looked severe.

'Thieves, the lot of 'em,' grumbled the woman. 'And what chance be there of me seein' a single silver penny for the loss? None, and me with four fatherless children to feed.'

'Oh, I think in this very particular case, mistress, Father Prior might consider it charitable to at least provide you with some recompense for your loss, especially as it is the abbey who has the right of the market, and takes dues from it.'

Bradecote was all reason, and smiled at Father Prior.

'Er . . . well, I can see you are in distress not of your own making and it would be . . . I will see to it that Brother Almoner gives you six pennies.'

'I always gets at least ten when I comes to Evesham.' It was the nearest the woman could come to haggling with the monk.

'I see, then eight, yes, eight pennies, for the abbey has to show charity to many souls.'

'Thank you, Father. And will you say a prayer for my poor 'usband, Brictric, as died last Ascensiontide?'

'I will.'

Tears forgotten, the woman beamed at the prior, then bobbed a curtsey to them both, and went out, followed closely by Serjeant Catchpoll. His words to her were softly spoken, but firm. Others, he said, would not be honest victims like her, but folk trying to get something for nothing, and would be claiming so much cast into the Avon that the river would divert into Bengeworth to go round the islet of goods. It would mean that the abbey came to see all requests as false, and good women, like her, would not be aided again.

'So what you does now, mistress, is go back to Badsey with your eight pennies and damp baskets, and just say trade was not so good today, it bein' so very hot. Understand?'

'I understands.' She did not know who he was, or what, but she understood the reasoning.

'Many folk stayed indoors if they could, and trade were a bit less than usual.' She showed she had the words ready.

'Good. Now, best you get them pennies, and if any tries to get toll off you goin' back across that bridge, tell 'em Serjeant Catchpoll, the lord Sheriff's Serjeant, knows what they is up to, and that it makes 'im unhappy.'

Catchpoll knew that there would be some men-at-arms within the garrison who had spent watches upon the walls of Worcester Castle, and everyone in the castle knew Serjeant Catchpoll. He had a strong feeling the lord Sheriff would not be 'unhappy' at all, but he could be as pleased as he liked with the commander of the garrison. The men-at-arms knew who was closest to making their lives a misery when next they came to Worcester, and it was not William de Beauchamp. He stepped back into Father Prior's chamber with the hint of a smile on his face.

'. . . and I will attend the service, of course.' Father Prior was giving details of Walter the Steward's funeral. The body had already been moved from the abbey church into the parish church of the Holy Trinity, which lay, unusually, within the enclave. It was a building of some age, the gift of Earl Leofric of Mercia, and his equally devout wife, the Lady Godgifu, in the time of the sainted King Edward, and if its exterior was not in the modern style, it was wonderfully endowed within. The abbey habitually provided the priest from among those who took their vows but felt the calling of a parish, and the current incumbent, Father Paulus, had been within the enclave, monk and priest, for thirty years.

'We will be there also, Father.' Bradecote made it sound for religious rather than investigative reasons and thanked the clerk once again before turning to leave.

Outside, he ran a hand through his hair.

'Holy Virgin, I hope I can remember all those trades again.'

'I listened close, my lord, and I reckon as I could put name and trade together for most. Odd to 'ear the name of Walter Horsweard again.' Walkelin had a good memory.

'It was, and it seems odd that his brother has fallen short on the last two Quarter Days.'

Bradecote was puzzled, and there was something niggling in his brain. Something did not fit. 'At some point, when the steward is buried, we will have to go to Bengeworth Castle, but what is likely to be important is this list. I get the feeling that these people will give us a clearer idea what Walter the Steward was doing, and thus the best chance of discovering who wanted to stop it, at any cost.'

The funeral of Walter the Steward was well attended, and although nobody shed a tear, or looked grief-stricken, faces were schooled into solemnity as they entered the cool of the church. As Catchpoll whispered to Walkelin, having heard about the man's character, it was a surprise that nobody cheered. Not for the first time, Catchpoll wished that for a few minutes he could be the priest, not for any religious reason, but because it would give such a good view of the faces of the congregation. Standing at the back, the sheriff's men could see the expressions as people entered and left, but otherwise they saw only backs of heads. The only faces looking towards them were those of the priest and the serene and shining faces of the Holy Virgin and St John the Evangelist, whose images, adorned in gold and silver, were set in niches either side of the chancel arch. Prior Richard, flanked by two accompanying minor obedientiaries, might have been expected to intone a prayer for one who had served the abbey for many years, but he simply stood in the chancel, apart from the townsfolk, facing the body and looking grave as the priest stood before them in blissful ignorance of what had come to light, and extolled the virtues of a man who had 'been devoted to the abbey and to this town'. A few feet did shuffle at that. Bradecote thought the prior had made a wise decision, since anything that showed the abbey's appreciation of what the man had done, would do nothing for relations between spiritual and secular in Evesham.

Bradecote wished that he could put the names on his list to more of the faces among the assembly, but other than the widow's family, Oswald Mealtere, with a placid, if not downtrodden, looking woman beside him, Adam the Welldelver, Hubert the Mason and Will Horsweard, memorable because of his hunched shoulders and limping gait, they were all simply townsfolk. He tried to imprint upon his memory any who looked different in demeanour to their fellows. To be sure, lack of grief was no sign of guilt in this case, but there might be an added tension if one had been the man to send Walter the Steward from the world in hot anger and was now seeing the stark reality of the consequences.

The widow looked pale, and even younger than her years, and had her mother at her side, though her father remained in the row behind. Was that to catch the girl if she fainted and fell back, as a physical as well as moral support, or keeping a lower profile? Walter's brother, William, was also at the front, but stood away from her and never as much as glanced towards her. He looked as if this was not a funeral but an investiture of his new position, and he stood the taller for it. There was no sign of the 'distress' he had shown before the monks the day before.

As Mærwynn followed the body out of the church for the burial, her mother took her alabaster-white hand and gripped it, possessively, as if reclaiming something that had been lost – or stolen. The graveside was in the full glare of the sun, and it beat upon the mourners, whose numbers had thinned, with some returning to their work. Walkelin saw a man with angel-blonde, wavy hair, wipe his forehead and murmur it was not half as hot as Walter the Steward would find Hell.

The soft monotone of the priest came to an end, a handful of earth was dropped into the grave by widow and brother, reduced by the summer's baking to a dust that landed with a patter rather than a thud, and the mourners dispersed, some to celebrate in private. Bradecote sent Walkelin in search of cool refreshment for parched throats, and he returned not only with a pitcher and three beakers, but a loaf of bread tucked under his arm.

'We needs to wait until everyone is back at their trades, so I asked for some bread as well. Also, I found out from a servant in the kitchens where the fuller, the dyer, the thatcher and the Widow Potter lives, so we has a start.' Walkelin had no doubt this would all be greeted with approbation, though Catchpoll's eyes narrowed.

'You did not ask outright, now, did you?'

'No, Serjeant.' Walkelin looked offended. ''Course not. I did it the "serjeantin' way" and they was none the wiser afterwards.'

'Just checkin' to be sure, but I did not think you would act green.' Catchpoll was placatory, which was unusual.

'Not now I am an underserjeant.' Walkelin was proud of his elevation, not so much because it gave him seniority over mere men-at-arms, though that was good, but because Serjeant Catchpoll had thought him worthy. He handed round the beakers.

Chapter Seven

The trio were leaving through the new northern gateway by the monk's graveyard when they were hailed, and turned to see a lanky novice hurrying towards them.

'My lord, Father Abbot asks if you would come to him. Something strange has occurred, and it is connected with Steward Walter.' The novice crossed himself.

'Of course.' Bradecote wondered what 'something strange' might be.

When they were admitted to the abbot's chamber, Prior Richard was also present, and a slight, nervous-looking man with angelic blonde, wavy hair. Walkelin would now be able to put a name to a face.

'My lord Bradecote, this is Aelred the Tailor, a man of good repute, who has come to us about the late Walter.' Abbot Reginald turned to the tailor. 'Tell the lord Undersheriff why you are here.'

'My lord,' Aelred bowed low, in a strangely precise way. Everything about him was neat, and his speech matched his demeanour. 'Walter the Steward had me make three fine tunics, with braiding upon the front and sleeves, a gown of the best wool, to be trimmed about the neck with fox fur, and a cloak with a squirrel-lined hood. These garments are almost finished, and all the cost, which is high, lands upon me. I came to ask if the debt passed to the abbey, if they had encouraged him to dress more finely to impress at manorial courts, or mayhap to William, the new steward, though I doubt he would be willing to pay unless the clothes can be adjusted to fit.'

'And we most certainly would not suggest an excess of adornment, not on anybody. It encourages the sin of pride.' Prior Richard was swift to divorce the abbey from any involvement, and also ignored the fact that both he and the abbot, whilst garbed as any other Benedictine, had habits made of the finest woollen cloth, whether the light one in summer or the thicker in winter, and the softest linen for undershirt and drawers. 'Our steward would not need to flaunt power or wealth hereabouts.'

'I see. You say he "had you" make these clothes, Master Tailor. Do you just mean he commissioned them from you, or did he exert some power or force upon you? Did he expect the price to be cheaper than their true value, for example?' Bradecote had detected a slight stress upon the words.

The tailor's eyes widened as if the undersheriff could read minds.

'It was made clear I must set aside other work to make them before everything else, my lord, and that the cost would be reduced by the amount already owed.'

'Owed? To the abbey?' Abbot Reginald was so surprised he let it show in his normally very even voice.

'No, no, my lord. I owe nothing to the abbey – always pay up on time I do, and to the full. No, no it – well you see—' The little man flushed and glanced at abbot and prior with a look of reproach. 'The abbey must have its reasons, I am sure, but—' He took a deep breath and then the words came out in a rush, 'I have been paying Walter, as best I could, to speak up against the wish to pull down my little house and build bigger, now that Evesham is growing so fast, and the rent would be more than I could afford, and besides, the place too big. He said all the rents would be rising for new occupiers. So you see, there was no choice.'

He was now looking at Bradecote, and so did not see the stunned look upon the faces of the Benedictines. Prior Richard blinked, then frowned.

'It is wrong to speak falsehoods, and how could you, when Father Abbot has spoken of your good repute? I do not know why you—'

'But all I say is true, Father Prior. I will swear it upon the bones of the blessed Saint Ecgwin, and may my hands lose their skill if I lie.' Aelred sounded desperate to be believed.

'How long had you been paying the steward to "protect" you from losing your home?' Bradecote did not doubt the man.

'Since Lady Day last year, my lord.' The tailor's shoulders sagged a little, as though the burden had been physical.

'And you never thought to come and ask here, yourself?' Abbot Reginald looked disappointed.

'No, my lord Abbot, for who would believe my word against that of your own trusted steward? That is what Walter said, and true it was.' Aelred responded swiftly, and with confidence that he spoke the truth.

Abbot Reginald put a long-fingered hand to his forehead and sighed.

'If the people of Evesham cannot bring petitions to us for fear of favour upon our appointees, we are in error.

My son, what cost has there been to you for making these garments, and the true cost, not what Walter offered?'

'In cloth, fur, braid and hours with my needle, a whole seven shillings and fourpence, my lord Abbot.' The tailor spoke the sum hesitantly, for it was more than two months' wages for most artisans.

'And Walter offered . . .?' Catchpoll wanted to know just how much the steward had wanted to pay.'

'Three shillings and sixpence.' Aelred hung his head. 'I paid three shillings a quarter to Walter, for his "help", but since Michaelmas trade has not been as good, and so I could not fulfil the sum.'

'The abbey will recompense you—' began Prior Richard, slowly.

'In full.' Abbot Reginald spared but a half glance at his deputy. 'You have been deceived, cheated and left wanting and in worry by one given power and credibility by this House. You should know, from me, that no plans have there been, at any time, for the taking down of existing properties, or casting out those who rent or lease from us. The new properties are on land owned by us but as yet unoccupied. If rumour has spread otherwise, then counter it with this truth, my son.'

'Thank you, oh thank you, my lord Abbot.' The tailor bowed several times, almost weeping with relief, and, after a brief, whispered conversation between abbot and prior, Prior Richard led him out to see to the provision of the silver pennies.

'I do not understand,' sighed Abbot Reginald. 'Our steward could have neither reason nor occasion to wear such opulent finery.'

Neither Catchpoll nor Walkelin knew what 'opulent finery' meant, but made a guess at 'rich man's clothes'.

'And if the steward demanded twelve shillings a year from Aelred the Tailor, and was also keepin' back some of the rent that were due as well, what did 'e plan to do with all that silver?' Catchpoll was trying to think of something and failing.

'And where was 'e keepin' it?' Walkelin did not think that in his own home would be wise, for wives tidied so much, especially a new wife, that Mærwynn would have been very likely to find it. He said as much.

'Yes, but we know that he controlled Mærwynn to such a degree she would not dare speak of it.' Bradecote had been wondering the same thing.

'Aye, but she would say now, now she is free of the man, so we should ask 'er.' Catchpoll was pragmatic.

'Unless she lies to keep it for 'erself. Might think as she deserves it, after what she put up with.' Walkelin saw a possible problem.

'And it still does not answer why.' Abbot Reginald, who felt slightly left behind following the way the shrieval trio's thought processes worked, sounded almost petulant.

'I think that, Father, is something we will discover only late in all this, but it will be found out. And best we set about asking a lot more questions, so we will leave you.' Bradecote nodded respectfully, and was followed by serjeant and underserjeant. Outside, he shut his eyes for a moment and sighed.

'This becomes more of a tangle, not less.'

'Sometimes that is the way of it, my lord, but we gets there in the end – usually.'

'And the greater the tangle, the more to work with,' volunteered Walkelin, who liked a lot of information.

'So we will begin with the one person on our list who at least is most unlikely to be our killer, the Widow Potter. Lead the way, Walkelin.'

The Widow Potter was a motherly-looking woman, with laughter lines about her eyes, and a face that exuded kindness and good humour. A strand of hair had escaped from under her coif, and was plastered to her forehead with clay slip, where she had tried to wipe it away from her eyes, and her apron was also adorned with smears and splashes. Two young men, whom she proudly named as her sons, were throwing pots upon wheels, and a younger lad was taking each completed beaker and putting it upon a tray, which would later go to the kiln.

The woman was respectful in her greeting but not overawed, and took the sheriff's men into the back of the premises, where the family lived in cramped conditions. However, it was clean and the widow said it was better they talk there, not least so that no clay could adhere to the lord Undersheriff's fine clothes.

'You went to the funeral this afternoon, mistress. Were you a friend of Walter the Steward?' Bradecote knew the question would not receive a positive answer, but was slightly taken aback when the woman laughed out loud and wreaked more havoc upon the cleanliness of her face by wiping her eyes as the tears flowed.

'Bless me, no, my lord, but then none there would say they was friends with the man, not if they is 'onest, and not even 'is brother, who will be a difficult man to deal with, now the stewardship lies with 'im. Pity 'tis that the position be inherited, since from what was said when I were young, their father was another such, and their oldfather also. Picked bad 'uns, did the abbot who chose the family, but there, nothing to be done about it now.'

'How was Walter bad, mistress?' Walkelin was playing the innocent.

'Could not keep that nose of 'is out of folks lives, day to day. Tried to tell me we could not fire our pots on any saints' days, and there be a lot of them in the year, unless we paid for exemption. We keeps the Holy Days and festivals, like everyone, but I asked our priest, and 'e said there were many more saints that the clergy celebrate with prayer during the usual Offices, saints we never even knows about. He laughed and said if we wanted rest from our labours on all of 'em we would never work more than three days together. So Walter the Steward was just tryin' to get even more money from us. I told Father Paulus all of it then, and 'e went and spoke with Father Prior, who said as Walter 'ad misunderstood. Misunderstood, ha! Knew what 'e were doin' all along.'

'So you did not pay.'

'Did not pay and told 'im why. Did not like that one bit, and blustered a lot.' The widow folded her arms at this point, and looked as she must have done at the steward.

'And why did you also not pay all your rent? It does not look as if your wares do not sell, for your sons are busy making many more.' Bradecote now tossed in the vital question.

'Not pay all?' The woman looked suddenly thrown off balance. 'But I always pays in full and on time, my lord. It will show in the abbey rolls.'

'Those show you have been lacking each Quarter for the last six, and by three shillings each time.'

The slight flush of anger fled from her cheeks, and she paled, her breath coming fast as if she had been running. She shook her head, and murmured 'Not so, not so'. Fearing she might collapse in a faint upon the floor, Walkelin pulled a stool towards her, and pressed her to sit upon it. She leant forward, her head drooping. Bradecote looked at Catchpoll, who looked at Walkelin. Her reaction was no act, and it was clear that she believed what she had said. It looked very much as though Walter the Steward had been extorting money from the abbey's tenants in varied ways, as well as cheating his employer directly.

'Mistress, silver is due to the abbey, but not from you. We have no cause to think you did not pay all that was required.' Bradecote spoke firmly but gently. 'However, we would ask you not to speak of this to others, not yet, until we find the extent of wrong-doing, and also take whoever killed Walter the Steward.' If all Evesham did not just dislike the man, but knew he had been a criminal as well, their chances of finding the killer were very small.

She nodded, took a deep breath and looked up at him. 'No crime is it to be glad the man be gone, though.'

'No, but the Law still needs the killer, for when a man has killed once, it is easier a second time, and Evesham is better without such men.' He thought that made it good sense without giving rise to panic.

'I can see that, my lord. I will not let out a word of it, not yet. And the abbey will not demand the money of me?'

'No, mistress.' Bradecote wondered how much silver the abbey coffers must forego in 'unpaid rent' that had been handed over but never reached them. The three men left Widow Potter to recover her composure, and moved on to find Grim the Thatcher, who was not at his home, but upon the roof of a house on the road down to the bridge. He had no good word to say about Walter the Steward but made no direct complaint about him. He was, however, as shocked as the Widow Potter to find that he was in arrears with the abbey. His first thought was that some clerk had made a simple error on the chequer cloth, but when it was explained that it was for several Quarters his face darkened, and he cursed the dead man.

What became clear, as Bradecote and his men worked through the list, was that whilst some men disclosed that they had been forced to pay more, for what now showed as spurious reasons, none knew that they were in default of their dues to the abbey. It did reduce the list of potential suspects.

'We can set aside the thatcher, the miller, the rope maker, the dyer and the Widow Potter. They may hope Walter the Steward burns in the eternal fires of Hell, but until now they had no reason to kill him.' Bradecote was thankful for small mercies.

'Aelred the Tailor thought that was where 'e was headin'', or wished it fervently, from what I heard 'im say at the funeral,' commented Walkelin. 'Though Aelred does not look a man as could drag the dead weight of the steward from where 'e fell to the well pit.'

'Looks can be deceptive, and a man fired up out of the ordinary could still do it.' Catchpoll had come across feats of strength, in both assailants and victims, that almost defied belief.

'Agreed, Catchpoll, though I would not put Aelred the Tailor high on our list. Will Horsweard, crippled as he is, is even less likely to the killer, but we will visit him, just to see if he was being pressured, before going to see Hubert the Mason, the fuller and lastly the neighbourly Oswald Mealtere and Wulfram Meduwyrhta. From what his son told us, we can be fairly sure the mason was paying the steward, though whether to advance his cause or not hinder it, we will find out. It will be interesting to see the mead maker's face when he finds out that not only was he forced to give Walter the Steward his daughter, but the man was keeping back part of his dues as well.'

'My lord, I knows we is tellin' folk not to speak of what we tells 'em, but I gives us no more than two days afore all Evesham knows, from babes at the breast to them on their deathbed.'

'I know it, Catchpoll. Time is not on our side, so let us get a move on.'

Will Horsweard looked about as happy to see the sheriff's men again as have a tooth drawn, but then his yard was busy, and there was a horse sidling about and giving the groom all manner of problems, just as he was trying to agree a price for its sale with a tall, lordly-looking man with a profile that showed a firm chin, and near black hair that curled up around the lobe of his ear as if cupping it. Catchpoll could sense Bradecote stiffen, and it was not at the sight of the horse dealer.

'My lord Undersheriff,' Horsweard made an awkward obeisance.

The lordly man, who could only have seen their

approach from the edge of his vision, turned with a strange mixture of smile and snarl.

'Ah, the lord Bradecote. Things have changed since we met last.' The man looked him up and down, rather as he had the horse, but with less enthusiasm. 'The benefit of a dead man's boots, eh? Not that Fulk de Crespignac was much of a man, not really. Trotting around looking important suited him, as it does you.'

Serjeant Catchpoll, whose grasp of 'Foreign' was not perfect, but certainly sufficient, had not regarded the previous lord Undersheriff in the same light as he did the current holder of the title, but insulting him insulted the role, and Catchpoll was very protective about the status of a sheriff's officer. His eyes narrowed.

'I enjoy riding, de Cormolain,' Bradecote did not rise to the bait, 'and the work exercises the mind as well as the body. '

'And does it make you feel more important, Bradecote?' The snarl became a sneer.

'Bein' Undersheriff *is* important,' growled Catchpoll, who looked like a dog who would dearly love to be let off the leash and rip the other man's throat out.

'It is to you, Catchpoll.' The lord, dropping into English, knew exactly who Serjeant Catchpoll was, but then so did every man who had fulfilled his service in Worcester Castle in the last twenty years.

'It is Serjeant Catchpoll.'

'And it is "my lord".' Having felt that he had put Catchpoll in his place, the man turned his attention back to Bradecote and reverted to Norman-French. 'If you spend too much time with this old fox, you will stink like a fox also, and what would your pretty wife think to that? I admit she was a nice prize for grovelling around with corpses, if you ignore who bedded her before you, but me, I think I prefer fresher fare, and to be my own man, not our lord Sheriff's lawhound.' He wanted to goad, and by insulting Christina, he found the chink in Bradecote's armour. A muscle moved in the undersheriff's cheek, and his hand moved involuntarily towards his dagger, but was halted by force of will.

'I had forgotten your tongue was far sharper than your sword, de Cormolain, but then I had forgotten you entirely, unimportant as you are. I am upon the lord Sheriff's business, and cannot afford the time to waste upon you, though know that I would take great satisfaction in cutting that sharp tongue of yours from your foul mouth.' Hugh Bradecote spoke slowly and deliberately, controlling his anger, just. It meant it was easier for Catchpoll to understand, and the serjeant was surprised by the degree of hatred in his superior's voice. The lord Bradecote was, though sometimes tetchy, not a man in whom hate was a prominent emotion.

'Master Horsweard, you may finish haggling over the horse later. First you speak with me, inside.' Bradecote returned to English, before de Cormolain could open his mouth.

The horse dealer had very little understanding of what was going on, other than the two important men within feet of him clearly loathed each other and might resort to violence at any moment. It drove mere dislike of having to speak with the lord Undersheriff and even worse, the lord Sheriff's Serjeant, from his head.

'Yes, my lord. Come this way.' He looked at de Cormolain. 'I am sorry my lord . . . the lord Undersheriff – important – please inspect the horse more.' He spread his hand to invite the sheriff's men into the cooler darkness of his house, and hobbled in after them.

'We wants to know if Walter the Steward got you to pay more 'n your set dues to the abbey.' Catchpoll felt they had wasted valuable time and did not beat about the bush.

'No, that he did not, but he wanted me to supply him with a good, but placid, horse come Michaelmas, and at half its value.'

'And why might you agree to that, Master Horsweard?' Bradecote focused on the matter in hand, forcing de Cormolain from his thoughts, though he was seething.

Will Horsweard said nothing.

'We have not time for this. Serjeant, ask him another way.' It was rare for Bradecote to even suggest violence when interviewing men.

'With pleasure, my lord.' Catchpoll smiled, very slowly and let the fear suffuse the horse trader's face.

'I-I bought two mules from a man who passed through Evesham early in the spring, very cheap. Turned out they were not his to sell. I sold them to the abbey, at a good price, and Walter the Steward learnt about the man, who was found guilty of horse-stealing and hanged in Moreton in Marsh, where he stole them. Recognised the animals from the description, he did, and said if I did not provide his horse as cheap as I bought the stolen mules, he would tell the lord Abbot, and all this,' Will Horsweard waved his arms about him, 'would be taken from me, and I would be sent before the Justices in Worcester. I did not know they were stolen when I bought them.'

'Just made a good guess, so offered a low price,' snorted Catchpoll.

'I did not kn—'

'Did the steward say why he wanted the horse? He used a beast from the abbey stables when he went upon abbey business, no doubt.' Bradecote saw no point in taking up the horse trader.

'I have no idea, my lord. He just said it had to be a quiet animal but look good. "A lord's horse"' he said. 'I agreed. I had no choice.'

'Very well. That is all for the present. Oh, and do not sell the horse cheaply to the Lord de Cormolain. He can afford a good price.' With which Bradecote turned on his heel and left, passing de Cormolain without a glance, and followed by Catchpoll and a very confused Walkelin.

It was fortunate that Hubert the Mason was working some way from where Will Horsweard lived, since it gave time for both Bradecote and Catchpoll's tempers to improve. Walkelin, wisely, said nothing, and judged both by their body language. When the lord Bradecote's stride shortened to its normal long length, and Serjeant Catchpoll lost his 'death grim' face, he relaxed.

Hubert the Mason was already preparing stone where the new well was going to be dug. He looked very wary at their approach, and was patently relieved when informed that his son was in no way suspected of the steward's murder.

'Good lad, our Simon,' the mason murmured, gruffly. 'Young 'uns gets a bit foolish, but – you mean what you say?'

'Would not say it else, Master Mason. Your lad favours 'is left, and the blow that killed Walter the Steward came from a right-handed man.' Catchpoll thought the explanation simple, but Hubert the Mason looked at him in awe.

'You can tell that?'

'Aye.' Catchpoll did not elaborate, since it helped if the man thought them clever. If he sat down and thought about it, he would see it was obvious, but then, most folk did not think about such things.

'And now we want to know why a man whose craft is in demand, should be behind in the paying of his rent to the abbey.' Bradecote sounded curious but not threatening.

'Why ask—you mean *me*?' The mason actually dropped his chisel. 'Must be a mistake, for I pays every penny owed, and on time.'

'Not for the last year.' Walkelin sounded as though the mason had disappointed him.

'I paid, I tell you, and—' Hubert stopped suddenly, realising his next words would sow a reason to want the steward dead.

'And you were payin' Walter the Steward more than just the rent.' Catchpoll played 'omniscient' again, and the mason's eyes boggled.

'You could not know.'

'Oh, we could.' The death's-head smile spread across Catchpoll's face.

'None knew. I did not even tell my son the whole of it.' The words emerged as a hoarse whisper.

'So tell us, Master Mason.' Walkelin's tone was inviting the man to unburden himself, not confess.

'The lord Abbot 'as been buildin' ever since 'e became abbot, back, let me think, yes, fifteen year ago, but the big buildings needs men used to churches and cloisters and all the decorated work too. Not for the likes of a man like me, with just my son alongside me. But there be work comin' that is in my line. A parlour for the holy brothers is planned, just a decent, plain chamber where they might meet with relatives come to speak with them, and such. The masons working in the abbey are more than busy enough, and it will not be part of the cloisters. I am the best mason in Evesham, and that is not a boast but a fact. The work should come to me. Walter the Steward said it would not unless I paid 'im, on the quiet, not to suggest otherwise. I paid, but, mark you, I did not kill the man. I swears that.'

'Very well. That is all for now, Master Mason.' Bradecote needed no more. They left him and went southward and then west along the lane towards the ferry once more, to Martin Fuller's premises, a good distance from other habitation. Bradecote turned up his nose as the smell hit him. Thankfully, Martin Fuller was one of the group who had not been coerced or blackmailed into giving the steward money, and was merely outraged that what had passed to Walter in rent had not all reached the abbey coffers.

'The bastard! The lyin' bastard! And kin too, since my wife's mother was sister to his! May he rot in Hell!'

'That seems to be the wish of everyone in Evesham we has spoken to this afternoon,' remarked Catchpoll. 'Thing is, we needs to find out who sent 'im on his way there, afore this became known.'

Walkelin had a thought, but decided this was not the time to voice it.

Bradecote, eager to leave the stench of the fuller's, decided they need not question further.

Only Oswald Mealtere and Wulfram Meduwyrhta remained, and having spoken once with them, they already knew that the steward had pressured the mead maker to give him his daughter to wife, using the same kind of threats as he had to others. It would, however, be useful to know if the maltster had suffered other than being left in debt to the abbey.

As they made their way back to where the track led down to the two feuding neighbours, Walkelin spoke up at last.

'I understands the townsfolk we speaks to about the steward demandin' extra silver all lookin' surprised and angry, but—' Walkelin paused for a moment, marshalling his thoughts into sentences.

'But what?' Bradecote demanded, tersely. He could feel the beginnings of one of his bad headaches, brought on by the heat, and that, on top of the stench lingering in his nose and the meeting with de Cormolain, shortened his temper.

'But would not that be a perfect reason for a man to fly at the steward's throat, there in the near dark by the well hole, my lord? It was said that Walter would not meet at another man's callin', so it must 'ave been the steward as demanded the two meet, and we is now but the day afore Quarter Day. Walter says he wants more, or another favour added on, and the man says no. That is when Walter says that the man is behind with the rent and 'e will see him thrown out of home and workshop if 'e does not submit. That makes the man snap, and start the fight. We sort of knows the rest.'

'Now that, Young Walkelin, makes very good sense.' Catchpoll nodded approvingly.

'It does?' Walkelin trusted himself but was astounded to receive such praise from Serjeant Catchpoll.

'Yes, it does, Walkelin.' Bradecote knew he had been too sharp with the underserjeant and added his commendation. 'It gives a good answer to the question you like to pose of "Why now?"'

'And it means 'tis very likely that someone is not as shocked as they sound, so we needs more afore we discounts folk completely. Oh well, idleness leads to sin, so we is headin' for sainthood at this rate.' Catchpoll gave a slow smile.

Bradecote managed half a smile and shook his head, which he then regretted doing.

Chapter Eight

As they crossed the bridge over the watercourse, they saw Oswald Mealtere walking homewards, and Catchpoll hailed him. He halted and turned.

'Yes, what now?' He sounded tetchy, and not at all respectful, which made Catchpoll growl, and remind him whom he was addressing.

'We want to know why you are in debt to the abbey, not having paid your rent in full over several Quarters.'

'I pay all, every time – my lord.' The man looked affronted. 'There 'as been better Quarters and worse 'uns, but I can always pay, and never a day late. Whoever tells otherwise spreads a falsehood, and I would confront the man, face to face.' He looked belligerent.

'It is the abbey's own Quarter Rolls that say so, and they do not lie.' Bradecote wondered if the maltster was on bad terms with not just Wulfram Meduwyrhta, and was by nature confrontational.

'I do not see how that could be, my lord. The monks is honest and godly, but must 'ave got muddled with all that scribblin'. I reckon as it is bad for the eyes.'

'Their records show you have paid less than you owe for over a year. A chance error could not be repeated four times.' Bradecote wondered how long it would take the maltster to reach the correct conclusion.

'Well, there is Osmund Rushman who makes baskets and sells floor rushes and loses much of 'is takin's at dice. It will be the two names next to each other and the numbers the wrong way around. Yes, that must be it.'

'Except we now know that Walter the Steward kept back money from quite a few of the abbey tenants in Evesham.' Bradecote, with the beginnings of a headache, decided he could not wait for the maltster to hit upon the answer.

'He what? But that would be stealin' from the lord Abbot as much as me. And from others too, you say?' Oswald shook his head, as if the thought needed to be cast from it.

'It was, and he did. You had no idea?'

'No, my lord, I did not. The grasp-fingered ba—! Of all the—!' Oswald's words were choked in his anger and his fists clenched. 'If I had I would . . .' – he now paused for a moment before completing the sentence, but it was not that he was lost for words – 'I would 'ave gone to Father Richard at the abbey and made complaint, good and loud.'

'Rather than strike 'im with a stone and cast the body in a well pit?' Catchpoll offered up the alternative.

'Cannot say as I feels sorry the bastard ended that way, but do not look at me for the man as did it. Peaceful in my bed I lay, and if others was cheated then there will be plenty for you to ask, my lord.' Oswald, very obviously ignoring Catchpoll, almost made it a challenge.

'We have asked.' Bradecote gave a small smile, which he hoped might dent the man's self-confidence. Only a momentary flicker in the maltster's eyes showed it had been effective.

'Then all I can say, my lord, is sometimes a question needs askin' more 'n once.'

'Oh, I quite agree, Master Maltster, I quite agree.' Bradecote tried to be reasonable. That this man was annoying him more was in part down to the headache, for sure. 'We will keep asking the questions until honest answers lead us to the truth.'

'I would swear a good oath I knew not about Walter the Steward and 'is cheatin' so many of the abbey's tenants in Evesham, not until you told me, my lord.'

'And would you swear as good an oath that you saw Wulfram Meduwyrhta coming down this track as dark fell the night Walter the Steward was killed?'

There was a heartbeat's pause before the maltster nodded, slowly, and only then did he confirm by speech. He looked the undersheriff in the eye as he did so, but it was a struggle. Bradecote dismissed him, and the trio stood and watched as he continued along the track to his home, well aware of their gaze upon his back.

'So, while it does not mean the mead maker is necessarily innocent, we can dismiss his definitely being up near Merstow green when Walter the Steward was killed.' Bradecote sighed.

'At least you got Oswald to show that he lied to us on that, my lord.' Walkelin was impressed at the way his superior had pounced with the question.

'Yes, but we are back to having many suspects with equal motive for murder.'

'Until we works out which of 'em is lyin' about not knowin' what Walter was up to, my lord.' Catchpoll was rather more patient than the undersheriff.

'And do you believe Oswald the Maltster, Catchpoll?'

'Hmm. Thing is, my lord, I just does not "feel" his honesty, though no reason could I give other than the man will end as bitter and miserable as 'is bent and bitter father.'

'My lord, the motive is not equal for all.' Walkelin did not quite say the lord Undersheriff was wrong.

'Because?' Bradecote did not treat the comment as presumptuous.

'Them as Walter only cheated by keepin' back some of their rents would not 'ave so great a reason to want 'im dead as them with more than one reason. Some was cheated and he also made them pay for a good word put in, or a bad one left out. And since Simon the mason's son saw how Mærwynn shrivelled to a shadow of the girl she were afore bein' wed, you would think the father would 'ave seen the same thing and been even more outraged. Add that to bein' forced to give 'er to Walter, and 'tis two reasons. If Wulfram discovered the rent thefts, then, of all in Evesham, he would be the man with three reasons to kill Walter the Steward.' Walkelin put the theory forward confidently, though there was a reluctance in his voice, which Bradecote noted.

'So why do you sound less than convinced by your own sound argument, Walkelin?'

'My lord, I-I think 'tis foolishness only, and a bit like Serjeant Catchpoll's not quite believin' Oswald.' Walkelin realised this might sound as if Catchpoll's gut feeling was foolish, and coloured, rushing his explanation. 'Not that Serjeant Catchpoll thinks foolish, but with me it comes down to the mead maker's home felt contented, and the man also, until we mentioned Mærwynn, and the reason for the marriage 'ad to be revealed before his wife.'

'So you are developing "serjeant's instincts" too, Walkelin.' Bradecote managed a thin smile.

'Proves I picked the right apprentice, since there's some

as never gets 'em, and no use would such be as serjeants.' Catchpoll was approving. 'Mind you, the problem with the "one, two or three reasons" lies in some men losin' their temper to killin' rage over the one, and long-sufferin' folk not liftin' a finger at three. 'Tis less likely, but possible, and we has to keep it in mind.'

'And we learn nothing while standing here. Come on, let us find out if Wulfram Meduwyrhta has two reasons or three.' Bradecote could feel the pounding behind his eyeballs getting worse, but they needed to have spoken with all the cheated rent payers by the end of the day.

The mead maker was not in home or workplace, but his wife directed them some way beyond the buildings, saying he was in the little channel that provided his fresh water for the mead making. The shrieval trio only saw him from behind as he rose to stand knee deep in it. They wondered what he was doing, until he turned at the sound of their approach, and they also saw his small daughter, wearing only her shift, waist deep, in front of him. He coloured, embarrassed at being found soaking wet and 'idle'. He pushed his hands through his wet hair to draw it from his brow, and then wiped the remaining droplets from his face.

'The wife wanted Win out from under 'er skirts, and 'tis terrible hot, so I opened the sluice and brought 'er to cool in the water.'

'And it cools you also.' Walkelin looked slightly envious, but the idea that the lord Sheriff's Underserjeant would ask official questions while paddling was unthinkable.

'That it does, indeed. Now, what need 'ave you of me, my lord Undersheriff?' The question was asked respectfully, and

Wulfram appeared curious rather than concerned.

'We wish to know why you have not paid all your due rent to Evesham Abbey for over a year.'

'But I pays each Quarter, on the day and the full sum, my lord.' A frown drew his brows together.

'And you paid it into the hand of Walter the Steward?'

'Yes, my lord, as has always been the way.'

'Then it seems you join others in Evesham, Master Meduwyrhta, who paid the full sum, but whose dues were only part paid into the abbey coffers.'

'You mean Walter kept back silver for hisself?' Wulfram was clearly quicker of thought than his neighbour. 'What reason could the man 'ave for that? If not the richest, quite, then for sure 'e were the most important man in Evesham, and knew it. Not countin' the lord Abbot, that is.' He shook his head. 'To cheat your wife's own father, even though we scarce spoke, seems to make it worse, and—' another thought hit him, 'he cheated the lord Abbot and all the godly brethren. Now that must surely mean his chance of Heaven be gone.'

'You had no idea of this before?' Bradecote thought it unlikely, unless the man was an extremely accomplished liar.

'Me? No, my lord. But then, I suppose all of us he cheated are now calling down curses upon Walter's soul, if you can curse a soul.'

'And you would call 'em the most, by rights.' Catchpoll had been watching Wulfram closely. The mead maker looked questioningly at him. 'Bein' as Walter forced you to give your daughter in marriage, with threats.'

'Tempted, I would be, though no doubt our priest would tell me to do so would harm my own soul for lack of charity.

Not sure anyone was ever in charity with Walter the Steward, 'cept the mother as bore 'im. Other than the monks, of course, but they is not like ordinary folk. Brother Petrus, the bee brother, says "Bless you" to every bee sting, and says as he prays for the hives every night. Now, I likes honey, but I would not bless the bee that stung me. Would you?'

Whether by design or just the way his thinking worked, Wulfram had drawn the conversation very much away from Walter and murder.

'You must not make bees angry,' announced little Win, whom everyone had forgotten, and who had found the grown-up talk boring until she heard about the bees. She knew Brother Petrus, and would sometimes watch him, from a safe distance, as he tended his bees.

'That's it, sweetin'.' Wulfram ruffled her damp hair. She shivered, for although the water had cooled wonderfully, simply standing in it had chilled her feet and legs. 'Now, we had best dry off in the sun afore you catches chill and Mother shouts at me, yes?' He smiled at the girl, who nodded vigorously. He put his hands about her waist and lifted her out, and told her to lie in the sun to dry. It was as if he had forgotten the law officers' presence, but as he made to step out, Walkelin offered a hand and smile, and he blinked, surprised, but took the hand in a strong grasp. As he stood on the grass, aware that he looked slightly ridiculous bare below the knee, and damp about the hem of his cotte, he went to tighten his belt under his belly, since he had loosened it when bending to play with the little girl in the water. The metal strap end, which Walkelin had noticed the day before, fell from the leather and dropped into the grass.

'Blessed thing 'as done that twice.' Wulfram shook his

head, and a few more droplets were flung from his hair. He bent and rummaged among the grass stalks to retrieve it.

'Not a good fit,' commented Walkelin.

'No, but then I fixed it on myself after I lost the one as were made for it.' The mead maker was not reluctant to reveal the loss.

'Well, if it fell off, the original could not 'ave been much good either.' Walkelin grinned.

'Ha! True enough, and I cannot think how it came to come away. I lost it early last week, and though I looked long and 'ard, it cannot be found. I ought to go and get a new one put on proper, but I 'as been that busy.'

'You may be in luck, Master Meduwyrhta, for I found a strap end just yesterday. I left it in the lord Undersheriff's chamber. A copper one, with the pattern of a leaf on it.' Walkelin was still sounding the helpful bystander, not the eagle-eyed underserjeant, but was actually watching the mead maker intently, There was a fraction of a moment when suspicion and then fear showed on the man's face.

'Alas, not mine, then. Mine bears three crosses.'

'But—' The little girl frowned, and would have said more, but her father pointed a forefinger at her, twirling it about and making a buzzing sound, then leant down to 'threaten' with the 'bee'. Distracted, she laughed. He looked up at Bradecote.

''Er . . . is there anythin' else you needs to know, my lord?'

'No, I think not. Thank you.' Bradecote was aware of disappointment that the man had lied to them, and was now much more of interest in the death of Walter the Steward, and at the same time was conscious that they intruded upon innocent domesticity. Catchpoll would say they could intrude on anything at need, but since there was, alas, no absolute proof that the strap end had been lost during the scuffle that ended in the steward's death, Bradecote, his head aching even more in the boring sunlight, felt that there was no point in probing deeper to get the same lie over and over.

They left father and daughter, crossed the narrow channel by a plank, which was obviously left to enable Wulfram to meet the beekeeper in the orchards, and walked back to the abbey with the slight shade afforded by the fruit trees until they reached the wicket gate set into the abbey wall, and passed into the enclave.

'So what does we do now, my lord?' Walkelin was eager to take the next step, but then remembered it might well be going down into Bengeworth and visiting the castle.

'I know what I wish to do,' Bradecote rubbed the bridge of his nose, grimacing, 'and that is seek out the abbey infirmarer and take whatever brew he thinks best to take the hammers from behind my eyeballs. I would go to Bengeworth fresh, rested and alert, and at present I am none of those things, so that is for the morrow. We seem to have made no clear progress, but it must be unlikely, short of an improbable Bengeworth connection, that the killer of Walter the Steward is not someone we have now met. I just wish one stood out.'

'The well delver keeps diggin' 'til 'e strikes water, my lord, and we keeps diggin' 'til the truth appears, much the same way.' Catchpoll was unperturbed. 'I would say we is but part way down as yet, so no need to fret about it. Better you gets a draught from the infirmarer, as you says, and lies quiet until the dinner hour.'

'And what will you do. Catchpoll?'

'Why, think with my eyes shut, my lord. A good way to

think, is that.' Catchpoll's response was instant.

'And since I does not want to disturb your thinkin', Serjeant, I will see what I can find out from the masons workin' on the church and cloister. You would think they would know a bit about Hubert, and have a view on Walter the Steward, which should tally with everyone else's.' Walkelin was hot and sweaty, but not tired, and he craved snippets of information to file away. The more they knew, the quicker they would find answers. Thus, the trio parted, with one still actively hunting.

The masons were a brotherhood unto themselves and did not tend to mix with the abbey servants or the Benedictine brothers. They had workshops in what would eventually be the calm space of the cloister garth and living quarters that were against the new enclave wall. Their work was far from silent, as mallet met chisel and chisel met stone with a sharp bite, but they were not given to chatter, not least because of the stone dust that resulted from their labours. When it came to hoisting the worked stone up the scaffolding to where it would be laid, there was the occasional warning shout or whistle to attract attention, but much 'conversation' was by means of clear signal by hand. The monks could not but be very aware of them, but could not claim they caused undue disruption.

A fair few were at height, even in the searing heat, and with the sun beating upon their backs and reflecting off the pale stone, back into their faces. Walkelin had no intention of climbing, and rightly assumed that the senior master mason would be directing from where it was marginally cooler, and where he would be easily found if any had questions.

There was a small area shaded by an oilcloth awning, and with a table set squarely beneath it, over which two men were talking and pointing at positions upon a vellum plan. It was the shorter man who seemed in command of the conversation, while the taller, though of similar age, mostly nodded, and perhaps sought clarification. Walkelin knew that, as the lord Sheriff's Underserjeant, he had the right to interrupt the meeting, but in doing so he would make himself like a bothersome fly, something to be swatted away. He chose instead to be patient and stood back in the entrance of the Chapter House, shaded from the glare and the worst of the heat, and observed, so still that an apprentice, coming past with a flagon to ease parched throats among his superiors, jumped as Walkelin swatted a wasp from buzzing about his head. The lad, spilling a little of the liquid, gave him a slightly reproachful look, and Walkelin raised a hand in apology.

'What is the name of the mason in charge?' Walkelin nodded towards the men beneath the awning.

'Master Bernard of Keynsham, master.' The apprentice, who looked no more than about fourteen, and was yet to fill out into youthful manhood, sensed rather than saw authority.

'Thank you.'

The lad stood for a moment, until Walkelin realised he was actually waiting for permission to move on and nodded dismissal. Walkelin was suddenly reminded of the first time he had been called 'master', also in Evesham, nearly a year before. It still felt odd, but at least he no longer showed surprise at it. Not showing surprise at things had been one of Serjeant Catchpoll's important 'serjeanting' lessons, though he did admit there were rare occasions when he was genuinely taken aback, and more where feigning surprise was part of the act to encourage a flow of information.

'One of the most important parts of bein' a serjeant is "bein' a serjeant".' It had been a statement that had needed explanation. 'Folk needs to look at you and see you fits what they expects a serjeant to be, and a bit more. So a serjeant never looks panicked, always looks as though they already know much of what will be revealed to 'em, unless playing the game of bein' "just a curious soul", and, though it takes time and practice, a serjeant needs to make folk see that crossin' him would be only just less terrible than Judgement Day.' It was the last part that Walkelin was still finding difficult, though he was getting better as his self-confidence as the lord Sheriff's Underserjeant grew.

The masons' meeting was ending, since the vellum was being rolled up. Walkelin emerged from his 'invisible' mode, and went, with unhurried tread, to the awning. The taller man had moved away and the other was tying a leather thong about the vellum roll. He had a lightly freckled complexion and fine hair that might have originally been somewhere between reddish and buttery gold but was now sun and time-bleached to a soft buttermilk colour. It had a wave which made it curl around his ears but had already receded from his brow and would be very like a monk's tonsure within a year or so. Walkelin thought him perhaps a few years shy of two score years and ten.

'Master Bernard of Keynsham?' It was only just a question.

'Aye.' The man looked at Walkelin, assessing him as he might a stone for dressing.

'I was wonderin' if you could tell me the way Walter the Steward, as is dead, treated you and your workforce. Did he like to tell you your craft as 'e did with others in Evesham?'

'I could, but I would ask first who you be, and why you seeks to know?' It was a reasonable question, and Walkelin smiled, and gave his name and position.

'Well, Underserjeant, I can tell you this. "Master Walter", and that was the name 'e called hisself, though to my mind a master be one as has mastered a craft, not set 'is own worth as high, tried to do as you say, off and on, but I told 'im to 'is face I would not stand for it. What did the man know of The Craft? Nothin' at all.' The master mason clearly felt that there was only one true craft, and others were lesser skills. 'I warned the men as well, not to obey just 'acos the abbey steward told 'em to do this or that, and always ask me first. After that we got not instructions but complaints, always small, always little things to annoy. Like bein' bitten by a flea, it were.' Master Bernard frowned. 'That was afore 'e began chastisin' the apprentices, whether it were for runnin' too fast, or walkin' too slow, carp, carp, carp 'e did, and threaten where 'e possessed no right.'

'Did you not go to the lord Abbot, or Father Prior, bein' yourself a man of importance?' Walkelin wondered.

'Thought of it, but here be a thing. For all that Master Walter were a man puffed up proud and with a nasty streak in 'im, the lord Abbot and the senior officeholders in this abbey thought 'im some wonder. You would think the sun shone from out his arse, truly you would. So I did not go to the monks, but gathered all the lads and made sure they knew the only voice they need heed be mine. And afore you asks, no, I did not kill 'im.'

'I did not ask, Master Bernard, but would ask if you knows the local masons, the ones not set up to build great churches and fine carvings?'

'Met with them once or twice. Courtesy brought them to see me, and courteous I were to them, as brothers of the stone. There's Osgod of Bengeworth, just across the river, and Hubert of the town itself. Good stone dressers both, but neither carvers, nor, as you say, able to take on a big task like this.'

'True. Hubert the Mason only has his son Simon to aid 'im, and still learnin'.'

'A son to follow on. Good is that, and one thing I lack, as Heaven 'as willed.' The master mason permitted himself a small sigh. 'So my "sons" are walls and corbels and sturdy columns, crafted to the glory of God.'

'And some men 'ave worse legacies in blood and bone, Master Bernard.'

'That they does, Underserjeant, that they does. Last time I spoke with Hubert he complained about the steward tryin' to count the stones bein' dressed for the well, and sayin' the abbey would pay by the number used. Good job 'e never tried that with me. Now, I should be aloft, checkin' the carpenter 'as set the form just right for the next arch. Be there anythin' more you needs to ask of me?' It was not said aggressively.

'No, and I thank you for your time.' Walkelin thought the courtesy worked both ways. He returned to the guest hall, aware that he had reinforced what they knew of the victim, but with nothing that would advance their investigation, and when he reported to his superiors after they had eaten, it was without providing anything revelatory.

* * *

Old Cuthbert sat alone with his ale, but then he usually did. Mostly he listened to the laughing, the friendly teasing and the ale-fuelled ranting, but it was also the place where he could rant, even if few listened. It was better than staying at home and ranting at the cat, which simply stared at him in a very superior way, then curled up on his lap and went to sleep. The talk on all lips was the murder of Walter the Steward, and the two themes that were common were how little the man was liked, and how the fact that he ended up at the bottom of a pit was, in a way none could prove, an indication that his soul was unlikely to reach Heaven without an exceedingly long time in Purgatory, if he got there at all. Instances were told of his pride, his intentional unpleasantness, even rumours that he had got rid of his first wife by starving her so she was too weak to fight off a cold, though a voice of reason said she began coughing in the autumn and did not die until after Candlemas, and no 'cold' lasted for five months. The voice of reason belonged to Hubert the Mason, who was still on his first beaker.

A man who was a stranger, but both loud and generous with his offer to buy everyone else ale, was questioning how it was that the lord Abbot had kept such a man as steward, and how divorced he must be from thinking about the people of Evesham who kept his abbey rich. Whilst some tried to explain the post was inherited, it was agreed that part of the problem lay in it being given to a kinsman by Abbot Walter, who was Foreign, and several anecdotes were told of the pride of the stewards since then, but as the ale flowed, murmurs did begin that the lord Abbot, godly though he obviously was, cared little for the folk of Evesham. Someone murmured as how Abbot Reginald was of lordly birth and with important kin, and would have no understanding of how ordinary souls laboured all their lives to keep their families fed and with a roof above their heads.

'And now 'e proves it with that great wall to keep you all out.' The stranger got up, staggering a little and spilling ale onto the table. 'The lord Abbot lives secure, in peace and comfort, while the good men of Evesham are bein' struck down in the street by unknown killers out for their blood. Who will be next?'

Ale-muddled heads did not ask how Walter the Steward suddenly counted as a 'good man'. Old Cuthbert, who was not as muddled as he would like to have been, waved his arm about, and his voice broke through the mumbles of agreement.

'Foolishness! 'Twere but one man as did the killin', and who else in Evesham invited such ill will as Walter the Steward? None! We is all glad enough 'e lies in the earth.'

'And 'ow does you know it were but one man, "Stinker"?' The appellation was habitual rather than an insult, having been coined long ago and, like the smell about his person, clung to him.

''Cos I saw, that's 'ow, as I let the cat in to keep the mice from my bed.'

'You should tell the lord Sheriff's men, Cuthbert,' came another voice, and Cuthbert's face contorted. 'Justice should be done.'

'Me? Help the Law? I knows what Justice does.' He raised his right hand, contracted forever into a fist. 'That be "Justice", robbin' a man of 'is trade, reducin' 'im to workin' with 'is feet. I spits on Justice.' He spat onto the earth floor.

'The lord Abbot might give a reward, though?'

'Hmm.' The response was non-committal. 'Might get more sense from the cat.' Cuthbert got up, pushing his empty beaker away with his left hand, and, with hunched shoulders, departed, muttering.

'So what tale lies beneath?' asked the stranger, curious.

''Tis two score years old or more. Old Cuthbert, though 'e were none so old then o'course, were a coppersmith, with plenty of custom and a comely wife.' The narrator was Oswald Mealtere. 'Then the wife were found strangled, down by the ferry. I think she 'ad kin the other side, but rumour had it not just kin, but a lover, and Cuthbert found out. Not a friendly sort, Cuthbert, and not enough oathswearers could be found, so 'e went before the Justices, and to trial by the hot iron. Found innocent, by the will of God, else 'e would not be alive now, but the right 'and, as needed for workin', well, holdin' the red-hot bar tightened it up into a fist as you see, and no more smithin' could Cuthbert do. Reduced to bein' a walker for Martin Fuller, since all a walker needs is two good feet and a strong nose. Would you want to earn your bread from stampin' up and down in a trough of stale piss all day? No wonder the man is bitter and twisted.'

Heads nodded as the drinkers imagined the agony of the glowing iron in their own palms, but then the conversation returned to a possible reward and whether it would be a blessing, which had its value, or silver, which would be far better. The drinkers agreed it would definitely be a blessing, and perhaps a prayer for the soul of a dead family member, since the monks were good at drawing money in, but not known for spending it on anything other than the abbey fabric, but not everyone remained to hear the decision.

Chapter Nine

Martin Fuller was making his early morning tour of his works. He liked the workplace tidy, even if some might see the tenter frames of drying cloth, wherever there was space that faced the summer noonday sun, as higgledy-piggledy. There was nothing he could do about the smells, but then, he could not smell them. Born and raised a fuller, his nose had ignored them from the time he could run about and get under people's feet. His workers would be arriving to be told the tasks of the day, though he knew old Cuthbert would already be at the stocks, preparing his day's treading, for treading was the only thing he could do with facility enough to make it more than charity to employ him. Martin had been in discussions with the abbey about making changes, and the Benedictines investing in a watermill to power the pounding of the cloth. It was the way forward, but would mean an end to employing Cuthbert. Mind you, by the time it was built, and he thought it was now more likely, Cuthbert might no longer be around.

Martin stretched, and began checking the frames where the cloth might have dried sufficiently to be taken down. He worked his way round methodically, and came to the area nearest the river, which was flattest and best for the treading. It was then that he stopped, his mouth opening to call to Cuthbert in the same moment he realised that Cuthbert would never hear him.

The fulling stocks, long wooden troughs, in which a man might walk up and down, trampling the woollen cloth beneath his feet, ran in a line. The first was filled with stale urine, the second with clean water, and the third had hot water with soapwort poured into it. Trampling the second was the preferred one in summer, and the third more popular in winter, Nobody liked the first, and Cuthbert was paid an extra half penny a day for doing it. He was already in the stocks, but not setting his next trampling of cloth into the bottom, but lying face down in it as though floating in a coffin. A wave of guilt flooded Martin; for he had just been thinking of Cuthbert as dead, and here he was. Then logic kicked in. He ran forward and grabbed the body by the shoulders, ignoring the fact that he was splashing stale urine from half Evesham over himself, trying to drag it out and onto the dusty earth, though it was difficult to move, and quite stiff. Voices hailed him, and two men who had just arrived together, rushed to see what had happened.

'Help me.'

There was a moment of indecision as both were not so keen to get elbow deep in the brown fluid.

'I said help!' The fuller yelled at them.

With their aid, the body was taken from the trough and laid upon the ground.

'Poor old Cuthbert,' said one of the men, wiping his hands on his cotte and then snatching off the straw hat that would keep the burn of the sun from his balding head. 'What a place to drop dead.'

Martin Fuller did not answer. The only people he had

seen dead were kin who had died in their beds and with the priest in attendance. Then the body was washed and laid out before it stiffened. Since Cuthbert was stiff, he could not have just 'dropped dead' after he had arrived for work.

'I doubts that he did,' he murmured, almost to himself.

'Well, he lies very dead, Master Martin.' The balding man was not really thinking.

'We should take 'im to the priest, but as 'e is, the smell will be bad.' His companion was being practical. 'A few buckets of water first, and then we gets the cart and takes 'im. At least there be none to grieve beyond that cat 'e lived with.'

'Should we raise a hue and cry?' The suggestion was half-hearted, but if the master thought the death not natural, then the Law might demand that they did so.

'No. First you, Harold, since you has longer legs and fewer years, run to the abbey and find the lord Sheriff's men as are in Evesham to find the killer of Walter the Steward.'

'Why, Master Martin?' Harold might be the most fleet of foot, but his mind had some catching up to do.

'I think someone killed Cuthbert.'

The workers stared at their employer at the suggestion being put so firmly, and several crossed themselves, as much praying for protection from some unknown killer as for the soul of the departed Cuthbert.

'But why would anyone kill Cuthbert?' The straw hat-bearing man asked, frowning.

'That is what the lord Sheriff's men needs discover, not us. Harold, get going. Ifan, find an oilcloth and cover the body. Then everyone get back to work.'

Thus dismissed, the fuller's workforce dispersed, though

he doubted they would put their backs into their labour. Martin Fuller himself remained staring at the corpse until the oilcloth was brought.

Hugh Bradecote had woken with a prayer of thanks for the skills of Brother Augustine, the abbey's infirmarer. His head was clear and he rose in a positive state of mind, though without any definite plan that would narrow down who had killed the unlamented abbey steward. The problem lay in the fact that they had spoken with everyone who might have had a motive to kill him, and their answers had all been good. He was not sure what new question might elicit something that would change matters, so they might as well go to the castle in Bengeworth and make it clear that harassing women coming to market was not going to be allowed to pass like the Avon's waters slipping smoothly beneath the bridge itself, whilst also finding out what interactions the garrison had with Walter the Steward.

Serjeant Catchpoll had slept the sleep of the just, according to his own words. Walkelin, by contrast, had been awake for some time, sorting the information in his head to try and make some greater sense of it. They broke their fast with bread and a small beer in the guest hall's small refectory, which also acted as sleeping quarters for the majority of those who sought the Benedictines' hospitality. What became clear when they entered was that the conversation stopped very suddenly, and everyone made studious efforts not to look interested in their presence. As they rose to leave, Walkelin heard a whispered 'brains left everywhere'. If the gossip, inaccurate and exaggerated, was running among Evesham's visitors, it must also be rife among the townsfolk. They would now have to deal with the supposition, exaggeration and third-hand 'evidence'.

The trio headed towards the new northern gate but were then found by the now breathless Harold. His obeisance was as much so that he could rest his hands upon his knees and gulp air into his straining lungs as a mark of respect.

'My lord,' he managed, on the third breath, 'Old Cuthbert – dead.'

This cryptic utterance did not have Bradecote thinking this information meant anything less than murder.

'Who is, or rather was, "Old Cuthbert"?'

'Walker at Master Martin's.'

'Martin the Fuller, yes?'

'Yes, my lord. Master Martin found 'im in the stocks, first thing, floatin' face down, and sent me to fetch you.'

'We will come immediately,' Bradecote saw Harold's shoulders sag, 'and no, I am not going to run all the way.'

Nonetheless, Harold was not able to fully recover his breath, since the lord Undersheriff had long legs and did not dawdle, even though the last place he wished to visit just after eating was the fuller's.

It was a very serious-faced fuller who greeted them down towards the ferry.

'My lord, I do not think I have called you falsely. I have tried to think of some way in which Old Cuthbert could have ended as he has, but only a foul deed seems to fit.'

'Then you did right to send to us. Tell us how you found him, and let us also see the body.'

Martin Fuller led them to the stocks, and the oilcloth-covered remains of Old Cuthbert.

'I always does the rounds each morn, to check the tenters are taut and the cloth progressin' well. Old Cuthbert tends – tended – to be the first to work, having nobody at home bar 'is cat. As I approached, I saw 'im lying' face down in the trough, and my first thought was as he dropped dead sudden and fell forward, but his arms lay straight down his sides, and nobody falls like a felled oak. I called for aid, and tried to get him out, and then I found he was not limp, but stiff and hard to lift out. I knows as a body goes stiff some time after the soul departs, so Old Cuthbert did not just die when he came to work.'

'Your thinking is sound, Master Fuller. There are several questions beyond the obvious one of why anyone would wish to kill an old man, and one is why meet him here, and kill him, and if they did not kill him here, why did they bring the body here from wherever it happened?'

'Is it a threat to me, to my business?' The fuller looked worried, for the thought had not occurred to him.

'Do you know anyone who resents you?' Bradecote did not think it a likely reason.

'None my lord, though some turn their noses up as they pass from the ferry, but I says to them, "Would you rather wear cloth that still smells of sheep and is not felted and warm? If no, then do not complain, but rather thank those who keep you warm and well dressed." Shuts most up.'

'And was Old Cuthbert well liked?'

'"Well liked"? Oh, I would not say that, but then he was not disliked, either. A bit of a loner and grumbler was Old Cuthbert, but his was not a happy life, so you could see why he was a miserable old bastard.'

'What had happened?'

'It were long ago, afore I was born. Cuthbert was a coppersmith accused of stranglin' his wife, and it went to trial by hot iron before the Justices, and 'e were proved innocent, but his hand was made useless for holdin' tools, or any other usual work, and my father took him on as a walker, since his feet were as good as any man's and the work does not appeal to most. Cuthbert worked, kept to himself, and once in a while would sit in the corner of the alehouse and listen to the world of happier men. Sad, when you think on it.'

'And you said as 'e lived with a cat for company?' Walkelin was linking information in his head.

'Yes. Talked to it, but said it never answered back, which was a good thing.'

'And where did 'e live?'

'Up by the green, this end.'

Walkelin did not add 'with a view of the well workings', but it was in his mind. It made a link between the two deaths far more likely.

'So let us look at the body.' Catchpoll knelt down with a low grunt as his knees complained, and lifted the oilcloth. The smell of urine was almost eye-watering, but although Catchpoll blinked the once, he gave no sign of his nose being offended by it. Old Cuthbert's eyes were open, staring unseeing and giving him a surprised look. It was one the serjeant knew well. Those who knew their life was coming to a close never looked startled, and most closed their eyes as for sleep. Those whose life was snuffed out unexpectedly, by natural cause or ill deed, did not have that calm acceptance. The skull felt intact and there were no signs of violence upon the face, though its overall bruised colour showed the man had lain face down in death for some hours. Catchpoll rolled the body over, took his knife and slit the back of the cotte open, since trying to remove it from a stiff body would be awkward. Martin Fuller turned away, feeling it unseemly to watch, and heard the serjeant's grunt of satisfaction. The back of the corpse was not discoloured by the settling of the blood after death, and what Catchpoll saw very clearly was bruising about the neck, with two bruises, almost an imprint of thumbs, overlapping over the spine. Someone had strangled Old Cuthbert with their bare hands.

'Well, that shows how 'e died, sure enough. I will look for a wound, but them bruises is dark, and I reckons they are much the same round at the front, just hidden by the blood gettin' back towards the earth. Whoever strangled him did it thorough, and trusted to a strong grip. Big 'ands they possess, not that we was thinkin' of a woman for this, and big for a man too, lookin' at the overlap.' Catchpoll laid his own hands with the thumbs over the two bruises, and his fingers did not meet at the front of the neck by the length of a little finger. Catchpoll was a wiry man, but of average height and size of hand.

'Since he has been dead some hours, it seems unlikely someone persuaded him to meet here, or come here, and then killed him. However, if he was strangled nearer to his home, then it is equally unlikely that his killer set him over his shoulder and carried him here.' Bradecote was thinking things through. 'So, something was used. Is there a handcart here that should not be?' He looked at the fuller.

'Not that I have seen, my lord, but I will look now. Once

I saw the body I was not lookin' at anything else.' Martin Fuller took it as an instruction and turned away, calling out to his workers to search for anything a body might be carried on.

'My lord,' Walkelin now felt free to speak, as Catchpoll, rather less gently than before, moved the body about and looked it over for any other sign that would aid them, 'when I spoke with those who lives by the well pit, there was a man described to me, a walker here, and with a cat, so it must be this man. It might be that someone hated 'is guts all of a sudden, but much more likely that 'e were killed because 'e saw somethin', or the killer came to think as 'e did.'

'It is the clear link, and, as you say, the chances of it being a random killing within days of Walter the Steward's death must be very small. We—' Bradecote stopped, as Martin Fuller hailed him.

'My lord – we found it!' The fuller drew close, solemnity replaced by excitement at having succeeded in his task. Coming behind him was a man pushing a small handcart. 'This does not belong to me and it turned up behind the giggin' and shearin' shed, where we naps the cloth or shears it fine. Tossed into the nettles is where we found it.'

'I wonder who is lacking a handcart this morning,' murmured Bradecote. 'I am sure we will find out, since the owner will be eager to cry "theft" to us. Thank you, Master Fuller. The body can go to the priest, and I suggest the handcart should be used again, and leave it with the priest. We will send its owner there when they make complaint to us.'

'Yes, my lord.' There was relief in the fuller's voice, for

once the corpse had been taken away, normality would soon return. Old Cuthbert did not deserve to die as he did, and a death was owed, but at least, thought the fuller, there were none to grieve, and God would look charitably upon his grumpiness, after all the trials he had endured in life.

The sheriff's men began to make their way back into the town, aware that this second death might bring to light just the piece of information that would lead them to the killer of both Evesham men.

They were nearly at the Merstow green when a very irate man came towards them.

'This will be the handcart owner,' murmured Catchpoll, suppressing a smile.

Oswald Mealtere had never shown them a smiling face, but at this moment he looked livid.

'There you are, my lord. I asked after you at the abbey and they said you had gone out the gate towards the ferry. 'Tis not in Hampton you needs to be, but right 'ere in Evesham, for someone stole my second cart last night. Will take more 'n twice the time to deliver my readied sacks of malt. I want the bastard caught, my lord, and justice meted out.' Outrage filled his voice.

'And in your mind that is more important than discovering the killer of Walter the Steward?' Bradecote spoke softly, and an interrogative eyebrow was raised.

'Well, no . . . but Walter cannot be brought back from the dead, and my cart can be found, if the bastard 'as not taken it out of Evesham to sell.'

'Now that is where we 'as gone wrong all this time, my lord, lookin' into foul killin' when we ought to be seekin' lost goods.' Catchpoll shook his head, and tutted, regretfully, then paused, and began again in a very different tone. 'You would not set such store by a lost cart if it were your kin with their throat cut in a ditch, or thrown down a well pit. You does not deserve your cart back, so sorry I am that we knows where it lies.'

'You do?' Oswald's face of wrath melted into surprised relief. 'Where?'

'At Martin Fuller's, where it was found among nettles.' Bradecote did not reveal everything about the handcart at once.

'So some drunken prank? Does not make it better, not by much.'

'What makes it far worse, Master Maltster is that it was not a drunken prank, but used to take the body of the man known as Old Cuthbert to be dumped into the fulling stocks.'

'No, surely not?' The maltster crossed himself. 'Miserable 'e were, but no wickedness did the man do.'

'Now, we want to know exactly where your handcart was taken from, last night, and when did you last see it? Was it at your malthouse?'

'No, my lord. I took a load up to Gyrth the Brewer and left the cart just over the bridge on my track.'

'Why leave it there and not take it home?'

''Acos I did not go straight 'ome to the wife, but went back to the alehouse to sup a beaker of ale or so and talk.' The maltster looked at the ground.

'Hmm, so you were in the alehouse, drinking the result of your own malt. I wonder why, since it costs you silver, and you must brew some for free at home.' Bradecote sounded suitably suspicious.

'Talk with the wife ain't like talk with other men. A man needs men's company sometimes.' The maltster looked a little sulky, and Walkelin thought Oswald's wife had not seen his absence the previous evening in the same light. 'Odd to think I saw Old Cuthbert, full of life there, and 'e left safe enough, not weavin' drunk.'

'You saw him?' This was an unexpected advance and it showed in Bradecote's voice.

'Aye, my lord. Sat in the alehouse. I goes there once in a while, since it looks bad if a maltster does not sup ale from 'is own malt.'

'So tell us about the evenin', first to last.' Catchpoll kept any excitement from his voice.

'Not much to say. Nothin' out of the ordinary took place, no arguments.'

'And the gossip?' Catchpoll had already made a good guess about the prime topic of conversation.

'All about Walter the Steward, but then that were natural. Been a long time since a death like that 'appened in Evesham, and none would say the loss of the steward gave rise to regret and sadness, neither.'

'So I says again, from first to last.' Catchpoll was dogged.

'If you must learn it all,' Oswald sounded as if this was wasting his time. 'When I arrived the place were not full, but busy enough. Old Cuthbert came in and sat in the corner, out the way, since none would choose to sit close, not with the smell that always clung to 'im. Drank a beaker of ale and listened, mostly.'

'"Mostly". So what did he say?' Bradecote pounced on the detail.

'Well . . .' Oswald looked less comfortable. 'Some

talked of whether we was all at risk, with killers about in Evesham, and Old Cuthbert said that were foolish 'acos nobody liked Walter and one man killed 'im. Someone asked 'ow Cuthbert could know that, and 'e said as 'e saw 'twere but one, when lettin' in the cat as lives with 'im.' Seeing the very grave look on the lord Undersheriff's face, Oswald was quick to play down this incident. 'The old man did not possess friends, but sayin' such a thing would make all listen and pay attention to 'im. I doubt not that all 'e saw were the uprights of the well hoist and dreamt the rest.'

'Can you give a name to any others in the alehouse, them as heard Old Cuthbert speak?' Walkelin was ready to file the names in his head.

'I will not thrust any man's 'ead into a noose just for bein' in the wrong place.' Oswald looked mulish.

'And nor do you by giving the names. What we want to learn is what each saw and heard, and among all there might be something to lead us to the right conclusion.' Bradecote did not sound threatening, but there was firmness in his tone. He expected a full answer.

'If you says so, my lord.' Oswald was still reluctant. 'The well delver were there, and Hubert the Mason with 'im, and Aelred the Tailor and Wilfred Fisher, and a stranger to Evesham, leastways new to me, the sort that likes to talk more 'n listen. Them is the ones I recall, but there was others too. Ask 'em and see what they say. None will say as I lies, my lord. None.'

'And we do not suggest they would, Master Mealtere. I suggest you go to the church and await your handcart, since the body is being brought to the priest upon it.'

'But it is m—' The maltster was on the point of refusing, but changed his mind. 'Aye, my lord. That would be charitable and Christian.'

'Then we will keep you no longer.' It was a curt dismissal, for the undersheriff was already thinking of where they must go next, which was the alehouse.

Since news of the death was still contained at the fuller's, Gyrth the brewer and alehouse keeper's shock was not surprising, and it took him some time to get past head shaking, tutting, and decrying the act as wicked and without cause. However, Bradecote curtailed his outpouring with a raised hand and a straight question.

'Was anyone at odds with the man, last night or previously?'

'No, my lord, not as such.' Gyrth looked a little guilty.

'Tell me about this "not as such".'

'It cannot be 'im, my lord, for the man is old and frail and could not kill a man.'

'Who, in Our Lady's name?' Catchpoll joined in.

'Siward Mealtere. The pair never liked each other, from afore I served a beaker of ale as a lad, in my father's time. Never knew the cause of it, but neither had a good word for t'other and would not speak to each other. Now nobody would sit next to Old Cuthbert from choice, 'im stinkin' somethin' ripe from 'is labours, but if the place were full, most would do so, reluctant like. Saw Siward Mealtere walk straight out again, more 'n once, and t'other way round too. But Siward ain't been within these walls for best part of a year, 'im findin' it difficult to see and creaky of bone, and Oswald, the son, says as 'e is

153

gettin' real tired of life and talks of the grave.'

'And Oswald Mealtere was here last night.' Bradecote made it a statement that could not be denied without a straight lie.

'Aye, but I does not think the son bore the grudge like the father.'

'And who else supped your ale last night, and was within when Old Cuthbert sat in the corner, for we knows that is what 'e did?' Walkelin still wanted names to file.

'A goodly number, since there be plenty to talk about, and if men wants to gossip they does it over ale. Hubert the Mason sat with the fellow who dug that well and now has to dig a new 'un. Aelred the Tailor came in quite late, and talked low and sort of angry with any as would listen, bemoanin' that Walter the Steward ordered fine clothes from 'im, puttin' back orders from other customers, on top of makin' 'im pay more than the abbey dues each Quarter. As for other drinkers, let me see, there was Will Fisher, though I 'eard 'im say as 'e were goin' to visit kin in Offenham today, Cuthwin Potter and 'is brother, never can recall the lad's name, and a couple of the abbey stable lads. Much of the talk were about Walter the Steward, and none of it bemoanin' the man's loss, I can tell you true. Most was wonderin' what need the man might 'ave for fine clothes. Struttin' about Evesham, mayhap? All was glad Walter 'as gone. Not that any would 'ave raised a fist to the man, but none would weep into their ale over 'is death, neither. Also, I remembers a loud man with silver to spend, one I could not name, the sort as likes to tell everyone the way to live their lives. Went on and on about the lord Abbot buildin' that great wall to keep apart from us ordinary folk, and with no thought to us bein' murdered in our beds. 'Twas that as made Old Cuthbert speak up.'

'And he said?' Bradecote wanted to know if the recollections tallied.

'My lord, Old Cuthbert said t'were foolish to talk of "murderers", which the stranger did, for it were but one man as killed, and 'e saw as much when 'e let in the cat as lived with 'im. Old Cuthbert lived on the west side of the green, so it might be true, but as likely 'e imagined it or just wanted folk to listen to 'im for a change.'

'When Old Cuthbert left, who left next?' Walkelin was focused.

'That I could not say, not for sure, for the hour were advanced and most thinkin' of their bed and wife, leastways someone's wife.' The alehouse keeper gave a wink and a chuckle, though it did not elicit any smiles in return. He then looked at the floor, embarrassed, but raised his eyes to give what he thought would be seen as something helpful.

'The Potter lads left last, with Aelred, for the younger one cannot take the ale so well yet, and needed a friend at either shoulder to aid 'im. A tongue lashin' will Widow Potter 'ave given the pair this morn, one for drunkenness and t'other for allowin' it.'

'Thank you.' Bradecote said no more, and the sheriff's men left, to be hailed by a boy of about ten summers, his nervous treble coming between gulping air. The child drew close and dropped to one knee and begged to speak with the 'great lord'. Bradecote had never been addressed in such elevated terms but kept a straight face.

'My lord, I bring a message from my uncle, Master Kenelm the Ferryman as cannot leave the ferry lest folk is stuck t'other side of the river.' This came out in as much of a rush as his laboured breathing could muster.

'Go on.'

'Uncle says as you needs to know that last night, when Uncle were abed, someone took the ferry across to Hampton on their own. Now it is known that Cuthbert the Walker is killed, 'e says it might well be the man as took the ferry did the killin'.'

'Thank you.' Bradecote turned to Walkelin 'Go to the ferryman and see if there is anything he can tell us, or indeed that the ferry can tell us. We will speak with the well delver and mason and meet you back at the abbey.'

Walkelin nodded assent and bade the child return with him, not that he needed a guide.

'Two violent deaths within three days, and the second man spouting that he had information on the first. Unlikely the two are not connected. Agreed, Catchpoll?'

'Indeed, my lord. And after a man kills the once, the second time is a mite easier, especially if they feels desperate. Sort of makes them think they can do no worse, and are forced into the next one. If I supped a beaker of ale for the number of times I has been told "I 'ad no choice" I would be senseless on the floor of that alehouse all this day and all the night followin'.'

'And yet, despite some of those we consider suspect for the death of Walter the Steward being present, it is quite possible the killer made their escape over the river, which immediately discounts Oswald Mealtere for a start.'

'Would t'were that simple, my lord, but think on this. A man could walk the other side of the Avon back to Bengeworth and come over the bridge and be in bed long afore the early cock crow of a summer night. Cannot be above a mile and a half at most, and the bank is clear for much of it, so not difficult even on a night with but a new moon.'

'Yes, but why do it at all, Catchpoll? It was near dark when the alehouse emptied, so about that time that Old Cuthbert was killed. What confuses me is why the body was not left, if not on the green, then just along the lane, in the hedge. What message was the killer giving by taking the corpse, at some risk, to the fuller's?' He shook his head. 'However, we then allow a little time for the killer to find the handcart and—Wait! Oswald Mealtere did not see his handcart was missing as he returned home, so either the killer took longer to find it or did not have to look at all, since it was actually Mealtere himself and he knew where he would find it anyway.'

'Again, my lord, you may say true, but we cannot be sure.' Catchpoll sucked his teeth. 'I would like to say it makes things clear, and if Oswald Mealtere killed Walter the Steward it follows very well, but it could be that half Evesham knows it as a place where 'tis left often enough, and more often when Oswald is sociable over ale.'

'But it does put the maltster to the top of our list.'

'That it does, my lord, and leavin' the body a good way from 'is own premises might give us a reason for it bein' moved so far. Let us see what news Walkelin can bring us, and what Adam Welldelver and Hubert the Mason gives up to us, then we can speak with Oswald again, and the wife too, though small chance is there she would say other than he slept soundly all night and came home early enough.

Chapter Ten

Walkelin did not dawdle, for he was eager to return and hear all that his superiors learnt without it being at second hand, but he felt a little guilty leaving the little boy with no chance to keep up, so ameliorated his pace a little. It did give him time to think upon the information they had gleaned that morning, and his conclusions were very similar to both his superiors. Oswald Mealtere looked most likely to be the killer, but to drag him off to await the Justices in Eyre would be to ignore other possibilities. There was also something he thought might solve the issue of the strap end, and a question niggling him which he wished to voice.

When he arrived at the ferry it was, as bad luck would have it, upon the other bank, and Kenelm was handing a woman into it, and a man in a wide-brimmed hat was already seated. Walkelin waited with every appearance of merely casual interest, though he was willing the ferryman's hand over hand progress to go the faster and he himself stepped forward to aid the woman to climb out. It was then that he saw the man stand up, and his mouth opened.

'Why, 'tis you, Master Sheriff's Man.' The speaker, who smiled, had one arm with the vestige of a hand bearing but two misshapen fingers, and the other arm tapering to nothing below the elbow.

'It is, and underserjeant I am now.' Walkelin smiled back and there was pride in his voice. 'How fare you, Alnoth?'

Alnoth the Handless was impressed that the lord Sheriff's officer could recall his name, though less surprised that his person stuck in the memory.

'Well, Underserjeant, very well. See, I still wears the boots I bought.' He indicated his feet with a stumpy arm. 'And prayers do I still offer for the lord as wore 'em afore me.'

The woman, who had been pleased that this young man had offered her a hand from the ferry, felt rather ignored, and her thanks were brief. Walkelin barely heard them, for Alnoth was speaking.

'And you is come to Evesham again and all for Master Walter the Steward as I hears.' Alnoth shook his head. 'In charity I ought to pray for 'is soul also, but it sticks in the throat to do so.'

Walkelin was torn. He needed to speak with the ferryman, and privately, but Alnoth was a man like himself, one who observed, and took in information. There might yet be something to be gleaned from his knowledge of how Walter the Steward had acted in Evesham these last few years.

'Would you await me under the tree yonder, and then we might walk up to the abbey, since I take it you seek lodgings there? I needs to speak with the ferryman first.'

'Gladly.' The crippled man went to sit beneath a youthful oak that had been an acorn when The Confessor died.

Walkelin turned to Kenelm the Ferryman.

'The lord Undersheriff thanks you for sendin' so quick to tell us what went on in the night. You saw nothin' until the dawn?'

'Saw, no, and I blames myself for thinkin' the sounds was my own dream. I could not tell the hour, though as I opened one eye the darkness were still full, and I felt the night not jaded, but I thought I dreamt the creak of the ferry in distress, callin' me, so to speak, and a gruntin' noise, a man not used to the work. All a dream I thought it, since we oft dream of what we does day in and day out, but now . . .'

'Just a grunt?'

'Well, I thought it sounded like 'e cried out, sort of in pain. Added to me bein' sure t'were a dream, makin' no sense.'

'And yet the ferry went over and a man took it.'

'Aye. Glad I am that Frawin, my mother's kinsman, came to cross early, and knows 'er.'

'Your mother?' Walkelin looked confused.

'No, the ferry.' Kenelm rolled his eyes as though his statement had been obvious.

Walkelin realised that Kenelm treated his ferry like a horse that needed to trust its rider.

'Have many crossed today?'

'Not so many as yestermorn, but some days 'tis quiet and some busy.' Kenelm was a man who took the blessings of each day one at a time.

'And may I look in the bottom in case anything remains that tells something of your ferry thief?'

'I saw nothin', but then I did not look. Your eyes is serjeantin' eyes and sees what plain folk does not see.' Kenelm was quite serious, and Walkelin knew it to be true.

Walkelin got upon his hands and knees, without any self-consciousness, and scrutinised the flat bottom of the ferry. He could not imagine what a man might have dropped that would aid in identifying him, but his job was to look, to see, and to report, even if there was nothing.

'How strong do you need to be to take her across?' Walkelin decided treating the ferry as 'she' would be a good idea. He had heard the Severn sailors call their boats 'she', so Kenelm was not alone.

'Just the once? Well, no insult meant, but with more in the arms than you possess, Underserjeant. Needs strength of forearm and of shoulder.'

'So it would need a man as works with the upper part of the body.' Walkelin was looking at Kenelm, who was quite skinny-legged, but whose arm muscles were visible through the linen of his cotte.

'Aye, and it takes time to learn the way of it, castin' the loop forward to catch on the crossin' rope and makin' it bite.'

Walkelin, who could see nothing beyond a snail in the boat bottom, stood, with a very slight wobble, and stared at the loop of twisted hemp, though not with any real hope. He caught his breath, feeling that Heaven had sent him a sign, for caught in the twist was something small and bloodied. He peered closer. It was a torn fingernail, and just seeing it made him wince, for it had been ripped from a finger with force. It would certainly have made a man cry out.

'Not yours, I take it?' He pointed at the scrap of another man's body, and then grimaced as he delicately drew it from between the twisted fibres. He no longer felt his stomach churn with the dead, but this was part of a man that still breathed, and it felt slightly wrong to hold it in his hand.

'How did you see that? No man as knew the ferry would catch a finger and a nail like that.' Kenelm drew his hand down the loop of rope in a half caress as though commending it for wreaking vengeance upon the thief. 'She bit 'im for layin' 'and on 'er.'

The portion of fingernail lay in Walkelin's palm, and he screwed up his nose in distaste. However, it was a possibly important find, for there could be few men in Evesham with a finger showing a damaged nail. He tried to assess which finger it might have come from, but only decided it was neither from a thumb or ear-cleaning finger, being too narrow for the former and too large for the latter. He then cast it into the river, since no further aid could it be. The lord Undersheriff and Serjeant Catchpoll would be content that any man who had been in the alehouse and lacked a fingernail would need oathswearers and appear before the Justices for the murder of Old Cuthbert, even if no confession could be gained for the death of Walter the Steward. It was only unfortunate that so small an injury would not stand out without looking carefully at hands.

Adam Welldelver was not a man who worried about things he could do nothing about. That he had spent two days shovelling earth back into the hole that had taken days to dig was just *wyrd* and now, as he levelled off the ground and prepared to move to the newly selected well site, he simply crossed himself and said a silent prayer for Walter the Steward to ward off bad luck attending his future diggings. The men who dug wells were not just men with spade and shovel but made it clear to 'ordinary folk' that it was also a slightly mystic art, and as it passed from father to son, it became something they began to believe themselves. It would be unwise to leave this 'well that was never a well' without a good, Christian prayer. Focused on the words in his head, the well digger had to be hailed a second time before he turned and saw the lord Undersheriff and lord Sheriff's Serjeant.

'If'n you wants me to take out the earth again, my lord—' He was all set to remonstrate, but Bradecote shook his head.

'No, Master Welldelver. There is nothing more to be known from that earth. However, we would ask what you could tell us about last night in the alehouse.'

'But that be days after the death.' The well digger looked confused. 'Words were said about 'im as died, and not sorrowful words, but nothin' as made a man the one as killed 'im.'

'That we understand, but a man who sat alone, one Old Cuthbert, was found dead this morning, and the death was intended.'

'Never!' The well digger crossed himself. 'I tells you, my lord, I will not choose to come to Evesham again. Not peaceable, not at all.'

'And they will not need many more wells once this next gives up water,' commented Catchpoll.

'True enough.'

'So what can you tell us of who was there and what was said, other than a lack of sadness at Walter the Steward's death?' Bradecote pressed the man.

'I could not name many, not bein' an Evesham man, though I sat with Hubert the Mason and we talked over a beaker or two. He—' The well digger stopped suddenly, and looked worried.

'Go on. Better we know and can set it aside, rather than you conceal and we have to think it something suspicious.'

'Worried about 'is son, was Hubert.'

'Well, we know the lad did not kill Walter the Steward, so do not be afraid to say more.'

This, thought Bradecote, was taking too long.

'Seems the lad used to be lovelorn over the girl as be now the steward's widow, and Hubert thinks if none stands trial for the death, then when the lad weds the widow, and 'e says 'e seems determined upon it, there will always be the rumour that young Simon committed murder.'

Catchpoll snorted at this foolishness, and commented that if the lord Sheriff's officers declared that Simon, son of Hubert, was not involved, that should be good enough for Evesham.

'I only says what Hubert said and you asked to learn.' The well digger looked a little affronted.

'So continue.' Bradecote's glance at Catchpoll indicated he should keep quiet.

'Not much more I can say, my lord. There was others there, o'course, but I could name none.' He frowned. 'One man did not fit in, not like one long known. Loud 'e were, like the cock on a dunghill if you asks me, though not crowin' proud about hisself, more determined to tell everyone what they should think. Sort of man as is used to tellin' folk what to do.'

'Can you describe him?'

'Not so as you would be sure to recognise the man at fifty paces, my lord. Not as tall as you, by my 'and's breadth,' he held up his hand, horizontally, to show them, 'though, come to think on it, 'is 'ands were much bigger 'n mine, and I saw no grey to what sprouted on the chin after a day. Oh, when 'e laughed, or rather pretended to laugh, mockin' the lord Abbot, which be a disrespectful thing to do, a tooth were gone, left side.' He opened his mouth and pointed to the tooth one back from the dogtooth. 'Not uncommon, but it might aid you.'

'Indeed. Thank you. Are you set to begin digging the new hole?' Bradecote ensured he did not sound as though the information was too useful.

'Aye, my lord. This forenoon will see first sod lifted, once the spare soil be spread around 'ere, so I wished it were cooler, but there.' The well digger shrugged, touched his forelock to Bradecote, and began stamping firmly over the freshly replaced earth. Undersheriff and serjeant left him to his labours and went to speak yet again with Hubert the Mason. It felt as if they were going round in ever-decreasing circles, being told half-truths and lies.

Hubert the Mason had put up a rough awning to keep the worst of the day's sun from his back and was dressing a stone from a pile which was all hewn to roughly the same size. He was not alone, for a young man they recognised was splitting larger lumps of stone to create them. Bradecote was surprised, since he had advised Simon to remain in Hampton.

'So you have returned, after all.' Bradecote raised an eyebrow and gazed at the youth, who blinked, wiped a dusty hand across his forehead to brush away a lock of curling hair, and nodded, blushing.

'I went over and fetched 'im, my lord. There's work to do.'

'Yet the stones that were going into the original well hole lie ready for use and the well delver has yet to set his spade to the earth here. It does not look an urgent need.' Bradecote sounded sceptical and the mason did not meet his eye.

'I reckons as this'n will be deeper and 'tis best to be prepared.' Hubert the Mason knew the excuse was lame.

'So you have fetched back your son even though only last evening you were bemoaning that if none is taken for the death of Walter the Steward, then suspicion will remain in Evesham that your son killed him. That seems strange.'

''Tis not true, not all of it.' Simon spoke up. 'Father did not come for me. I came back 'acos I-I wanted to see Mærwynn.' It came out in a rush, and the lad glanced at his father's angry expression.

'Which be a fool thing to do, and I told 'im such,' grumbled the mason. 'Will lead to talk.'

'No, for I went to 'er father to ask after 'er first, and she be back with the family already. Stayin' in that place, Walter's "prison", would make 'er more ill, so Mistress Meduwyrhta says. But none other than me knows she is 'ome, not yet.' Simon wanted to show he was not just a rash and lovelorn swain.

'Is she now?' Catchpoll nodded at the information. 'Glad will 'er mother be for that.'

'Aye, and Wulfram says as once the time is passed to . . .' Simon stopped for a moment, not liking to think of Mærwynn in Walter the Steward's bed – 'to show she does not carry the steward's child, then if I work's 'ard with father then Wulfram will not refuse me when I asks again to wed Mærwynn.' He looked almost belligerent, daring both father and sheriff's officers to tell him he could not do so.

'And you does not fear gossip?' Catchpoll sounded vaguely curious, no more.

'No, Serjeant, 'acos you and the lord Undersheriff will take them as killed Walter the Steward, even though I would like to shake that man's 'and afore you lead 'im away.'

'Well, we likes to 'ear that folk feel confident of our success.' Catchpoll controlled the urge to laugh, but then asked a serious question. 'When did you return?'

'Came over the ferry first thing. Odd it were, for Kenelm stood upon the Evesham bank and a kinsman took me across. Someone took the ferry over in the night. Very strange.' Simon shrugged and dismissed further thought on the incident, not knowing that it proved his statement true without further corroboration.

'And when did you hear of the killing of Old Cuthbert?' Bradecote looked at father and son together.

'The old man as smells of piss and shouts out 'is door that 'e does not want the well near to it?' Simon looked stunned. 'Dead?'

'Yes, after leaving the alehouse. You were there, Master Mason. Was anything said that might hint at who killed him.' Bradecote wanted the mason to know his presence was undeniable.

'Nothin' my ears caught, my lord.'

'So you did not hear him say he had seen that one man alone killed Walter the Steward?'

'No, my lord.' The man was a poor liar.

'What do you fear by admitting it, if you had nothing to do with the death? Most of the alehouse would have heard him.'

'You spoke with me afore and I want nothin' more that links me with any killin'.' Hubert looked sullen. 'The only thing I ever raise my 'and to is stone, and with my mallet, though the steward tried me sorely. I killed none, my lord and there's the end to it.'

'And we accept that, but we need to have the truth spoken to us, not half-truths and lies. It just makes our task the longer and harder.' Bradecote's admonishment was softly given, but the mason hung his head nevertheless.

'Who else did you see in the alehouse?' Catchpoll did not expect any revelation.

'Aelred the Tailor, grumblin', though 'tis not like the man, to be fair. Then others as Walter the Steward took dues from but did not put into the abbey's coffers. Seems there was many of us,' Hubert gave a grim laugh, 'and fools we all felt. Oh, and Oswald Mealtere, who said little and looked into 'is beaker more 'n most. Mayhap the same trick were played on 'im, but 'e did not like to admit it.'

'That we shall ask him. We need trouble you no more, Master Mason.' With a nod, Bradecote turned away, and he and Catchpoll went to speak again with the maltster.

They encountered Oswald Mealtere pushing his purloined handcart over the little stone bridge, for which Bradecote gave silent thanks, since it would enable raising the question of his father's antagonism towards Old Cuthbert without the irascible old man interrupting. When hailed, Oswald looked visibly annoyed.

'Does I get no peace, my lord? What possible need has you to speak with me again this day?' The man glowered at them and winced as he stopped and straightened.

'Not keen others know you lost silver to Walter the Steward, we 'as found.' Catchpoll jumped in first.

'Ha. Why share it? Does it feel better to be one of many?

No. Best just forget the lot.' Oswald shrugged as if dropping a cloak from his shoulders.

'You did not tell us that your father and Old Cuthbert were so much at odds that your father would not even sit next to him.' Bradecote changed the line of question.

'Who would want to do so, my lord? Smelt of piss, no fault to 'im, but 'tis true.'

'Yet we hear that there is some old grudge between them.' Bradecote felt the word appropriate, having heard how the maltsters, father and son, kept a grudge alive for decades.

'Whatever the cause, it be so old I cannot tell you the source of it, and Father never leaves the 'ouse these days. To suggest 'e killed Old Cuthbert would be madness. 'Tis impossible.'

'We is not suggestin' that,' murmured Catchpoll, softly.

'Then—wait! No! You think after all this time I did it, as some sort of revenge? Why would I do it now if the reason existed?'

This thought had already occurred to both Bradecote and Catchpoll, but there were too many lies and half answers coming to them, and they needed to be able to sort it all out.

'Agreed, but what if what you told us afore were but 'alf the tale? What if Old Cuthbert really did see one man kill Walter the Steward and that man stands before us right now? Knowin' your father loathed 'im would make the act the sweeter. An old score paid off when your father sits too blind and weak to end it for hisself.' Catchpoll almost purred the accusation.

'Not so.' Oswald Mealtere paled and shook his head. 'That somethin' lay betwixt my father and Old Cuthbert I knew, but never did Father speak of it, and the "fault" did not lie with 'im. Words was said, many years past, and not forgotten, but I bore no grudge against the old man. Life was not kind to 'im, and why did I need to add to that? No reason. I will swear a good oath and would undergo any ordeal, knowin' I be innocent of the death of Old Cuthbert. God hear me.' He crossed himself.

'Then we will speak with your father to discover what began the grudge, lest others shared it.' It sounded sensible enough, but Bradecote was hoping the old man, in his anger against the world, might be more forthcoming than the son.

'Worry an old man as awaits nothin' more than the grave?' Oswald sounded accusatory.

'The more we knows of what runs through Evesham to fester in the present, the closer we will be to Walter the Steward's killer.' Catchpoll clearly agreed with his superior's decision.

'And none in Evesham would thank you for that, only for takin' the man as killed Old Cuthbert. Father could 'ave done neither. Leave the man be.' The son was defensive, but his words fell on deaf ears. Undersheriff and serjeant strode down the gentle slope to the house, followed by the maltster, still complaining, and Catchpoll opened the door without knocking.

A woman was shelling peas into a bowl, and looked up, startled. She had a weary and wary face, one which spoke without words to Catchpoll of a life spent placating a house filled with anger and little kindness.

'Be calm, mistress. This is the lord Undersheriff and—' Catchpoll, seeing the woman's surprise turn to terror, realised that his second announcement had rendered the first useless. If she was afraid of the men in her house, she was even more afraid of men with power. She dropped the pea pod she was shelling, and dipped in a curtsey so low she stumbled as she rose afterwards.

'I—' She got no further, stopped by a look from her husband and his terse words.

'The lord Undersheriff does not need to speak with you. Go and feed the hens.'

Since she fed the chickens early each morning, this was clearly just a command to get out. She nodded, made a second obeisance to Bradecote, and dashed out.

'A good wife for some things, and a fair cook, but no wit to speak of.' Oswald dismissed his spouse in a tone of some contempt.

'Why come they back?' Siward Mealtere, huddled before a small hearth fire that made the room even hotter than the June day outside, peered in the direction of Bradecote and Catchpoll. He did not sound worried, just annoyed.

'We needs to know what cause lay between you and Old Cuthbert, so strong as to keep you from words even after as long as half a lifetime.' Catchpoll spoke a little louder, on the assumption that since the old man's words were loud, his hearing was as limited as his sight.

'Ask the bastard yourself.'

'I would, but he lies dead.' Catchpoll's response was instant, to catch the natural reaction. That it was a cackle of laughter and a clapping of hands was not what he had expected. 'He died by intent and 'is body left face down in the fuller's stocks.'

Siward Mealtere laughed the louder, and rocked to and fro with the spasm of it. Bradecote, watching the son,

Oswald, saw that he was as surprised as they were at his sire's emotions.

'It is not a matter for rejoicing, Master Mealtere.' Bradecote was severe.

''Tis to me, my lord. Has shut his lyin' mouth at last. Left in a trough of piss! Could not 'ave imagined a better end.' The old man sounded gleeful.

'Father.' Oswald's tone made the word a warning, but it was waved away. His father chuckled and looked rejuvenated by the news. He stooped the less, even if his eyes were as milky as ever.

'So what did Old Cuthbert say as was a lie?' Catchpoll put no threat in the question.

'Nothin' as need be spoken of again,' came the swift response, and although the eyes could not twinkle, the voice held triumph. 'The past lies buried from now on and can rot.'

Whatever Siward Mealtere meant by these obtuse utterances, it was patent that they meant as little to the son as to the sheriff's officers, and, not without a deeply felt reluctance, Bradecote mentally crossed Oswald from the list of those who might have killed Old Cuthbert, and thus also Walter the Steward.

Alnoth had been waiting patiently for Walkelin, seated upon the grass beneath the spreading boughs of the oak tree. When Walkelin approached he rose with a nimbleness that surprised the underserjeant, since he had no good hands upon which to lean and push up. Instead, he bent his knees and leant back against the tree, bracing his back and pushing up from the ground so that he rose like a growing plant to stand before him.

'You looked like a hound upon a scent, down in the ferry,' commented Alnoth, grinning. 'If you had given voice I would have laughed out loud and counted it the funniest thing seen since a man with no charity in 'is soul and no coin for a man as needs it, tripped and fell flat in a fresh horse shit outside St Peter's Abbey in Gloucester.'

'Come you from Gloucester this journey?' Walkelin smiled at Alnoth, knowing that the man was not being other than friendly.

'Indeed, and from Pershore afore reachin' the ferry, and Kenelm as gives me free passage, God be kind to 'im. The news of Walter the Steward is a big surprise, but however much I ought to pray for 'is soul, as I said, I fear it will not be felt from the heart in my case.'

'You are a watcher of men, Alnoth, and I values that. What would you say about the man?'

Walkelin wondered if anything new might be learnt that would progress the hunt for his killer.

'First, I would say as the man was one with two faces, one to the lord Abbot and Father Prior, and another to all of us as 'e felt beneath 'im. Never came across a man with more pride and – self-worth. If you told me Walter the Steward were a king's bastard, I would believe it, and we all knows King Henry, God grant 'im rest, were a king as fathered more 'n any could count, so as to make Earl Robert of Gloucester just chief among bastards.' Alnoth was about to continue, but stopped, his mouth half open, and frowned. Walkelin pounced upon this hesitation.

'You recalls somethin' strange?'

'Aye. Last Michaelmas, I think, I stayed at St Peter's in Gloucester for their fair, and folk was generous, so I could buy a new oilcloth to keep out the worst of winter rains if no shelter could be found. I watched over a stall while the woman sellin' apples went to buy linen for a coif, and I would swear a good oath that I saw Master Walter the Steward, but for the fact that 'e wore a cap of soft coney fur and a cloak trimmed the same, like a great lord, and strode about like it too. A man, a man with the manner of a grovellin' clerk by the look of 'im, bowed and scraped before 'im and this "Walter" fair glowed with pleasure at it. Never saw me, o' course, but then the likes of Master Walter never saw me, just wanted me out the way. Oft I waited in the courtyard at Evesham Abbey and Master Walter would send a groom to tell me to leave and not trouble Brother Almoner, but the grooms did not like 'im either, so would tell me as they was told to say, but then let me lurk quiet in a sheltered corner until Brother Almoner was free to see me.'

'Are you sure this man in Gloucester and Walter the Steward was one and the same?'

'Sense says no, Underserjeant, but my eyes is good and, as you says, I watch, and my oath would be good to say yes.'

'That is both interesting and fits with somethin' else learnt of the steward.' Walkelin felt he could trust his instincts with Alnoth, and would have revealed something of what had already been learnt of the steward's desire for rich clothes, but he feared that Serjeant Catchpoll would berate him for letting out knowledge that should still be kept privy. Instead, he asked for any aid that the crippled man could give.

'You speak the truth when you says folk do not see you,

not all of 'em, nor do they keep quiet when you might listen. I ask you, in the name of the lord King's good laws, that if you learn anything about the death of Master Walter or of Old Cuthbert the—'

'Old Cuthbert too?' This time Alnoth clearly regarded the news as bad. 'Now there be a poor man as I will pray for, though some might laugh at me. Suffered, did Old Cuthbert, and I understand sufferin' and not bein' able to do those things others do and be a master of a craft, though I were always like this, and poor Cuthbert came to it through mischance. When I first came to Evesham, ooh, when I numbered no more 'n fifteen summers, so a score years past, Cuthbert, none so old then, showed a little kindness to me, and I learnt the tale of woe as brought 'im to be but a walker of cloth. Cuthbert 'ad a fair wife, the sort other men covet, and Cuthbert feared she were unfaithful. Told 'er that the life of a woman without virtue would mean no wife of Evesham would speak with 'er, and the lover would in time replace 'er, though 'e, Cuthbert, would always cherish 'er. She said she would tell the lover no more would she meet, and it were after that she were found dead, strangled. The gossip meant it seemed Cuthbert might 'ave done it, and the hue and cry took 'im up and the lord Sheriff's Serjeant, not the one as does it now, came and took Cuthbert to Worcester and the Justices. Despite the rumours, all Cuthbert's tithing swore for 'im, bar one man, and Cuthbert told me once it were that man as killed 'er when she said 'im nay.'

'Did the man have a name?'

'Aye, Siward Mealtere. Cuthbert were proved innocent, but the ordeal by hot iron cost 'im the use of 'is right 'and. A coppersmith needs fingers and good 'ands, and Cuthbert could not continue. When 'e said what 'e believed about Siward, Siward denied it all, and said Cuthbert's mind were as twisted as 'is right 'and, and would never speak again with 'im. Most forgot the grudge, but not the pair o' them.'

'Why did Siward not face questions?' Walkelin felt the Law had let a man down twice if Cuthbert had been right.

'I does not know, but mayhap folk did not like to think too much about the speed they took up Cuthbert, and wanted it all forgotten, or Siward's wife swore 'e were loyal and in 'is own bed the night of the killin'. I does not know, Underserjeant. There was some of the wife's kin as always blamed Cuthbert, even after God proved 'im innocent. It were all a long time ago when I learnt it.'

'Well, the more we knows, the easier it will be to find the truth, friend. One more question, since you knows Evesham well. Where do folk go for strap ends for their belts?'

'Let me see, mmm.' Alnoth considered the question. 'Them as shows off wealth might go to a silversmith, but most ordinary men would go to Theobald the Coppersmith as works just off the marketplace, east side. I can tell an interestin' story about Theobald . . .' Alnoth was clearly happy to have someone to talk with, and since they were both going to the abbey, Walkelin was quite content to listen to him.

Chapter Eleven

Ansculf, the serjeant of the guard, looked the man up and down, then spat into the dirt.

'That is what you are worth to me – one spit.' His voice was little more than an angry growl, but the man-at-arms flinched. Those men who came to the castle when their lord did service soon learnt from the small permanent company that getting on the wrong side of Serjeant Ansculf was a very bad idea.

'Sorry, Serjeant.'

'"Sorry"? Oh, I will ensure you is sorry, Croc, every night for the rest of your lord's service in this midden-stench castle, when you does the night watch without bein' allowed near the guardroom all the night long. If you gets within three paces of it, I will see you whipped. Understand?' Ansculf only wished it was cold enough for the night guard to need a brazier in the guardroom to make the punishment worse.

'Yes, Serjeant.'

'Good. Now get out of my sight. The rest of you misbegotten bastards as do not even deserve to 'ave mothers. When I says—'

'But Serjeant Catchpoll w—' A voice spoke up from the back, but almost immediately thought better of it.

'Serjeant Catchpoll is not your serjeant. 'Tis me, and you

does as I says, not that death's head on legs. Fools, the lot of you, if you fears Catchpoll more than me.' Ansculf snarled, angered that Catchpoll had influence even when, for most of these men, he was a figure rarely encountered.

Ansculf was in his late thirties and looked upon Serjeant Catchpoll with a mixture of respect and loathing. What he wanted was to be feared by men-at-arms as much as Catchpoll, feared more than their lords or the lord Sheriff himself, since most men-at-arms were ignored by the Foreign-speaking lordly class unless it was to pass the highest sentence for desertion. In Ansculf's view, a man-at-arms needed to treat a lord like a bear, something to be avoided and, if encountered, not looked in the eye, but he needed to fear the serjeant like a wolf, for the wolf would hunt him down if he felt like it. Catchpoll was like a wolf. Ansculf would never want Catchpoll's position as lord Sheriff's Serjeant, because it involved collecting taxes and all the ferreting around with the undersheriff, just to bring folk before the Justices. As Ansculf saw it, Catchpoll lacked independence, and what Ansculf enjoyed was freedom to do much more what he wanted. Bengeworth was undoubtedly a miserable place to inhabit, but he saw it as a place of opportunity, since most lords came for a month, drank a lot, and left, just doing enough to keep the lord Sheriff content, which gave him free rein to interpret William de Beauchamp's wishes as he thought might eventually make him serjeant at Elmley Castle itself. He had been at Bengeworth for half a year, effectively running the castle, and treating Evesham as a place besieged, to be entered for reconnaissance and occasional raids.

'I told you to make sure all that comes into Evesham over

the bridge pays a toll to the castle in goods or coin, and now I finds Croc, and no doubt others, is lettin' all sorts of folk pass for free. Bein' an old woman or a fair maid does not mean they goes over without payin'. Useless soft-hearts, the lot o' you.'

'But will it not just mean folk come in from the west over the ferry to avoid the bridge, Serjeant?' A young man-at-arms with more brains and a little more courage, asked the question, and for a moment Ansculf did not reply. Then he smiled a very wolfish smile

'Well, that depends on whether the ferryman agrees to take a little toll for us or not.' Ansculf picked three men, since he felt a show of might would make refusal even less likely, and told them to wait while he went and spoke with the lord de Cormolain.

Rahere de Cormolain was paring his nails and yawned when the serjeant suggested 'a visit' to the Hampton ferry.

'I take it you are not suggesting I go?'

'No, no, my lord.' Ansculf was almost shocked. The last thing he needed was a lord to be present and feel it was his own success. 'This is work for me and a couple o' big lads. The ferryman is a reed of a man and will bend to our – your – biddin' easy enough. I just thought as if we does not take the toll there also, then folk will avoid the bridge and use the ferry, even if it is longer.' The serjeant stole the man-at-arms' idea as a matter of course.

'Yes, it makes sense. Well done. I just want my period of service to be the most profitable the lord Sheriff has seen these last five years.'

'I am sure we can see to that, my lord.' Ansculf was

now more confident that the men would not be swayed by sympathy or hard luck stories at the bridge. 'I will tell Baldric where I have gone, and he should be able to cover the guard.' He spoke slightly casually about de Cormolain's senior man-at-arms, giving the hint that Baldric was not at the same level.

'Yes.' De Cormolain drained his cup. 'And send a servant to bring me more wine as you leave.' He dismissed the serjeant with a wave of his hand, like shooing a fly away. Ansculf swore softly under his breath, but obeyed, and hoped de Cormolain got a sore head from the wine.

Walkelin felt very hot, and he mopped his brow and the back of his neck with one hand. Alnoth, his few possessions gathered into a bundle on his back, and wearing a floppy-brimmed hat, scarcely seemed to notice the heat at all, and was happily talking about how much he liked visiting Evesham, and reminiscing about an anchoress who had lived in a small dwelling on the abbey's land, when he had first come to the town. Mother Placida had been the name by which she was known, and he heard she had been a well-born lady before she was called by God to abandon the world for a solitary life of simplicity and prayer. He had sat outside her humble home and asked for her prayers, which he was sure would carry great weight in Heaven, her being so godly, and she had not only prayed for him, but even passed out to him some of the food that was brought to her, through the little hatch in the door, and which was enough to sustain life without sating all hunger.

'I never saw more 'n the godly soul's soft, white fingers. She came years afore, and the abbot of the time let 'er live in the abbey enclave, but 'twere too noisy and busy, so then the abbot gave 'er a spot away from the brethren and bustle, down beyond the orchards, just above the flood point of the riverbanks. Aid were given, since she could not know the way of makin' somewhere to live, but she directed the way of it, like a little tower in daub and wattle, with a thatched roof. And only one window to let in light, up so she could not look at anythin' but Heaven. She lived there for nigh on a score years and ten and were old when I first came. When she died, and they opened the door, they found 'er scarce more 'n skin and bone, arms crossed over 'er bosom and 'er wooden cross, like she laid 'erself out ready.'

Walkelin, half attending, asked if she had lived beyond Wulfram Meduwyrhta.

'Aye, most 'ave forgotten the good soul, but not me. I puts 'er in my prayers as she put me in 'ers, though mine are poor offerin's.'

They had reached the main gate of the abbey by this point, and an abbey servant, crossing the courtyard, hailed Alnoth and began to ask if he had heard the 'good news', then realised he was with the underserjeant and coloured. Walkelin shook his head and smiled, then left the handless man and went to the lord Undersheriff's chamber in the guest hall.

His superiors had discovered nothing new from the others named as present in the alehouse, only corroboration about the stranger ranting about how the lord Abbot wanted to forget the folk of Evesham who looked to the abbey as overlord, and the fact that Old Cuthbert had said he knew only one man was involved in the killing of Walter the Steward. The younger Potter brother, who looked ale-sick, could not remember anything at all, and his brother Cuthwin admitted he had not paid any attention to much more than the inside of his ale beaker. At this, his mother had heaved a big sigh and threw him a reproachful look.

Walkelin found undersheriff and serjeant with a jug of small beer and some fresh bread, which they offered to share with him.

'Thank you, but first I must tell you what I discovered at the ferry.' Walkelin sounded eager, so he was not about to say there had been nothing useful.

'Go on, then. Spit it out afore you chokes on it.' Catchpoll was not going to appear all ears, on principle.

Walkelin told them all that Kenelm knew and then revealed the discovery of the fingernail.

'So when we finds a man with big 'ands and a very sore finger end, we knows who stole the ferry and most like killed Old Cuthbert.' Walkelin could not prevent a touch of pride entering his voice.

'Very true, though we cannot just demand to see the hands of every man in Evesham.' Bradecote's commendation was muted.

'And even if we could, no proof would it be, of itself, since a man might give a reason for a damaged finger, and no way could we show a particular nail belonged to one man, even if you had been fool enough to bring it back with you.' Catchpoll sounded even less cheered.

Bradecote nodded in agreement. A scrap of coloured cloth that might match a tear had some value, but even finding hair of a certain colour only pointed to all those who shared it. He gave himself a mental shake, since being pessimistic would not advance their chances. He strove to feel as positive as Walkelin, who continued his report.

'Alnoth said somethin' else, my lord. He said that Old Cuthbert once told 'im Siward Mealtere killed 'is wife, but none believed 'im.'

'Well, one old man did not kill the other, and it did not seem that Oswald knew why the two were at odds, nor did I notice any damaged finger this morning, so I am not sure it aids us, other than knowing why Siward spoke as he did about the past being in the past.' Bradecote felt the information was merely an explanation of what they had encountered.

'However, we also learnt information about "the stranger", and that is that he is not as tall as me, young enough to lack any grey to his chin, and is missing a tooth.' He indicated which one.

'Then, my lord, what if "the stranger" with the missing tooth is also lackin' a fingernail? Small chance could there be several men that lacked both in Evesham, right now.' Walkelin, having been a little downcast at his superiors' initial reaction, was now his normal self again.

'Seems we is seekin' a man lackin' too many parts,' murmured Catchpoll. 'Let us pray the man lacks a little brain too, and makes hisself clear to us.'

'But Walkelin is right that if both things apply to one man it is very likely he is the killer.' Bradecote nodded approvingly. 'And the likeliest place to find him is Bengeworth Castle, which we have put off visiting for too long.' He pushed a beaker towards Walkelin. 'Since this "stranger" was clearly trying to stir up the drinkers against Abbot Reginald and the abbey in general, I am much inclined to think he was sent by de Cormolain as part of the campaign to make life difficult for the Benedictines.'

'But that the man should then kill an old man he did not know still sounds too great a step, my lord.' Walkelin frowned.

'I know, Walkelin, but since there have already been goods cast into the river, and thefts from the enclave, the risk is that eventually some eager subordinate casts an innocent traveller into the river and there is another death. Better we stamp on this now.'

'And the lord de Cormolain will not like that.' Catchpoll murmured, already anticipating his superior's answer.

'No, he will not, which is why I like the idea even more.' Bradecote's mouth lengthened into a grim smile. 'I never thought the day would come when I would enjoy entering Bengeworth Castle.'

If Catchpoll secretly thought life would be the easier if the lord Undersheriff never got round to prodding the hornets' nest that was Bengeworth Castle, he did not show it. That there would be any connection found between the men there and the death of Walter the Steward had seemed highly unlikely, not when so many within the town had very valid reasons for hating the man's guts, but Bradecote had wanted to eliminate any possibility, even before the description of 'the stranger', and especially when he found that the current vassal lord on duty was Rahere de Cormolain. Catchpoll did not like the man either, but could effectively forget his existence, since they encountered each other so rarely.

Hugh Bradecote strode through the castle gate with an air of authority that meant the gate guard straightened without knowing who the tall, lordly man was. The man did not recognise Catchpoll and Walkelin as individuals, but they exuded such an air of 'serjeant' it did not matter. Heads turned, and one man, a little brighter than the others, disappeared to find the guard commander, Baldric. Walkelin, having exchanged a whispered word with Catchpoll, hung back, hoping to survey as many men in the bailey as possible for a combination of missing tooth and missing fingernail. Bradecote, however, made straight for the constable's chamber, the lone stone building, which had once been an abbey tithe barn and been roughly adapted to become the commander's lodging and squat keep, and entered without knocking, with Catchpoll in his wake.

Rahere de Cormolain was lounging in the one high-backed seat, his feet upon the trestled table before him, and a cup of wine in his hand.

'That is all I need, you sniffing about and playing "lord Sheriff's right-hand man". You are meant to be looking for a steward-killer, so why come here?' De Cormolain sounded as bored as he looked, and his voice had the slow precision of a man struggling to avoid slurring his words. He liked to mock Hugh Bradecote and felt aggrieved that he had come when he was not clear of thought and barbs would be hard to find.

'For two reasons. The first is that there has been another killing in Evesham, of a man who left the alehouse last night, and one man present was a stranger to all the others and made much of abbot and abbey having no interest in the lives of the townsfolk, just taking their silver and leaving them to be attacked and killed. There are not many strangers about, leastways none as would have a view on abbey and town, and it sounds just the sort of trouble-stirring that might give "amusement" here, since there have already been thefts of abbey property and illegal taking of toll from those bringing goods to sell at market. Requiring you to desist from those illegal acts is the second reason.'

'"Requiring"?' De Cormolain looked daggers at Bradecote. 'Ha! You have no authority to "require" me to do anything. Besides, I have no knowledge of any toll taking or thefts and have given no orders for such things. My men would not disobey me, for they know I am not one to displease if they value the skin on their backs. and nor are they given leave to drink in the town.' He focused, thrusting the fogginess of drink from his brain.

'If you spend your day with wine as your companion I would be surprised if you knew anything of what is happening, but you are still responsible as constable.' Bradecote made no attempt to conceal his disdain. De Cormolain's fingers gripped the cup more tightly, but he did not rise to the insult, which prompted Bradecote to go further.

'You know, I was wrong. Actually, there are three reasons I came.'

'So the third is?' De Cormolain knew, as he asked the question, that it was to step into the trap.

'I knew it would annoy you.' Bradecote smiled, and could almost hear de Cormolain's teeth grind, which made the smile even broader. De Cormolain threw the wine cup at him, though he ducked and laughed, then his face grew serious again. 'If you know nothing then you are not fit to sit in that chair, and if you did, then you are responsible for what is done by your subordinates.'

'You sound so righteous, must be all the Law you swallow

to spout to make you sound important. But you are a fool, Bradecote. Do you think I care about Evesham, its abbot or the people who scrape a living there? Would I put myself out just to annoy them? No. I am here, as I am sure you have been in the past, in vassal service to William de Beauchamp, your overlord as he is mine. This is *his* castle, built at *his* command, manned at *his* command. Do you not know that he and the abbot are at odds as sheriff and abbot have been since our fathers' times? Are you that blind? No? Then have you not considered that whatever little nibbles at the abbot's authority begin here, they stem from our overlord's wishes.' De Cormolain saw that this hit home, even though it was only a flicker in Bradecote's eyes. It was his turn to smile. 'Are you going to make this complaint to him, and do you not already know how he will respond?'

Bradecote had a very good idea how William de Beauchamp would respond. Catchpoll had already warned him not to interfere at Bengeworth. It was not that he had ignored the command, but that he had set it aside, because he, Hugh Bradecote, was a vassal not just of William de Beauchamp, but now of the Law. The trouble was that the Law was unbending but not irascible and vindictive, and William de Beauchamp was both. Had it been worth it? His heart told him yes, because the Law had to be upheld by all, but his head anticipated trouble.

'When it comes to murder, the lord Sheriff will not stand idly by.' He thought that at least probably true.

'But all you come bleating to me about is that you connect a man who is a "stranger" in Evesham with this castle upon a guess, a possibility at best. You have no proof of any such connection and all the other matters are not yours to interfere with. You are just an undersheriff, and the main part of that is "under". You cannot countermand the lord Sheriff and woe betide you if you try.'

'And you cannot breach the King's Laws with impunity.'

'I have not done so,' de Cormolain stuck his chin in the air, 'and you cannot prove otherwise, Bradecote.'

'Not yet, de Cormolain.' Bradecote turned on his heel, his expression stony, and Catchpoll followed him out. They collected Walkelin by the gate and the trio left the castle and went over the bridge up into Evesham without another word being spoken. Walkelin, having drawn a blank by nonchalant observation, was trying to think if there was a way to discover if any of the castle men were lacking a particular tooth and a fingernail without some sort of parade, to which the constable was not going to give permission, and Bradecote and Catchpoll were both wondering just how upset William de Beauchamp would be with each of them when he found out what had been going on, despite his instructions.

Ansculf decided it was better he and the men he took with him walked to Hampton rather than rode, since it was not far and leaving a man to hold the horses, or tying them up, looked somehow a less threatening precursor to his 'little talk' with the ferryman. He had picked three men, not that he needed three to intimidate, and they were big but not bright, and not likely to have such a thing as a moral qualm. As he led them, tracing the loop of the Avon, he was thinking of all the different ways he could be 'persuasive', which put him in a very good mood. As they came to stand on the Hampton side of the ferry he was smiling, and Kenelm, mid-river and coming towards them with two old women deep in gossip in the boat, was thinking no more than the four of them would be a full load to his craft. The old women climbed out, thanked Kenelm and wished him a fair day, and passed the men with one cautious, sideways glance.

'Good morrow. Good job there are no more o' you, or else you would need pick straws to decide who waits to come over second.' Kenelm smiled. 'A penny covers all.'

'Ah, you mistake, Master Ferryman.' Ansculf had decided to commence by being smooth, to accentuate the later threat. 'We are not wishful to cross.'

'You are not? Then why stand upon the bank there?'

'Well, we 'as a problem, or rather the lord Sheriff 'as a problem, and you look just the man to solve it.'

Kenelm looked a little worried. The name of the lord Sheriff wanting him, specifically, to do something, was of concern, as Ansculf intended. Not that Kenelm had encountered the lord Sheriff more than to ferry him across the river, without mention of a fee, on a few occasions. He normally went from Elmley to Bengeworth, or approached from the north.

'In what way?'

'There is a toll to pay to the castle by those crossin' the Bengeworth bridge with goods into Evesham, and pity of it is some is reluctant to do so and would rather walk their load all the way round to this ferry and cross.'

'No toll were there afore, at the bridge.' Kenelm had heard a few grumblings but had thought perhaps it was just an increase in the toll paid at the market to the abbey. It made sense that it might be so, with all the building work in stone that had already gone on for years.

'Well, toll there be now, and the lord Sheriff dislikes it

bein' avoided. Howsoever, there can be a neat answer to the problem. You will take the toll for 'im, on top of the *fourthing* for the crossin', and we comes each week's end and collects it from you.' The smoothness now had a vein of threat running through it.

'But that will not work, master.' Kenelm thought it wise to sound respectful. 'You cannot know the number that crosses who would 'ave used the bridge and what would be owed, and nor is I goin' to be given more each journey, even if I says why. More like I will be tossed in the river.'

'That risk will be yours to take, and as for the sum, well it will be far easier to just charge everyone as crosses and pass the toll to us. Only fair that them crossin' into Evesham the west side pays as does them on the east.'

Kenelm folded his arms and looked obdurate.

'Been ferryin' since I were tall enough and strong enough, like my father afore me, and his afore that. Never been no toll, and never an unfair price to bear folk across. Not right to start now, and nor will I.'

'Wrong answer. I asked nice, and so now I tells. You do as I tells you.'

'My overlord is the lord Abbot. I will go to—' Kenelm got no further, since two of the men, at a small nod of the head from Ansculf, grabbed his arms and held him, while the third hit him in the midriff, winding him. It was an act Ansculf would have enjoyed himself, but his hand was sore.

'Wrong answer again. Disobeyin' the lord Sheriff's wishes be a bad thing and leads to bad things.' Ansculf was warming to the task. 'You will obey.'

Kenelm, unable to speak and still doubled over, shook his head, and the man who had hit him, lifted his head by the hair.

'More, Serjeant?' The man asked the question in a rumbling voice, and, at the nod, punched Kenelm in the face. Ansculf laughed and drew a knife from his belt.

'Then no ferry, and no food on the table.' He stepped into the flat-bottomed boat and took the loop of rope that connected the ferry to the crossing rope, wincing slightly as he gripped it. He began to cut the fibres, sawing at it and hissing with discomfort as he did so. There was something almost personal in the action. As the last twist frayed and gave up, he stepped back onto the little landing stage, and the ferry, untethered, was stolen gently by the current and began to float downstream. 'Now everyone must use the bridge and pay toll. I think I prefer this way.'

Kenelm looked bloodied, bruised, but most of all distraught. He groaned, not at the pain, though pain there was, but at the loss of his ferry. Ansculf laughed, and nodded to the men, who let go of Kenelm so that he fell forwards, hitting his forehead on the timbers of the landing stage and rendering him senseless. They left without another word.

When Kenelm came back to consciousness he tried to think, even as the blood dripped from his nose and pooled on the planking. He was still short of breath, his head reeled and his thoughts were jumbled. He was overcome with inaction. A chiffchaff, on a bough nearby, seemed to chide him for not moving. For some time his body needed to recover. Before he could stand, a hand was placed upon his shoulder, and for one moment he wondered if his assailants had returned.

'Kenelm, what 'as happened? Where be the ferry?' It was a confused but friendly voice. The hand moved, and a second joined it to haul Kenelm upright.

'Sweet Virgin, who did this? Who would want to—' The man was all concern.

'Find 'er. 'Tis all I asks. Downriver she be gone, not long. Please, find 'er. I will do well enough.' The words were a little muffled by a split lip, and Kenelm spat blood into the water's edge.

The man looked about, for a moment thinking that Kenelm meant a woman passenger lost from the ferry, then realised it was the ferry itself that was missing. On seeing a woman approaching, the Good Samaritan called out urgently to her, promising Kenelm he would get aid and bring back the ferry. It was not only a charitable act, but practical for one that lived on the Hampton bank, since the ferry was part of everyday life. The woman, taking his place with Kenelm, soothed as she would a hurt child, and Kenelm felt suddenly too overcome to push her away. He just wished the man God's speed.

Ansculf was feeling pleased with the result of his visit to the Hampton ferry, although it was very hot and rivulets of sweat were running down his spine beneath his cotte, and his hand throbbed. No sooner had he dismissed the men with a small word of praise and more of warning to keep their mouths shut about what they did, than Baldric came to him and said that the lord de Cormolain wanted him straight away. Ansculf frowned. It did not sound as though this was to praise him. He entered the slightly musty gloom of the hall and wondered if de Cormolain had moved at all during his absence.

'You called for me, my lord.'

'Yes, you are to ride to Elmley Castle, immediately, and if the lord Sheriff is not there, go on to Worcester. You are to tell him that his undersheriff has been "requiring", and you are to stress the word, that the occupants of this castle do not take any action that creates problems for Evesham Abbey, counter to his own commands, and that I request that he come, most urgently, to make the situation clear to the lord Bradecote that it is he, and not the undersheriff, whose word is to be followed.'

'But I am the castle serjeant not a messenger, my lord, and I am just come back from—'

'I care not. You are the only one I can be assured will deliver the message properly. Go, and ride fast. If you do not return with the lord Sheriff on the morrow, at the latest, I will see that you are removed from the post of castle serjeant, if the lord Sheriff does not do so first. Understand?'

'Yes, my lord.' Ansculf felt hard done by.

'Repeat back what you are to say, first. It is important that the lord Sheriff comes straight away.'

Ansculf, in a slightly sullen voice, did so, and went to find the swiftest horse in the castle stables.

Rahere de Cormolain decided that the man need not know that it was also better he be absent from Evesham, at least until the overarching 'protection' of William de Beauchamp was visible. It had occurred to him that Ansculf, who was a man who relished handing out violence, might just have taken his orders too far when keeping abbey and town at odds, especially if he had drunk too much in the alehouse. It was a situation de Cormolain would rather face with his overlord present, since he wanted to be able to distance himself from any responsibility and to see Bradecote's face when told to leave it all alone. Rahere de Cormolain smiled and pushed the cup of wine away.

Chapter Twelve

By the time the trio entered the abbey enclave again, Bradecote had come to terms with the fact that his actions might have put his position as undersheriff in jeopardy. He had done what he thought right and the rest was, as Catchpoll would say, '*wyrd*'. If he was fated to be removed and become again just a minor vassal lord, well it would mean more time with his wife and children and his manors, which was no bad thing. The part of him that insisted it would be, he silenced firmly.

Catchpoll did not fear for his position, and was sanguine about the lord Sheriff's wrath, since he had felt it on enough occasions in well over a score years, but he did not like to think about having a new undersheriff when Bradecote was the best he had worked for, and indeed with. He knew that they, with Walkelin, made a very efficient team. He wondered what it was that lay between the lords Bradecote and de Cormolain, and when Walkelin went off to find the grooms who had been at the alehouse the previous evening, and seek out the coppersmith, the serjeant took the chance to ask the question.

'You can say 'tis nothin' I needs to know, my lord, but you both act like tom cats in a sack when put together. Cannot say I likes the man, not one bit, but with you, well, 'tis more.'

'You do not "need" to know, but it is a fair question, Catchpoll, and I will tell you this much. His sire and mine were at odds from long ago, over the same woman – my mother. De Cormolain the Elder even sought to "win" her by taking her from her family and wedding her by force, but my father intervened. I think my father nearly killed him, and from then on, if the de Cormolains could serve us a bad turn they would, openly or by underhand ways. Son is like sire, and not only has he repeated his father's lies about my mother, God grant her peace,' Bradecote crossed himself, 'but we both hold land at Himbleton, and he is ever trying to encroach, or claim encroachment. It is like having a horsefly about one's head, and like a horsefly, I wish I could swat him away forever.' He paused. 'It does not mean I would try and implicate him in a crime without cause, if that is your fear.'

'Never entered my head, my lord, but not many men rouse you to anger, or you them, just on sight. Thing is, though, the lord de Cormolain might well claim such to the lord Sheriff.'

'I know, but there is nothing I can do about that now. I still think that the unknown man in the alehouse is likely to have come from the castle, but we have not heard anyone say they saw Walter the Steward meet with anyone, or speak of the castle, so why would he arrange to meet a castle dweller by the well hole?'

'Mayhap the steward wanted to get silver from the castle as from the townsfolk and knew somethin' about the man?' Catchpoll did not sound very convinced.

'But the constable changes regularly, and brings his own men-at-arms as garrison, so there would be no time to gain such a hold over someone.'

'There's some as is the lord Sheriff's own men. I heard as the serjeant died of a fever midwinter, and the lord Sheriff promoted a man from Elmley Castle, but I does not recall the name. Did not seem important, since they would not be servin' in Worcester and gettin' under my feet.'

'At least that means we are only looking at a small number of the permanent garrison, which is in our favour.' Bradecote was cheered by the thought.

'And also at the men directly in the service of the lord Sheriff, who will like our interfering even less. If we can prove that you are right, the lord Sheriff will hunch 'is shoulders and grumble, and if we cannot . . .' Catchpoll did not need to finish the sentence. If Hugh Bradecote pointed a finger of suspicion at William de Beauchamp's own men without it being almost impossible that it could be anyone else, then de Beauchamp would more than just snarl.

'Since we cannot think of a reason why one of the garrison would kill Walter the Steward, the lord Sheriff would dig in his heels and say it simply could not be one of his men and that it must be a townsman.' Bradecote ran his long fingers through his hair and sighed. 'What have we missed, Catchpoll? That the man who claimed to have seen the first killing is then also killed must mean both deaths are connected, but I cannot see why a man-at-arms would kill the steward, nor a townsman kill Old Cuthbert. The most likely was Oswald Mealtere, but you saw his face when his father gloated over Old Cuthbert's death.'

'Aye, as surprised as we were, even shocked, and if 'n that were an act, I never saw one better. Truth rang from 'is offer of an oath also.'

'It is all there, and yet all hidden still, and I do not know how we ask again and do not get the same truths and also the same lies, for lies have certainly been told.'

'Which might aid us in the end, my lord. Lies, said over, oft show little cracks we can open like Hubert the Mason with mallet and bolster. What makes things difficult is when folk speak "true", and would swear an oath, yet be mistaken. But we gets there in the end, my lord, and the morrow brings a fresh dawn and fresh chances.' Catchpoll's was sometimes a patient philosophy.

'Over all the years as the lord Sheriff's Serjeant, how many times has no answer come, and nobody been taken to put before the Justices in Eyre, Catchpoll?'

'Some, my lord, but I could not give a number, for a tally would be of no use. I cannot go back and change the outcome, just as I cannot bring the dead back to life. Only God in Heaven can do that, and if we misses some, well He will not, come the Reckonin'.'

'Well, tonight I will pray God gives us aid before that.' Bradecote was sincere.

There was a firm but courteous knock upon the door and Walkelin entered, returned from a fruitless questioning of the servants, but more useful information from the coppersmith.

'The coppersmith put a strap end on a new belt for Oswald Mealtere a few days ago but cannot swear whether 'twere the day afore Walter the Steward died, or the one after. The coppersmith's favoured decoration be a leaf and 'tis rare for any to bear anythin' else. Wulfram Meduwyrhta buys from 'im, but 'as not done so in two years, and the coppersmith does not think 'e asked for a special shape. So the strap end I found could belong to either of 'em, or many men in Evesham. The grooms that visited the alehouse could tell me nothin' of use, but we can be sure that the man missing a tooth does not come from among those recently at the abbey, my lord. I knows it were not likely, but every path we can shut off makes it easier to find the right one.'

'Now you are sounding like Serjeant Catchpoll.' Bradecote gave a small smile.

'Well, it shows as I learns well, my lord, and Serjeant Catchpoll cannot find fault with me if I sounds just like 'im.' Walkelin looked all innocent eagerness.

'Hmm. Since you sounds like me, what does you make of all we knows?' Catchpoll was not going to actually say Walkelin's view was of equal value, not out loud, but he knew it was these days, for the most part.

'Nothin' fits together neat, not yet. We 'as many pieces, but they sort of do not make a pot. In fact, they looks like different pots, or when a man gets a knock on the skull and sees two of everythin'.' Walkelin paused. 'We still does not know what Walter the Steward did with the coin kept from the abbey and forced from the townsfolk, other than— There, I ought to 'ave said afore!' Walkelin clenched his fists in annoyance with himself. 'But all the thoughts were about the ferry.'

'Then sit down and tell us now.' Catchpoll did not approve of Walkelin getting agitated over something he could not alter.

'I met Alnoth the Handless at the ferry, and we walked together up to the abbey after I spoke with Kenelm the Ferryman. Alnoth found the boots and clothes of the lord Osbern de Lench, last summer.'

'I remember.' Bradecote nodded.

'Well, Alnoth goes from place to place, and seems to follow a way from Gloucester to Evesham, since there's shrines and pilgrims and a good chance of charity and work for a day at the markets and fairs. What Alnoth said was 'e saw Walter the Steward, though dressed far finer, in Gloucester last Michaelmas. Was sure it were Walter. So why did the Steward of Evesham visit Gloucester lookin' "lordly" and where did 'e keep the silver as paid for those clothes and the ones ordered from Aelred the Tailor? Could we 'ave been lookin' at this the wrong way?'

'How?' Bradecote frowned, but it was with interest, not annoyance.

'What if the man as killed Walter found out about Gloucester, by chance, and sniffed about to find out the way Walter got 'is wealth? Suddenly, that man can threaten Walter who is used to threatenin'. It is the killer as arranges the meetin' after all, and demands a share of the silver. Walter refuses and the man tries to make 'im say where it lies. They fight, and Walter gets clouted with the stone and dies.'

'It could be as the man already knew a little by bein' one made to give more on Quarter days.' Catchpoll could see the logic of Walkelin's idea. 'Not a great leap to think 'e were not the only victim.'

'And that would help us, since some have only now discovered their rents were not all paid into the abbey coffers, and were not threatened and made to pay extra as well. A good thought, Walkelin.' Bradecote was approving, but cautious. 'The trouble is, that if that was the reason for the killing, it makes it very unlikely Old Cuthbert's killer came from Bengeworth, since the two connect.'

'If the killer found the silver, and it must be quite a sum, would they 'ave left Evesham, or kept quiet until we leaves and all is quiet?' Walkelin pondered aloud.

'A missin' townsman would raise too much talk and gossip. No, Walkelin, if what you say be so, man and silver remain.' Catchpoll's experience told him it could not be otherwise.

'So the killer will keep a close eye upon the place and if we gets close, may well panic.'

'The trouble is, Walkelin, that since last night the alehouse was full of gossip about Walter the Steward and fine clothes, any men in Evesham he took from will have worked out that he had a lot of stolen silver pennies hidden somewhere. If we go hunting for a hoard, many eyes will watch us. But it was a good idea,' Bradecote saw the underserjeant's shoulders droop a little, 'and we may be fortunate. We should at least bear in mind as we go about Evesham that there must be a place that Walter could use and be confident it would remain a secret.'

'And since Mærwynn is back with 'er kinfolk, the steward's place lies empty. Might be wise if we was to look within afore others beats us to it.' Catchpoll could just imagine it being ransacked by eager hands.

'Unless . . . No, I was thinking that the new steward would have already moved in, but I doubt he could have moved all his goods and chattels since yesterday, when there was no sign in his home that anything was being put in chests in preparation.' Bradecote looked thoughtful. 'It might be too obvious a place, but if Walter cowed Mærwynn so much he could have commanded her never to look within a certain cask or chest and would have been obeyed, even over a young wife's curiosity. We would also look foolish if we hunt all over Evesham and it was hidden there all along. There is time before the evening meal for us to go and be thorough.'

'My lord, could Mærwynn have been curious and looked in a forbidden place once Walter lay dead?' Walkelin could not see her doing so while he breathed, but his Eluned had told him several times when he had tried to sound 'man of the house' that nothing made her want to do something as much as it being declared forbidden, other than by the priest, of course.

'Possibly, but we can go and ask her after looking for ourselves. It also has the benefit of us doing something rather than brooding on our lack of progress.'

The sheriff's men went out into the heat of the mid-afternoon with a purpose.

As they reached the door of the steward's house, the Welsh neighbour was at her own doorway, in conversation with another woman, whom she nudged as Bradecote approached, and they dipped respectfully. On seeing Walkelin, however, the woman looked far more at ease and friendly, and gave him a '*Pnawn da*' and a smile.

'No quieter now than when the poor wife were alone in the place,' she commented, as Catchpoll opened the door. 'Be noisier once the new one lives within, him having a full brood of family. Take a bit of getting used to, it will. Came round a while ago to look it over. Surprised I was he did not bring the wife, though. 'Tis a woman makes the *tỹ* a home, not the man.'

'Did he leave with anything, mistress?' Walkelin, about to follow Bradecote within, stopped and looked at her.

'Not that I saw, though I was not looking.' The woman blushed a little at the soft lie. 'Other than a scroll of vellum under one arm, that is.'

Walkelin thanked her in her own tongue, smiled, and went into the cool gloom of the interior to pass on this information to his superiors.

'The only way it could connect with the silver is if it is a map of Evesham and has the place where the silver is buried marked upon it,' suggested Walkelin.

Catchpoll, already checking a chest containing two thick blankets and a linen sheet, slightly darned where a toe had gone through it, looked up.

'Unless Walter split the hoard and set it in different places there would be no need to mark a map. A man remembers where he leaves silver wealth.'

'But it is interesting that there are other documents still here, and we have no reason to think either Walter or William can read. What lie here are maps of abbey holdings right up onto the Cotswolds and in three shires beyond Worcestershire. So why one particular map?' Bradecote thrust a rolled vellum back into a long box. 'It is worth asking him when we have finished here, and before visiting Mærwynn the mead maker's daughter.' It was only as he said it that Hugh Bradecote realised he had not called her 'Walter the Steward's widow.' Perhaps, he thought, he was instinctively extracting her from a relationship that had not been of her choosing and brought her nothing but harm.

'Nothin' shows a rich man, beyond what you would expect of the Evesham Abbey steward,' noted Catchpoll, 'and most men with money likes to dress up the wife and show 'er off in the best cloth and silver brooches, but this one kept the girl within, other than to go to church, and none said she dressed too fine for that.'

'I do not think he had any intention of showing off to Evesham. After all, it would make everyone ask how he could afford it, and if he still lived here, as the steward – Walkelin, tell us again what Alnoth the Handless saw.' Bradecote, about to check behind a small tapestry that hung on an otherwise bare wall, turned and looked at him.

'He said he saw him at Michaelmas, all dressed in fine clothes, a cap of coney and a coney-trimmed cloak, and acting like a great lord. There was a man with 'im, a man Alnoth said was like,' Walkelin drew the word from his memory, 'a grovellin' clerk.'

'I think Walter was trying out being someone else.' Bradecote half shut his eyes, imagining.

'But who, my lord?' asked Walkelin.

'Oh, I do not think that matters. He would have called himself something like "Geoffrey fitzWalter", and pretended he was a rich man, perhaps a merchant rather than a lord, since he would have no men-at-arms, one thinking of taking property in Gloucester. He might even think that he was so clever at getting what he wanted he could be a merchant. Once he had proved to himself, and some clerk in Gloucester, that he could be this new man, he returned to increase his wealth, and plan for the day when he simply disappeared from Evesham. I doubt he would have taken his wife, if she still lived, since with a new life he might aim for a wealthy widow and get richer that way.'

'I sort of hopes that proves true, my lord, since Walter ended in a well pit without ever gettin' to carry out the plan.' Walkelin smiled at the thought. It felt just.

'It makes it less likely he hid the silver here, but let us be thorough.' Bradecote found nothing behind the tapestry other than the wall, and they carried on the search.

Whilst it proved fruitless, they were happy that it excluded the house from their possible list of hideaways and went directly to the house of William the Steward, though they knew he might be at the abbey or collecting the dues, since it was Midsummer Day and thus a Quarter Day. His wife in fact directed them to the new well site, where they found him in agitated conversation with Adam Welldelver, whose arms were folded firmly across his chest, and who had a calm, obstinate look that was clearly infuriating the new steward. Hubert the Mason had straightened his back and was watching with interest.

'But it needs to be four paces eastward,' cried William, almost spitting with ire.

'You can say that all you likes, Master Steward, but what is just below the ground four paces eastward is solid rock, and I cannot dig through that. This 'ere be the nearest place where a spade can cleave the earth, and that is where I be diggin'.'

'But I want the street to be straight, so that when the town grows it will be a crossroads with the well in the middle.' It was almost a wail.

'You can want whatever you please, but what you will get will be a well right in this place or no well at all.' The well delver did not raise his voice in the slightest.

'You do not underst—'

'No, 'tis you as does not understand. You can draw pretty lines on that there vellum, but them is just lines, not a real place. Earth be real, rock be real, and a well you needs, so I digs where I can to give water.'

'I—'

'Ah, Master Steward. We was lookin' for you.' Catchpoll sounded so cheery the steward might have almost thought they wanted to invite him to sup ale with them. Then, as the steward turned round, he saw Catchpoll's death's-head smile, and he knew there was nothing convivial intended.

'I must finish—' the steward began.

'No, no, we 'as finished right enough, Serjeant. If you wants to speak with Master Steward, you get right along with it, and let me get back to my spadework.' The well digger's smile was at least genuine, for it meant the problem he had with the steward would be taken away.

'You "must" nothin', not when the lord Undersheriff needs to speak with you.' Walkelin took the steward's elbow, not in an arresting grip, but firmly enough that the man knew that complaint was useless. Catchpoll, who had been ready to say much the same thing, was both pleased and a little put out that Walkelin had beaten him to it. It did at least show the underserjeant was being suitably defensive of the position of lord Undersheriff. Walkelin had come a long way.

With Walkelin's pressure at his elbow, William the Steward stepped a little away from the well digging and Hubert the Mason, who had been watching the 'argument' between steward and well digger with silent amusement.

'We want to know what the roll of vellum contained that you felt the need to take it from the steward's house today.' Bradecote did not beat about the bush.

'Roll of vellum? Why, that was the map, the plan, that my brother put forward for the new building in the town, and that I persuaded the lord Abbot to change. Walter kept it, and I think he was still hoping to get my changes removed. I found marks on the plan, the streets I planned crossed and scratched over. Walter never could see what Evesham should be.'

'And you took nothing else from the house?' Bradecote almost glared at the man.

'What would I take? My family is moving in at the week's end and what is there is now ours, not that I think it a great inheritance.'

'Especially since your brother was keeping so much back from the abbey dues.' This was said smoothly, and William looked not angry but peeved. 'Do you know where he kept it?'

'No, not that I would say if I did, you will think.' The peeved look became more pronounced. 'Come back in half a year, and if my wife is fur-wrapped and with servants, then you can accuse me of finding and keeping what Walter hid like a squirrel burying nuts for the winter. What he did has put doubt in heads, and I will have every burgess in Evesham demanding to see proof that their rent has been put into the abbey coffers.' His annoyance looked genuine, but, thought Bradecote, that might equally stem from frustration at having looked and found nothing in the house, and having no idea where to look next.

'Well, if you does come across all that silver as belongs to others, be sure to let us know.' Catchpoll's cheerful tone remained, in part to irk the man.

'Of course,' snapped the new steward. 'Now, if there is nothing more, my lord, I have work to do.'

'Nothing at present. Carry on.' Bradecote made sure that the dismissal came from him.

William the Steward, clearly fuming, gave a nod so curt that Walkelin wondered if his neck might snap, and turned around again to remonstrate with the well digger, but Adam

Welldelver had climbed into the beginnings of his well pit, which meant he was only visible from mid-thigh upwards, and he was bent forwards as he thrust spade into earth. Looking down and arguing with someone in a hole would look foolish, thought William the Steward, so he stalked off.

'Glad I am I does not live in Evesham,' came the well digger's voice, and a chuckle accompanied it.

'We will leave you to work in peace,' Bradecote responded, and looked also at Hubert the Mason, who nodded and resumed his work. His son, whose absence had been noted, was seen approaching, leading the donkey and cart with more stone.

The sheriff's men headed southward, across the Merstow green and then from the lane towards Wulfram Meduwyrhta's holding. They saw two women taking up the day's dried washing from some bushes beyond the house and nearer the tumbled-down dwelling and went directly towards them. Whilst Wulfram's wife was one of them, they were surprised to see that the other was Oswald Mealtere's put-upon-looking spouse. Since the husbands would not so much as exchange the time of day, it seemed odd that the women were close enough to be able to speak with each other.

As they drew close, Mistress Mealtere seemed to shrink. Both women set down their baskets and dipped in an obeisance to Bradecote, and authority in general. He looked from one to the other. Both blushed.

'So the feud does not extend to the womenfolk.' He smiled, but the seemingly innocuous comment caused panic in the maltster's wife.

'Do not say anything to my Oswald, my lord, I beg you. If 'e knew. . .' She shuddered.

'What lies between the menfolk be between the menfolk,' declared Mistress Meduwyrhta, determinedly. 'We knew each other afore we was wed, and just sometimes we gets to speak, quiet, when they cannot see. We tells 'em we argue over the best bushes, but we do not. 'Tis best they do not know, my lord.'

'That I understand, and no word of it will come from us. I am here to speak with your daughter, mistress, and thought it would be she who was with you.'

'Mærwynn 'as taken 'er sister to watch Brother Petrus with the bees. Little Win likes to watch, but far enough away not to be stung. They is all in the orchard yonder.' Mistress Meduwyrhta pointed across the narrow channel, now a drying ditch, and up the gradual slope to the east. 'You can cross on the plank. 'Tis strong enough for a man,' she added, helpfully.

'Thank you.'

They left the two women staring after them, both as still as Lot's salt-pillar wife.

Mærwynn, who had a little more colour than when Bradecote had seen her last, had her arm about her little sister, and was crouching down to be at her level as the child told her about the bees, while Brother Petrus tended his skeps. Bradecote was surprised, because the Benedictine was not garbed in the usual dark habit but wore a pale linen 'shift' and a broad-brimmed hat draped over with a thin veiling that was tucked into the cord about his waist. He was swinging what looked like a battered censer, as though involved in a service before the high altar, but then set it down and took up a pair of small bellows to direct the curls of smoke over and into the hives. The little girl, seeing Bradecote fascinated by what he saw, raised her voice and told him that 'Brother Bee' sang lullabies to the bees and sent in the warm smoke so they would be sleepy, and wore a 'pale gown' because the bees did not 'see' it as they did something dark.

'And they loves him as he loves them, but sometimes a bee forgets and stings, and then the bee dies. Brother Bee wears his funny hat so they do not sting and do not die. A very kind man.'

Mærwynn squeezed her sister's shoulder, and apologised to the lord Undersheriff, but Bradecote shook his head and addressed the little girl.

'Thank you for telling me. I do not know about bees, but you do.'

'Brother Bee tells me things when I asks questions. Never says I am in the way, neither.' There was a swift and slightly reproachful glance at her sister before she looked at the undersheriff. 'I likes honey. Does you?'

'I do. Will you watch Brother Bee while I speak with your sister?'

The child nodded and smiled, and wriggled from her sister's hold and would have skipped forward had not Brother Petrus turned at the voices and waved, but motioned her to sit, and with a finger placed in front of where his mouth would be, under his veil, to be quiet. Bradecote and the other sheriff's men moved a little further from the beekeeper and child, and Mærwynn, who was now looking worried, went with them.

'Do not be frightened. We only wish to know if' – there was a moment's pause as Bradecote thought better of saying 'husband' – 'Walter had any place within the house that was secret, perhaps where he told you not to look?'

'Told me not to do many things, my lord, every day, but no place did 'e keep privy for 'imself alone.' She looked away for a moment, but it was to smile at her sister.

'You have heard he took silver from townsfolk and did not hand over all their rents?'

It was her turn to nod, a bigger version of the little sister.

'And you have no idea where he might have hidden his hoard?'

'No, my lord. If I did, I would tell Brother Petrus, and then 'e could tell the lord Abbot. 'Tis silver as belongs to the Church, and to take it would be such a sin as I could not atone for.'

Mærwynn had clearly not thought of the sums that were owed to those from whom they had been extorted.

'If any place occurs to you, tell us, for we will see it returned.'

'As you wish, my lord.' She would clearly have preferred to go to the beekeeping Benedictine but would not disobey so mighty a personage as the lord Undersheriff.

'Can you tell us whether Walter went to Gloucester on abbey business last Michaelmas?'

'I cannot, my lord, for we was wed just after the holy day. All I knows he were away upon abbey business until the day afore, but then Walter often went to the abbey manors, up to Maugersbury and Stow as well as those in this shire, but 'e never told me other than 'e would be away for two days, three days, and not to put any meat or fish in the pottage until 'e returned.' Mærwynn could give them no more.

'Then we will leave you to your bee watching.' Bradecote gave a nod of dismissal and thanks, and Mærwynn went to sit upon the ground with her sister. The beekeeper raised a hand in benediction, and the three men skirted through the orchard, avoiding the beehives, to take the 'garden door' into the abbey enclave.

When they entered the abbey courtyard, it had a sleepy air and lacked the bustle of earlier in the day. A groom was leading a chestnut cob to the stables, and a youth, clearly on 'extra duties' for some misdemeanour, was sweeping horse droppings onto a shovel as slowly as possible. Alnoth the Handless was waiting to speak with Walkelin, though he hung back a little so that he need not present himself to the lord Undersheriff. There was only so much power with which he felt comfortable, and Walkelin was a friendly soul who did not exude cold, hard authority. Alnoth would have been surprised to know it was an appearance he was trying to learn for certain situations, though so far Serjeant Catchpoll usually said he just looked like the carved statue of a martyred saint.

'Underserjeant.' Alnoth's call was barely more than an urgent undertone, but Walkelin heard, glanced round, and then made his excuses to his superiors, promising to join them very shortly. He went to where Alnoth was leaning back against the western wall of the gateway, a place now in shade as the day advanced and the gateway blocked the sun's burning rays.

'The afternoon went well for you, Alnoth?'

'Indeed, Underserjeant. A kindly woman gave me a little bowl full of cherries, and I earned two silver ha'pennies for watchin' stalls. But, you did not tell me that Master Walter the Steward kept silver that belongs to this abbey.'

He sounded disappointed in Walkelin. 'Must 'ave been that made the man look so fine in Gloucester last year.'

'I am sorry. I would have told you afore, but I was not sure what Serjeant Catchpoll and the lord Undersheriff would want known.' Walkelin sounded genuinely apologetic.

'All Evesham wants to know where that silver lies now, but that be mostly 'acos 'tis the latest gossip, and in truth, they should be talkin' more of poor Old Cuthbert, and seekin' to aid you to find who killed 'im. Silver cannot be more important than a soul.' Alnoth sighed, and Walkelin felt that Alnoth would have made a good monk.

'You speaks true enough, but findin' the silver will end the gossip, and them as ought to possess it will get it back. Then we might find folk quicker to aid us over Old Cuthbert.' It was a subtle way of saying that if any word came to Alnoth's ear of the hoard, he should let Walkelin know of it.

'Mmm.' Alnoth frowned, chasing a thought that jinked like a chased hare and eluded him for the moment, and Walkelin was not sure whether he should have made himself clearer.

When Catchpoll asked later whether anything new had been learnt, Walkelin could only say that Alnoth would do what he could to help them in finding Old Cuthbert's killer.

Chapter Thirteen

Bradecote looked up as Walkelin entered the small chamber.

'We have been trying to work out where Walter the Steward might have hidden his ill-gotten silver, Walkelin, as well as working back through all we have been told to try and find the lies, or those things mistakenly given as truth. That a killer will lie is what we expect, but we are being muddled by innocent folk misleading us.' Bradecote looked to Walkelin as the repository of information, for his head seemed to file it away most accurately, and he was good at retrieving it. 'Sense says the hiding place must not be where all could get to it, and if not his house, then we are looking at abbey land. The trouble is that he might even have hidden it on one of the abbey holdings outside Evesham.'

'Not to my mind, my lord.' Catchpoll wore a 'thinking face', but not the one where his eyes were also closed. 'A man like Walter would always worry that someone might come across it by chance if it lay somewhere else where 'e could not check upon it when the fear touched 'im.'

'Yes, you are right, Catchpoll. I ought to have considered that.'

'Which means that it would be most like somewheres

213

down this bit 'o the ground as lies close to the loop of the river, and not where folk pokes about day to day in their work. So it will not be inside the walls as they stands.'

'And not where the masons is at work either, my lord,' Walkelin offered.

'But there are those two ruins before the orchard, that Prior Richard told me had once been for knights who owed service to the abbey but had been told they need only pay in coin. Not much stands, but we have seen before how a hearthstone can prove a good hiding place with a hiding hole dug beneath. We should go and look there after the evening meal. There is also—'

What Bradecote was about to say remained unspoken, for an urgent knocking on the door interrupted him, and what was reported drove all thought of stolen silver from their minds.

The man who stood before them had come from the Hampton ferry, if not at the run, then at a fast walking pace, which meant sweat stood upon his brow and he needed to catch a breath between sentences.

'My lord, Kenelm the Ferryman lies near senseless and beaten bad on the far bank. They got the priest to 'im, but the good Father thinks Kenelm needs care and prayers but not the Last Rites.' The man took a deep breath and then continued. 'And the ferry be cut loose and gone downstream, though two men 'as gone and rowed downstream in a boat to catch it. I came across in a coracle.'

'Did someone steal his takings of the day?' Bradecote wondered if it would be a sum that would inspire a violent robbery.

'That I does not know, my lord. Kenelm were not yet clear of mind when I left.'

'We will come immediately.' Bradecote sent Walkelin to see to the horses being saddled. The tired messenger could be carried up behind Walkelin, rather than run himself into a red-mist exhaustion trying to keep up with the fresher sheriff's men. If there was nothing bigger than a coracle to convey them across, they would leave the horses and cross one at a time, if there was no alternative.

Within a few minutes they were trotting out under the abbey gateway, their faces so serious that a woman who saw them crossed herself and told her neighbour she thought there had been another killing in the town. When they reached the ferry, a rowing boat awaited them. The priest, certain that at least the lord Sheriff's Serjeant would come to see what had happened, had found another man with a small fishing craft which was more stable, and larger than a coracle, and might take two in safety, and three if the passengers sat still, and sent him over to await whoever came down from the town.

Bradecote, not liking the idea of an overburdened boat tipping him into the flow of the Avon, suggested he and Catchpoll cross, but Walkelin, not wishing to be left holding the horses on the Evesham bank, persuaded the man behind him that he could fit in the coracle, being thin and with joints that bent easily. Thus, all three sheriff's men crossed the river, and the horses were left tethered and under the eye of Kenelm's young nephew.

The priest still sat with Kenelm in the little wooden hut that was the ferryman's shelter when he thought the crossing traffic would be more from west to east bank, and the ferryman looked both pale and bloodied, and a rough bandage had been wrapped about his head. He was crouched upon the ground, his head resting forward in his hands, which in turn rested upon his raised knees. It was almost a foetal position, and he did not lift his head as they entered.

'How does he, Father?' Bradecote addressed the priest.

'Well enough, my son,' the priest assessed Bradecote as lordly by garb and voice, but it did not change his demeanour, 'though his head still spins and he will not allow himself true rest until his ferry is safely back where it belongs. I have no doubt at all that it will be found, for two men rowing will be faster than the current, and the only delay will be towing it back upstream, against the flow.' The priest was softly spoken, and exuded calm.

'Can you tell us who did this, Kenelm, and for what reason? Had they crossed from the Evesham side with you and then attacked you rather than pay the fare?' Bradecote looked down at the man, not expecting much in response.

Kenelm moved his head slowly, shaking it in slow motion and groaning a little as he did so.

'Bastards came down this side, and I thought they wanted to cross.'

'And they did not. What did they want, friend?' Catchpoll, who had been offered a log end to sit upon, crouched down with a groan not unlike that of the injured ferryman, thanks to his arthritic knees, and put a hand onto Kenelm's arm.

'To take more 'n just, and give it to them,' Kenelm managed, in something between a growl and a groan.

It sounded as though someone had taken the idea from Walter the Steward.

'And you refused.' It was the obvious assumption, otherwise they would not have cut loose the ferry, even if Kenelm had been 'persuaded' by blows. Catchpoll was not surprised.

''Course I did. The ferryman asks a fair price and no more. They wanted me to add on the toll.' Kellen raised his head, outrage giving him strength.

'What toll?' Bradecote frowned. 'No toll is due on the ferry.'

'Same toll as at the bridge.'

Understanding dawned on Bradecote.

'So they were from Bengeworth garrison.'

'Aye, the lord Sheriff's men. Said as folk was avoidin' the toll on the bridge and walkin' round to use the ferry, but no change in numbers 'as I seen, and no toll were there afore now on the bridge.'

Catchpoll swore under his breath, and Kenelm took it as vindication of his stance.

'I thinks the same, Serjeant Catchpoll.'

'Can you describe or give a name to any of them, and how many were there?' Bradecote wanted to be able to identify the culprits before Rahere de Cormolain.

'Four, my lord, and no face did I know. Three was just the bullies, big men. Fourth was in charge and only one as spoke. Enjoyed it all, though 'e left the blows to the bullies. Laughed, 'e did, and 'twere 'im as cut my ferry loose, may 'e rot in Hell,' Kenelm groaned again then added, 'and "Serjeant" was what one called 'im.'

Catchpoll made a growling noise.

'And what did the serjeant look like?' Walkelin wanted detail.

'Not so tall above the usual, but big in build. Brown locks.' Kenelm shut his eyes tight and tried to see the man in his mind more clearly than through the mist of anger. 'Lacked a tooth. Saw that when 'e laughed.'

'Top or bottom?' Walkelin did not care that he sounded eager.

'Top, left side, as I recalls. Nothin' more I can give you.'

'Nor need you, friend. We 'as enough.' Catchpoll got up, slowly.

'Your ferry will be restored to you, and any damage will be paid for by those at the castle,' declared Bradecote. 'You were right to refuse, and I am sorry you suffered for your honesty.'

'As long as my ferry be found, my lord, and she 'as taken no worse 'arm, I will not complain.'

'Well, we will see justice for what has been done.' Bradecote looked at the priest. 'Can he be taken across to lie in his own bed?'

'Indeed, he can, my lord, but after you have gone across. There are willing hands to row all as needs this evening, and the ferry fare will still be Kenelm's, not,' he raised a hand, 'that any fare was due for you doing your duty by the Law.'

'Then we will leave now and hope to reach the castle before the gates are barred for the night.' Bradecote nodded to priest and ferryman, and the temporary ferrymen, in rowing boat and coracle, took them once more across the Avon.

It was only when they were alone and had collected their horses that Catchpoll gave vent to his ire.

'A serjeant to act like that. Gives all serjeants a bad

name.' He spat somewhere past his horse's right ear.

'But the serjeant I saw early this afternoon was not lacking a tooth and was grey at the temple and the lazy sort.' Walkelin knew it could not be that man.

'And de Cormolain said none of his men were allowed into the town, which was a lie, since the serjeant with a missing tooth is clearly our "stranger" in the alehouse.' Bradecote would never trust de Cormolain, but the blatant lie still stung.

'Depends the way you sees it, my lord. The serjeant Walkelin saw would be the lord de Cormolain's man, not the lord Sheriff's, the garrison serjeant as stays all the time, not the one as comes with each lord. Which makes things more – difficult.'

'He would still be under de Cormolain's command during his tenure, and there is no difficulty if we have proof enough, Catchpoll.' Bradecote was determined.

'Easy to say, my lord, but the lord Sheriff thinks 'is own way.'

'True, but if faced with our proof—'

'And if the serjeant is missin' a fingernail too, my lord,' added Walkelin, interrupting.

'Indeed. That is plenty enough to give cause to put the man before the Justices in Eyre for the killing of Old Cuthbert, and while the lord Sheriff might be more than happy to annoy Abbot Reginald of Evesham, he cannot be seen to set aside murder by one of his own men.'

Catchpoll wished he was as convinced as his superior, but they cantered up into Evesham and then trotted down the hill to cross the bridge and into the gateway of Bengeworth Castle.

The duty guard, somnolent of a summer evening, were present in body, but not in mind. Three were playing at dice on the dusty earth of the bailey, just out of sight beyond the corner of the gatehouse. The two actually in the gateway were lounging against the day-warmed wood of the palisade. One caught sight of the three figures just in time to straighten as they swung left, and, recognising them from earlier in the afternoon, he made no effort to challenge them. They ignored him, for which he was grateful, seeing the look on the lord's face and that of Serjeant Catchpoll.

Rahere de Cormolain was thinking of his bed when Bradecote entered, without knocking and with Catchpoll right behind him. Walkelin had been ordered to cover the gate to ensure that no man left the castle.

'Not again.' De Cormolain covered his eyes as if by doing so he could make Bradecote disappear. 'Is not one pointless visitation in a day enough for you?'

'You can be sure I would not return to this damp hole without good cause, de Cormolain, but good cause I have. This afternoon, Kenelm the Ferryman, who mans the crossing from Hampton, was attacked by men from this castle, and his ferry cut loose.'

'And you think me the one wine-addled? I most certainly did not send anyone to the ferry. Why would I?'

'The ferryman is sore of body and head but could tell us what happened. Four men, one of whom was addressed as "Serjeant", came to the Hampton side. Kenelm thought they wanted to cross, but they did not. What they did want to do was get him to take silver beyond his crossing fare to match the "toll" due at the Bengeworth bridge, because some might avoid the bridge when bringing goods to market. They said it was the lord Sheriff's wish.'

'I have not had any instruction from the lord Sheriff about the ferry at Hampton, and if I had then you would need to speak with him. I would enjoy watching you try and treat him as you do those Catchpoll here takes up. Do you have any idea who he would pick as your replacement?'

De Cormolain smiled, unpleasantly. 'You come here, at a day's end, to spout accusations that can be nothing but foolishness. My serjeant has been here all day, and from what he told me after you left, your "Serjeant's whelp" was asking him questions this afternoon about drinking in the town, and I said that none went without my permission.'

'But this were the lord Sheriff's man, my lord, the garrison serjeant, not yours.' Catchpoll was respectful but guarded.

'And the garrison serjeant is away from Bengeworth at present. You did not see him this afternoon because he was not here and I do not know when he will return, for he is gone to the lord Sheriff upon garrison business.' De Cormolain turned back to Bradecote. 'Has it not occurred to you that any small band of greedy men could claim to be in the lord Sheriff's employ to give power to their threats.'

'But they knew of the toll being taken here, at the bridge,' countered Bradecote.

'Many do, since it was brought in.'

'At the lord Sheriff's direct command?'

'At his wish, shall we say.' De Cormolain yawned. 'The ferry will be found, I take it?'

'Almost certainly.'

'And the ferryman is not like to die or be crippled for life. So a man was threatened by four unknown men who claimed connection with the lord Sheriff. That cannot be proved, the lord Sheriff's garrison serjeant is not even in Bengeworth, and I did not, I swear to you, order him to Hampton at any time. You are just trying to put pressure on this garrison because you and I dislike each other. There is no proof you can bring to show otherwise.'

'There you are wrong, de Cormolain. We have a description of this serjeant that is quite distinctive, since he lacks an upper tooth on the left side.'

'But Serjeant Catchpoll lacks an upper left tooth and you have not thought to arraign him before the Justices.' De Cormolain shrugged. 'It is not so very rare.'

'And—'

'We 'as enough to be sure, my lord, and to make it beyond doubt to the lord Sheriff,' Catchpoll interrupted his superior without compunction, and Bradecote, realising why, made no complaint.

'I somehow think your "sure" may not be the same as his, Serjeant.' De Cormolain was apparently unruffled.

'I want all the garrison in the bailey to answer our questions, whether the garrison serjeant is present or not.' Bradecote felt nothing more could be gained discussing the absent serjeant.

'You can "want" all you please, but I am not turning out my men upon your whim.' De Cormolain was beginning to lose his temper. He was tired, annoyed and needed to think.

'I do not speak as myself but as representative of the lord Sheriff and the lord King's Law.'

'Ah yes, the really not so very high, and only moderately mighty lord Undersheriff. Behold me quaking.' De Cormolain was mocking.

Hugh Bradecote was also tired, and had missed the evening meal, so he was hungry and in no mood to back down. His hand went unconsciously to his sword hilt.

'The Law is patient, my lord.' Catchpoll was looking at de Cormolain, but his words were as much for his superior. He had no doubt that Bradecote, even a tired and hungry Bradecote, could best a man who, if the state of the table was anything to go by, had not only been drinking in the afternoon, but continued after his own dinner, and with enough ease to make it look an unfair contest. It would complicate matters even more. Far better they withdrew, even if de Cormolain felt that a victory, since the last word would be with them on the morrow.

Hugh Bradecote stiffened, but did not look at Catchpoll.

'The Law is . . . better than the men that serve it. Oh, go to bed, Bradecote, and see sense in the morning.' It was, very intentionally, an insulting dismissal, and de Cormolain liked that.

Bradecote did not, but he could almost feel Catchpoll's eyes on his back and knew that what he wanted to do and what was best diverged.

'I will be glad to get to bed, de Cormolain, thank you, and I will be seeing the same sense come the dawn. I wonder if you will.' It was the best he could do to counter the man, though it fell far short of what he would have liked. At least de Cormolain's laugh did not sound as confident as it would have otherwise done. 'And I will set a watch upon the gate so that none can slip away before my return.' Bradecote did not have the resources to do so, but he doubted de Cormolain was clear-headed enough to think things through, and he could at least leave Walkelin, very obviously, until after full darkness fell.

When undersheriff and sheriff's serjeant had departed, de Cormolain swore. Ansculf had been too open and heavy-handed and had better hope that William de Beauchamp would stand up for him in the face of damning evidence, since he would be the only one to do so.

'I will be damned if I will let him drag me into all this,' de Cormolain muttered. 'Let him get himself out of the mire.'

Bradecote knew he had been too close to letting his anger overcome good sense, and he was annoyed with himself. He forced himself to set his anger aside to think clearly and had swift but quiet words with Catchpoll and Walkelin, who made a short report while their horses were brought.

'My lord, somethin' were different from the first visit. Nobody tried to leave, but many eyes watched me, and they looked – nervous. If the garrison serjeant be the one we seek, it may be that the men as went with 'im carried on to Elmley or Worcester, but then others know they went off sudden and did not return, which looks strange. The lord de Cormolain's serjeant also did not come nigh me, and I thought 'e would ask why we was back.'

'So we have very good grounds to say that Kenelm the Ferryman's attackers are from the castle, and that whoever killed Old Cuthbert is their leader, but it gets us not much closer to laying hands upon the man. I have told de Cormolain I will set a watch upon the gate, in case the underlings are still here, which means, I am afraid, I need you to be seen to be outside until it is full dark and quiet. We will ensure the porter at the abbey gate knows you will return late, so you can get to your bed eventually.'

'I understand, my lord, though I wish as we 'ad eaten afore we came.'

'Your rumblin' gut will make sure you keeps awake,' offered Catchpoll, but then relented and said he would try and secure at least some bread to eat before he laid his head to rest.

The trio then gave a performance in the bailey, with Bradecote ordering Walkelin to give his horse to Catchpoll and to remain outside the castle to detain any who might leave overnight. Walkelin looked suitably 'obedient but none too pleased' and stationed himself very obviously opposite the castle gateway.

Bradecote and Catchpoll, the latter leading Walkelin's horse, did not say anything until halfway up the hill to the abbey, and it was Bradecote who broke the silence.

'You were right, Catchpoll. The Law is patient, but its patience is not without end. I nearly let my own feelings get in the way of the Law. Tomorrow will be different.'

'Aye, my lord, but unless the garrison serjeant returns, we are matching a description with an unknown. Will the man lack a tooth? I am sure that 'e will, but it needs to be seen for the accusation to be made without doubt, and with the lord de Cormolain sayin' as the man was not in Evesham at the time.'

'Do you believe that, Catchpoll?'

'Not as such, my lord. My thought would be 'e were sent off out the way, but it could be mighty difficult to prove just when, and whether 'e went by way of the ferry first.'

'And my fear is that de Cormolain will send to the lord

Sheriff and tell him it would be best not to send back the garrison serjeant at all.'

'Well, the lord Sheriff was never one to like to be "told" anything, so we 'as that in our favour, and worryin' about the morrow will just cost us sleep and do no good.'

'You are right, Catchpoll.' Bradecote managed a small smile.

'As always, my lord?' Catchpoll ventured.

'I would not go that far, Serjeant.'

The abbey gate had been shut, for the hour was late, and the sun had finally dipped below the western horizon, but since it was known that the lord Undersheriff was not yet back and within, there was a gatekeeper on watch to let them in. They dismounted, and Catchpoll led the horses to the stable to find a groom, while Bradecote spoke with the gatekeeper. Both were surprised that in the guest hall a tired servant was waiting with the welcome news that there was not only bread and cheese, but cold chicken from the abbot's own table should they wish to eat. Catchpoll ensured a portion was wrapped in a cloth and left on Walkelin's cot.

The only person who had given up waiting to see them, and taken to his bed, was Alnoth the Handless.

Alnoth was a man who was content with his own company, and found joy in simple things, such as being warm, fed, and able to sit of an evening and listen to the birds singing before the melodies ceased in July. When the evening meal was over, he had gone to listen to Compline in the abbey church, and then, since it was still warm and the evening light was soft and golden, he walked within the abbey land, into the orchard, past the near-silent bee skeps and on to the tumbled-down retreat that had been home to Mother Placida. He was accompanied part of the way by Brother Petrus, the beekeeper, who was giving up sleep before the Night Offices to check one of his hives that gave cause for concern. It had seemed to him increasingly 'out of sorts' the last few weeks, and he was concerned that the numbers of bees within it had dropped. If the queen was ill or too old to produce more bees for the colony, it might cease to be viable, and the bees might simply go away.

Alnoth left him to his hives and carried on to the anchoress's old cell. If he had possessed hands, he would have touched the wall in remembrance, but instead he leant back against it on the south side, where the heat of the sun had warmed it through the day, and closed his eyes. The memories flooded back; he had sat at the base of this wall and heard the swallows on the wing, the blackbird in the orchard asserting his territory, the trilling wren in the bushes where the women of two households always laid their washing, and Mother Placida's voice, low and intent, using the words of the Office he had just attended. Her voice was the one thing absent, yet it drifted into his mind, as a benevolent ghost of sound. He smiled, and then sighed, and quietly said the *Nunc Dimittis* in her memory. Assuredly, he thought, hers was a soul that had departed in peace.

His mind had drifted, and the disconnected thoughts that swirled in his half-dozing state passed around each other in a soporific dance until two touched. He opened his eyes and a frown appeared on his brow. Walter the Steward had hidden his stolen silver somewhere others would not find it, and he had seen the man at the anchoress's decaying home several times over the last two years. He remembered it because he had been coming to sit as he was now, and decided against it, since the steward was a man who was full of his own worth and power and would no doubt order him away. He had once done so when Alnoth was walking through the orchard, claiming he would steal the fruit, though how he was meant to do so without hands to reach the laden branches, and no power in a two-fingered grip on a stick, Alnoth could not imagine. He had assumed it had simply been unfortunate that Walter the steward was making rounds of the demesne just at that hour, but now another reason raised its head. Could he have been adding to his hoard, or checking it lay safe? Yes, now he considered it more, he had actually seen him coming out of the doorway, and most folk did not enter what felt like a tomb, although the anchoress had been too frail to dig her own grave within its walls, as Alnoth heard some did. She had been buried in a quiet spot at the edge of the monks' burial ground, keeping her bones in the chaste seclusion in which she had lived.

Alnoth still had not wanted to trespass in what he felt was a holy place, however fallen down it had become. It may not have been consecrated by a priest, but the anchoress had consecrated it by her presence within the walls for so long. At the same time, Underserjeant Walkelin had said that if the stolen silver was returned to the abbey, there was a better chance of finding out who killed Old Cuthbert. Alnoth was torn, so he had prayed for guidance. Into his mind came the memory of Mother Placida's shapely white hand proffering food through the little hatch in the door. He felt it was a sign. Yes, he could open the hatch without disturbing the serenity within, and at least see if there was anything inside.

When his eyes had adjusted to the low light, he could see nothing obvious, and yet something was not right. The chamber had been unoccupied for years, and the floor rushes had rotted to dust, but there were holes in the thatch, new since his last visit, which should have meant remnants of the reeds upon the floor, yet there was nothing but a hearthstone and bare earth. He felt, rather than knew, that someone had trespassed. He would tell Underserjeant Walkelin, and if it was nothing, then at least the underserjeant would not chastise him for making the suggestion.

As the sun set he returned to the enclave, and asked after the lord Sheriff's men, but was told they had ridden out and not returned. He waited a while in the shadows, half dozing, until he heard horses' hooves upon the cobbles, but there were only two riders. Alnoth, unwilling to speak of his suspicions other than with Walkelin, took them to his bed and kept them close. They could wait until morning, or the underserjeant's return.

Oswald Mealtere's wife had spent much of the evening keeping quiet, which was always the safest thing to do in her house, and had lingered over scrubbing out the bowls from the evening pottage. Her husband was in a foul mood, which was not uncommon, and arguing with his father. Their son, whose nature was more like that of his mother, had offered to go and put the chickens into the coop for the night, and she knew he would remain outside as long as he could.

Siward Mealtere was on the defensive, as his son harangued him.

'What lay betwixt Cuthbert 'n me be no business of any other, even you. 'Tis enough that you know 'e would be as pleased at my death as I be at 'is.'

'But to crow of it before the lord Undersheriff, Father . . .' Oswald shook his head.

'Ha! No risk to me in that, and the Law be so keen on truthfulness. Well, I did not lie and say I regretted the death.'

'Our strife with Wulfram Meduwyrhta I understands, aye, and agrees with. You never said why though, with Cuthbert. No need would 'e 'ave of our malt, and even afore 'e lost wife and trade, there—'

Siward held up a hand, not so much in an action of halting, as protecting himself.

'You leave 'er out of it.'

'I did not bring the woman into it, just—oh, I gives up. Your skull be as full of clouds as your eyes.' Oswald had thumped the table angrily, and grimaced, though his wife looked thoughtful. 'I needs none of this. Every mouth in Evesham spouts questions about Walter the Steward's silver, 'cept it were never 'is to keep, and where it might be kept close and safe. A good sum of it be mine, but all will pass to the monks, I doubts not, if whoever finds it speaks up. The bastard steward deserved all 'e got. That is what I will always say. Not even content with what 'e took, 'e wanted more, and—' Oswald, pursed his lips and shook his head, vehemently.

His wife realised that she would be sharing the bed with a still irascible husband, and tried to say something that might reduce his anger.

'The lord Undersheriff spoke with Mærwynn about the silver this afternoon.'

'How could you know that?' Oswald turned, and his voice was dismissive.

'I was out with washin' when Mærwynn and little Win came to their mother, and the little girl's voice carries.'

'Hmm. So what did she say?'

'I only 'eard what the child reported.'

'And that be what I meant, foolish woman.' Oswald scowled.

His wife, who had in fact still been talking with the mead maker's wife, made a vague report, to avoid showing how close she had been.

'She said about them askin' Mærwynn if she knew if the silver were kept close in the steward's 'ouse, and Mærwynn said no, and somethin' about bees and Brother Petrus.'

'Did she now? Well, that may just be interestin'.' It was the nearest Mistress Mealtere would get to praise, but she had just been thankful that it seemed to make her husband less angry and more thoughtful.

Chapter Fourteen

William de Beauchamp passed a poor night, though that was more down to eating too much than the news from Bengeworth, according to his lady, who turned her back to him and huffed as he tossed and turned to try and get comfortable. He woke, unrefreshed, with the first glimmer of dawn, his head fuzzy, and then could not get back to sleep. He decided that if he was awake, then so could everyone else be, and so rose, roused his servants and called for his horse, and the men from Bengeworth, to be ready to ride out in short order. It was more pleasant to ride before the day became hot, and he had no desire to break his fast, so they would not get the chance to do so either. That there were grumbles among those who followed him, and stifled yawns, did not interest him.

Ansculf did not yawn, and nor did he grumble. He was worried, though he concealed it from his companions. In a foul mood, their lord could be unpredictable, other than you could guarantee that he would not be charitable and understanding. The garrison serjeant was not sure whether the fact that they rode in silence was a good or a bad one, and secretly hoped that venting his ire upon the lord Bradecote, or on the lord de Cormolain, would, like excising a boil, ease the lord Sheriff and leave nothing more than disinterest in a mere serjeant. If that was not the case, his life was about to become very difficult.

It was only a few miles from the castle at Elmley to the loop of the Avon that snaked about Evesham and kept it from Bengeworth, and the majority of those who dwelt in the latter were only just opening their shutters and doors when William de Beauchamp and his entourage reached Bengeworth. The look upon his face made those inhabitants of the community that saw him make so deep an obeisance that their faces were nigh unto their knees, and they crossed themselves thereafter, pitying whoever it was who was on the receiving end of his wrath, even if one of the garrison, who were distrusted and disliked. He rode into the castle sitting lance-straight in the saddle, his reins-bearing hand upon the pommel, the other imperiously upon his hip, and entered the hastily opened gate to find the duty watch assembling in a rush. He ignored them and came to a halt in the middle of the bailey. A man ran forward to take his horse at the bit so that he might dismount, though he remained in the saddle, and received not so much as a glance.

Rahere de Cormolain did not give the appearance of rushing, though his heart rate had increased at hearing his overlord was at the gate, and he had fumbled getting his sword into its hanger as he strove to look more 'garrison commander' and less 'man only recently risen from his bed'. Once he set eyes upon him, he did not think it was because William de Beauchamp had come to heap praise upon his head. He was worried, but composed, and made a bow that was deferential but not grovelling.

'My lord, I am hon—' He got no further.

'Send a man to find my undersheriff, and bring me wine. Now.'

While he disliked being addressed like a common servant, a flood of relief surged through de Cormolain like the wave of the Severn Bore rushing upstream. It was Bradecote who was in trouble, not he himself.

'Immediately, my lord.' He turned to Ansculf, who had also dismounted, and was hovering just out of the lord Sheriff's line of sight. 'Ansculf, go to the abbey and fetch the lord Bradecote. If he is not within the walls, have the monks go out and search for him, as a matter of urgency.'

Ansculf did not respond immediately. He thought it would be better if he remained in the background and did not show his face in Evesham town for a while. He stared at de Cormolain, part of him hoping that he would realise it would be better to send another.

'Yes, go, and make sure Serjeant Catchpoll also comes before me.' De Beauchamp would have words with his serjeant for not making his commands sufficiently plain, as well as with his undersheriff for ignoring them.

'As you command, my lord.' Ansculf had no choice but to obey swiftly. He remounted and wheeled his horse about, clattering out under the arch of the gateway as though chased by hellhounds, though he amended his pace as he crossed the bridge and rode up into the town, realising that he had no power to command the lord Abbot of Evesham's monks, and it was a matter of debate as to whether the lord Sheriff did either.

De Cormolain, irritated that the garrison serjeant had not leapt to obey without the added command of de Beauchamp, overcame his temper and strove to sound emollient. 'I am sure you would prefer to come within my lodging, my lord, and the best wine will be brought to you there.' He indicated the duty constable's lodging. It looked what it was – makeshift and half-hearted, and no lord who performed his service to de Beauchamp there enjoyed a single day of it.

De Beauchamp sat silent for a moment, as if considering the offer, though in reality he just wanted to keep de Cormolain off-balance. Then he grunted and dismounted slowly.

'Very well.' It was grudging. He followed in de Cormolain's wake until the garrison commander stepped aside to let him enter the chamber first.

William de Beauchamp himself had never stayed in this castle, since his own seat at Elmley lay only a few short miles away, and in fact he had never actually been within the 'keep' since instructing it to be adapted from a draughty barn. He halted in the doorway and sniffed.

'What is the foul smell?'

'It is the damp, my lord.' De Cormolain tried not to sound annoyed that the man who sent him to this place, and lived under an hour's ride away, had never discovered this for himself before. 'It is here and in the barracks also, though the hot summer has dried them out a little more than the stonework.'

'Then give thanks you are not on duty here in the winter.' De Beauchamp wrinkled his nose and went towards the dais and the seat that was his right.

'Indeed, my lord.' De Cormolain had done a month in midwinter three years previously and had feared he would take such an ague from it that he might never recover. He sent a servant scurrying for wine and, in a low voice, the best goblet, and invited his overlord to be seated. Suggesting he might make himself 'comfortable' would sound foolish. There was an awkward silence until the wine had been brought, and the servant dismissed. Then de Beauchamp took a long draught, ran his tongue along his lips, with his gaze never leaving his vassal lord, and spoke.

'So Bradecote is getting in your way.' It was a statement, not a question. 'As you are getting in the Abbot of Evesham's way.'

'My lord, I have done only as you instructed me. Whenever opportunity arises, my men disrupt the townsfolk and villagers bringing in goods, make incursions over the abbey wall to show its uselessness, and sow discord among the townsfolk, which has been the easier since the steward of the abbey was killed a few days past. Bradecote is here to sniff into that, but it was beyond any possible remit to have Serjeant Catchpoll threaten the garrison if they continue to harass those who want to cross the bridge by exacting a toll.'

'You have been doing that?' De Beauchamp looked vaguely pleased. Money coming to him always pleased him.

'Why yes, as it complies with your instruction my lord.'

'An instruction that has never been given, de Cormolain, just remember that.'

'But you—'

'I have no knowledge of any unlawful acts by members of this garrison, nor, of course, as lord Sheriff, would I condone those acts.' De Beauchamp's tone was colourless. There was a pause. 'Have the countryfolk been complaining loudly to Evesham's overlord, the high and mighty abbot?'

A touch of eagerness entered his voice.

'I believe so, since that must be how Catchpoll learnt the details of a recent reported incident.' De Cormolain now comprehended that his lord was approving of his actions but would deny any connection. 'There is no link between anyone here and the dead steward, and while Bradecote might want to poke his nose in just to annoy me, it should have ended with a few questions and him trotting off to root around for answers elsewhere.'

'You do not like him, do you.' Again, this was not a question.

'No, my lord. Never did and never will, and nor does he like me.'

'Very well. But remember that he is my vassal, not yours, and so you will not go beyond your "dislike".'

'As you command, my lord.'

'Exactly. As I command.'

'And what happens now, my lord?'

'I wait, and the longer I have to wait, the less happy I will be.'

De Cormolain made a silent prayer that Bradecote would be hard to find in Evesham.

The lord Sheriff's men had risen before the bell tolled for Prime, with the intention of appearing before the castle gates as soon as they were unbarred for the day, though Catchpoll had needed to shake Walkelin by the shoulder to rouse him after his shortened rest. As they were about to leave by the gate in the new enclave wall, however, Walkelin was hailed by Alnoth the Handless, who had been heading towards the church to sit in the south transept and listen to the Office. Alnoth beckoned the underserjeant with his vestige of a hand, and Bradecote indicated he would wait until the man had spoken with Walkelin. It was clear that Alnoth did not feel confident enough to approach the lord Undersheriff. Walkelin greeted him with a cheerful 'good morrow'.

'I tried to see you yestereve, Underserjeant, but no sign of you could I find.' Alnoth's voice had a hint of excitement within it.

'No, Alnoth, my duties kept me from the guest hall and my rest until after nightfall.'

'At least I can tell you now.' Alnoth did look as if his information was bubbling up within him and he was glad to give it release. He took a deep breath. 'I think Walter the Steward broke the sanctity of Mother Placida's retreat and buried 'is stolen silver there.' It came out in a rush of words.

'Why do you think so?'

'I went to sit outside it in the evenin', and I remembered seein' the steward several times by it, for it made me keep away to avoid bein' shouted at. And – and then I felt encouraged to look inside.'

'You have found it?' Walkelin was understandably excited.

'No, but I looked within, and it was not . . . right. These long years after the godly soul's death, and with the roof part fallen in, it should 'ave looked unloved, untidy. I expected little bits of thatch upon the earth, a broken rafter. The floor was just – the floor, as though it had been swept, not recently, but certainly only months past.'

Walkelin tempered his excitement. This was an

impression, a 'feeling', nothing solid upon which to declare to the lord Bradecote that the missing silver was found, and even if it had been where the steward had hidden it once, there was no proof it still lay there.

'So there was no bag or sign of anything bein' kept there?'

'No, but – mayhap Walter the Steward buried it and just moved the earth about so it did not look fresh?' Alnoth sounded a little less sure himself now.

'Thank you. Wait here and I will tell the lord Undersheriff and Serjeant Catchpoll what you have said. I do not know if we will look straight away, but I am sure we will look at it some time today.'

'If you enters, you must promise to say a prayer for Mother Placida. If Walter the Steward went in for bad reasons, 'e would not say a prayer, and – well, look what 'appened to the man.' If Alnoth did not think the place cursed, he certainly felt that treating it with less than great respect for its previous occupant would bring down wrath from Heaven.

'I promise that,' Walkelin answered over his shoulder, as he returned to his superiors.

'Well, was that fruitful?' Bradecote had noted a spring in Walkelin's step.

'I think so, my lord, though it is not certain. Alnoth remembers Walter the Steward bein' at the anchoress's old cell several times, and when Alnoth looked inside, 'e said as it did not seem as long abandoned as it should.'

'It is worth looking into.' Bradecote paused for a moment, wondering whether he needed to have Walkelin with them at the castle. It occurred to him that if he and Catchpoll met with opposition, Walkelin alone would not change the outcome. At the same time, he knew that Walkelin had been instrumental in collecting the information that had led them to a castle occupant being the man they sought for the death of Old Cuthbert, and he deserved to be there. He came to a decision. 'Go with Alnoth and take a "serjeant's look" in the anchoress's home, not a townsman's glance, and if the silver is there, bring it back to Abbot Reginald. Whether there or not, join us at the castle.'

'I will not linger, my lord, but will look well.' Walkelin nodded, turned and strode purposefully back to where Alnoth the Handless was watching the three men. He did not see the man who entered the new gate on horseback and went straight up to Catchpoll.

Ansculf was not sure whether he was lucky or unlucky to espy Serjeant Catchpoll straight away. The tall, lordly-looking man with him must be the undersheriff that the lord de Cormolain disliked. There was a risk they were looking for him after the little 'affair' at the ferry, but he had been sent by the lord Sheriff, and that cloak of protection should hold. He came forward boldly.

'You are the lord Undersheriff, my lord?' Being bold did not mean being offensive, not yet.

'Yes. And you are?'

'Ansculf, my lord.' Anculf thought better of giving his rank. 'The lord Sheriff commands that you attend him at the castle, Bengeworth Castle, right away. I am sent to bring you to him.'

'Well, I will hardly get lost going down the hill.' Bradecote chose to sound casual, since if William de

Beauchamp was at the castle, it was not going to be a courteous visit, and it was a matter of pride that he should look calm about the summons.

'No, my lord.' Ansculf was a little taken aback at the response. 'But you will come with me.' It ought to have sounded the way it did when Catchpoll took someone in, but somehow it had a pleading inflection.

'We will have our horses saddled immediately. Serjeant Catchpoll, see things are not delayed.'

Catchpoll caught not only the tone and being addressed as 'Serjeant Catchpoll'. He did not think for one moment that his superior was treating him as an underling. What the lord Bradecote was really saying was 'let Walkelin know we need him'. Walkelin's account of what he heard and found at the ferry would be vital in showing the lord Sheriff that what his undersheriff, and by association, his serjeant and underserjeant, had done was right.

'Aye, my lord.' Catchpoll nodded and, whilst not running, disappeared swiftly into the stables. Bradecote was left looking at the messenger. He had not seen this man before, but then he had not taken note of any of the current garrison. Perhaps it was the word 'garrison' in his mind that made him glance at the man's right hand. He was holding his horse's bridle at the bit with his left, across his body. It seemed . . . odd. The right hand hung at his side, and about the middle finger was a linen wrapping, bandaging it. Bradecote did not allow his gaze to linger, but his confidence rose.

Catchpoll returned, ostensibly from the stables, and leading Bradecote's steel grey and his own horse. Bradecote could see a groom holding the bridle of Walkelin's permanently idle mount, Snægl, just within the stables' entrance. It proved Catchpoll had understood him perfectly.

'All ready, my lord.' Catchpoll handed the grey's reins to Bradecote and mounted his own horse.

The trio trotted out through the gate and turned to the right to descend to the bridge. As they did so a man stopped dead in the street and stared at the man whose name he did not know. It did not mean that he did not recognise him, however.

Walkelin was in a hurry but knew that he could not rush what he needed to do. Alnoth, unaware that his companion was torn, was telling him how much the abbey had changed over the last few years, with claustral additions, the removal of the knights' houses, and the new wall. They had just reached the orchard edge when a stable boy caught up with them and passed on Catchpoll's instructions.

'My friend, I am sorry that I cannot go with you to—' Walkelin decided saying the place in front of the lad was feeding curiosity, so changed his words, 'see the place you mentioned. You can be sure that I will come back as soon as the lord Undersheriff can spare me.'

'I shall await you here, Underserjeant. I am too late to hear Prime, and I can give thanks for a new fine day as well in the sunshine as in a church.'

Walkelin gave him a pat upon the shoulder and then ran back to the narrow gate into the enclave to seek his horse. As he went the same way to reach the bridge he passed the bandy-legged well digger, hurrying down the hill, and was hailed by him.

'I saw the man,' Adam Welldelver gasped, pointing

across the bridge. 'Leastways I think 'twere the man in the alehouse that made such a fuss. Could not see the tooth, or rather, where it should be, but it looked very like 'im.'

'Then climb up behind and come with me, Master Welldelver. You may well be just the man the lord Undersheriff needs.' Walkelin reached down a hand, and Snægl made a huffing sound as the added weight landed upon his haunches.

'Beats me why a man would want to ride a beast,' muttered the well digger, bumping up and down and with his hands gripping Walkelin's belt. Walkelin just laughed and consoled him with the fact that they were only going a few hundred paces.

'Would rather 'ave run than 'ave my bones shook out o'place.'

'You gets used to it. Now, you is to say nothin' and stay back until I calls you, when we is inside the castle.'

'Is that where we is goin'? Not sure I likes that idea, from what folk says about it.'

'Well, you are aidin' the Law, so there can be no reason to worry.' Walkelin knew that was not actually true, but he told himself it ought to be, and was thus not a real lie.

Bradecote and Catchpoll, closely followed by Ansculf, who wanted to look as if he was preventing their escape rather than leading them in, trotted into the castle bailey, and could immediately feel the change in atmosphere occasioned by the lord Sheriff's presence, even if he was now out of sight. The men-at-arms were indefinably more martial, the grooms more attentive, and even the lad bearing two buckets of water towards the kitchen staggered faster, and thus slopped more water over his feet and into the parched dust.

They dismounted, handing their horses' reins to the men who scurried forward to take them, and Bradecote led the way to the keep. At the last moment, Ansculf nipped past him to open the door for him. This was not out of courtesy, but so that he could announce to his overlord that he had completed his task, and since there had been no delay, he knew he could not be castigated. As soon as he had done so, he intended to remove himself and keep well out of the way. He began to step back, pulling the door closed after him, but Bradecote's clipped command stopped him.

'Stay here.' It was said softly enough, but was pure command. Ansculf looked surprised and then unsettled, which was enough to make Catchpoll edge himself so that he could put his hand upon the door edge and prevent it moving further.

'My lord, I have fulfilled your command and I have duties . . .' Try as he might, Ansculf could not keep a note of entreaty from his voice.

William de Beauchamp, who had been feeding his wrath, or rather lubricating it with a rather inferior wine, which was claimed to be the best within the castle, was focused upon how much he was going to enjoy berating his undersheriff. Bradecote had, as far as he was concerned, attempted to upset his plans to cause annoyance to Abbot Reginald and, in consequence, ruined his night's sleep. That the connection was at best tenuous was not relevant. Neither Bradecote nor Serjeant Catchpoll were slow of wits, so must be anticipating an unpleasant interview, which made Bradecote's giving the garrison serjeant a command,

and looking not the least concerned, both an irritation and distraction. De Beauchamp fought down the desire to simply ask why the serjeant should remain, and let his face settle into the angry expression which had become almost that of default. He growled, letting the rumble build within his chest before letting it loose, and glared at Bradecote.

'Tell me, Bradecote, how it is that you think you are superior to me.'

'I do not think it, my lord, nor have ever thought it.'

'Then explain to me why you came to Evesham and straight away disobeyed my instructions to ignore the Abbot of Evesham's complaints about my castle.'

'My lord, I did not visit the castle until yesterday forenoon, and that was concerning the killing of a man in the town the previous night.' Bradecote sounded confident, which annoyed his superior even more.

'I do not care what the reason was. The fact is that you took it upon yourself to "command" de Cormolain here not to raise a toll at the bridge. He is my vassal, as you are, and you have no authority over him, no right to issue commands.'

'Indeed, my lord, but as I explained to him, I did not do so as another vassal lord of yours, but as a vassal of the Law. I had heard from Abbot Reginald of various incursions and depredations by men of this castle, but it was not the reason I spoke out. A woman coming to market had been assaulted, and her goods thrown into the Avon. Not only was that unlawful, but it would be all too easy for a repeat of the action to end up with a body in the river, not just baskets of fruit, and then there would be a death to investigate.'

This was not the answer de Beauchamp had expected, and he needed a moment to consider it. In the meantime, he turned his gaze upon Catchpoll.

'And you let him do this, Catchpoll? Did you fail to make my requirements known?'

'No, my lord, I passed on your instructions right enough, but what the lord Bradecote says is true. 'Tis an easy step for a mindless man-at-arms to go further than jostlin' and takin' a woman's means to earn silver, and push folk into the river and see 'em drown. Makes more work for us and the Justices.' Catchpoll was respectful but firm. He would not budge from that view and looked William de Beauchamp squarely in the face.

'You are not employed to do as little work as possible.'

'No, my lord. I does what needs doin'. This needed to be stopped afore it got worse, but in truth we failed, and failed twice.'

'How?' Curiosity supplanted de Beauchamp's anger, and Catchpoll glanced at Bradecote, wondering if the undersheriff would want to explain himself. Bradecote's barely perceptible nod gave him the go ahead.

'Well, my lord, this "chargin' a toll" seemed such a good idea that an attempt was made to spread it to cover anyone coming into Evesham over the Hampton ferry. Kenelm the Ferryman rightly refused to charge folk extra and give that to the castle. Not only was it wrong, but there would be no way 'e could prove the sum and might end up bein' told to give more and losin' the crossin' coin. When Kenelm refused, they gave 'im a beatin' and cut the ferry loose.'

'But why assume that it was men from the castle and not just – men seeing an opportunity?'

'Because, my lord, Kenelm heard the man who loosed his ferry addressed as "serjeant". When I came to the castle yesterday, the garrison serjeant was not here.' Bradecote took Catchpoll's place in the conversation.

'I told you I had not sent him there,' De Cormolain interjected, and it sounded just what it was, distancing himself from any blame.

'It does not mean he did not go.' Bradecote did not so much as glance at him. 'My lord, the serjeant in question lacked an upper tooth on the left side. If you tell your serjeant here to open his mouth, you will find that he too does so.'

'Open your mouth.' William de Beauchamp wanted to remain in control of what was going on but felt it slipping from him. He did not like it.

Ansculf opened his mouth, in as much as his lips parted.

'Properly.' It was no way to put the lord Sheriff on his side.

Ansculf bared his teeth. The gap next to his upper left dogtooth was obvious.

'You are a fool, Ansculf.'

'My lord I was only—'

'You were not ordered to the ferry but took it upon yourself to make a decision which reflects upon this castle and upon me. You will return to Elmley where I can keep you under my eye, and another will take your place here. What is more, I will send two weeks' wages, due to you, to the ferryman in compensation.' De Beauchamp looked at Bradecote. 'The matter is better dealt with swiftly, and this is fair. The ferryman took no lasting harm I take it?'

'No, my lord, and it is. However, there is more.' Bradecote

kept any note of triumph from his voice. 'A man known as Old Cuthbert, a man once proven innocent by God at the ordeal, but thereafter unable to ply his craft and reduced to being a walker in a fuller's troughs, was strangled two nights ago when he left the alehouse in Evesham. He said he had seen something of the killing of Walter the Steward and was silenced. We have spoken with those present and accounted for all but one man. This man was "a stranger" to the locals and was loud in condemning the Abbot of Evesham for not caring about the townsfolk and letting them be killed, while he lies safe behind his new wall. There is no reason we yet know why he killed the steward, but we can be sure enough that he killed Old Cuthbert for us to arraign that man before the Justices in Eyre.' Bradecote paused for a moment, just for effect. 'The man was described to us as shorter than me, brown-haired, without grey in his beard, and lacking an upper left tooth. What is more, the body was found at the fuller's next morning, down by the ferry, and the ferry was taken in the night over to the Hampton side by someone not used to the work and who lost a fingernail in the process.' He now looked at Ansculf. 'What happened to your finger?'

'I lost the nail, but the finger had got caught in a door.' The answer was prompt enough, but lacked conviction, for Ansculf knew that when he was forced to show the finger, they would see the nail had not fallen off but been ripped from the bed.

'Show us.' Catchpoll looked grim.

Ansculf glanced at the door, wondering, for one brief moment, if he could make it in time to escape, but as he did so the door opened, and Walkelin entered, followed by a short, bandy-legged individual.

'My lord, I bring before you Adam Welldelver, as drank in the alehouse the night Old Cuthbert was killed, and who identifies this man', he pointed at Ansculf, 'as the stranger who spoke out against the lord Abbot and seemed intent on raisin' bad feelin' against the abbey.'

''Tis the man, I will swear a good oath, my lord.' Adam Welldelver bowed low and offered the information, thinking it marginally less frightening than actually being addressed by the lord Sheriff of Worcestershire, especially as he looked now, which was mightily displeased.

'We will see the injury.' De Beauchamp could see no reason for the garrison serjeant to have killed two Evesham men, but the evidence seemed good enough to present him before the Justices in Eyre, unless he could find oathswearers to vouch for him.

Ansculf could not escape with Walkelin between him and the door, and trying to fight his way out would be pointless. Walkelin and Catchpoll took his arms, and then Catchpoll, with no attempt at being gentle, unravelled the bandage from about the finger.

'That's day fresh, my lord, and not a nail as fell off after a blood bruise.' Catchpoll, if anything, sounded even more displeased than the lord Sheriff.

'I obeyed my lord's commands, nothin' more,' shouted Ansculf, in desperation.

'And I am not his lord,' murmured Rahere de Cormolain, loudly enough for de Beauchamp to hear him.

'I am, but no command from me ever said to raise tolls on the bridge, or the ferry, and assuredly none to kill innocent men.'

Knowing William de Beauchamp well, Bradecote,

Catchpoll and Walkelin knew there would have been no specific order to do so, but he might have approved the toll raising.

"Twere just an old man, and one not happy with 'is life, an old miseryguts. Did 'im a favour in many ways.' Ansculf clutched at anything that might improve his situation, though his throat felt tight as if the noose were already about it. 'Besides, 'e killed 'is wife, long ago, so none so innocent a man.'

'God proved his innocence in the ordeal,' snapped Walkelin, outraged that the man had suffered for that proof and yet could still be blamed.

'And I am none so young,' Catchpoll growled, his face inches from Ansculf's, and his hand grasping the injured one so that Ansculf's eyes watered at the pain, 'and just at this minute I am not happy, either, but that be 'acos there's a stench in front of my nose, the stench of a rotten serjeant, and nothin' smells worse to me. You befouls the rank. I 'ave seen your sort afore in my time, bullies as liked to use the cloak of "orders" to step so far beyond the Law they was no better than outlaws. They just liked power over folk, and the power to end a life felt just too good.'

'I wanted to be better than you, more feared than you,' Ansculf declared, part defiant and part pleading.

'You got it all wrong.' Catchpoll shook his head, but his eyes still glinted fiercely rather than in sorrow. 'Bein' "better" comes down to 'ard work and experience, and keepin' to rules in 'ere.' He tapped his temple with his free hand. 'Bein' "feared" is not an end, just a means to keep folk safe, leastways when you is a Sheriff's Serjeant. Best to think of it as fear actin' as the voice inside that tells you not to do somethin', and warns of what 'appens if you does it. You just wanted folk to be frightened, not raise that voice in their 'eads.'

'And why did you kill Walter the Steward? Was it just because he was the abbey's man?' Bradecote, who had been thinking as well as listening to Catchpoll, needed the question answering.

'I never killed the steward. Only saw the man twice as I remembers, and the night 'e died I played at dice with the lord de Cormolain's serjeant until long past dark, and the night watch will swear I checked 'em late afore I went to my bed.'

'You only saw Old Cuthbert the once,' commented Walkelin, 'so that part counts for nothin'.'

'Aye, but 'is wife were distant kin of my mother, and the family said it must 'ave been 'im as killed the wife. Never thought much to it, nor recall the woman's name, but then the story came out in the alehouse and, it seemed fittin'. Suddenly I could not only make more fear in Evesham, and anger at the abbot, but I could avenge my kin.' It sounded an excuse more than a reason, a man grasping at a straw to validate his act.

'Like Walkelin says, God found the man innocent. You cannot claim justification because a family story said he was guilty.' Bradecote dismissed the mitigation with a wave of his hand, while his mind was grappling with the knowledge that, despite all the odds to the contrary, the two killings were definitely not connected and they were not one step closer to finding the killer of Walter the Steward. 'My lord, I admit I thought our duty in Evesham done, and the killer of one was the killer of both, but against all likelihood, it seems there were two men responsible and we hold but one. Will you take this man in charge?'

William de Beauchamp sniffed and looked thoughtfully at Ansculf. The man was a fool, and a killer, and a liability.

'I will take him to Elmley today, and then await you in Worcester, since I hardly think you will take the second man before tomorrow.' It was grudgingly said. Deep down, de Beauchamp 'blamed' his undersheriff for the very success for which he should be praised. It was – inconvenient.

'Thank you, my lord. Then we will make it known in the town that a man is taken for the death of Old Cuthbert, though most were keen his killer should be taken, and less interested in who killed Walter the Steward, who had been keeping rents due to the abbey for himself and forcing silver from townsfolk with threats.'

A part of William de Beauchamp delighted in the loss to the abbey, imagining Abbot Reginald's chagrin when he found out.

'I still expect you to find him.' That, thought de Beauchamp, was at least a small payback for the inconvenience Bradecote had caused.

'Yes, my lord. We will be about it immediately.' Bradecote bowed, and Catchpoll and Walkelin followed suit. They went out, with the forgotten well delver in their wake.

'I do not know why you keep Bradecote as your undersheriff, my lord,' commented de Cormolain.

'Because he is good at what he does, and he does not fail.' De Beauchamp looked at his vassal. 'I dislike failure. Remember that.'

'Yes, my lord.'

Chapter Fifteen

Adam Welldelver said he would rather walk back into the town, so the three sheriff's men were free to discuss what lay before them as they rode over the bridge and up the hill.

'It seemed impossible that the two deaths were not connected and must mean Walkelin's idea about the hoard is correct,' bemoaned Bradecote, still contemplating that although he had proved himself in the right, his overlord was not going to thank him for it and might make his life awkward.

'Well, in one way they was, my lord,' Walkelin reminded him. 'Old Cuthbert was, most like, a witness to the killin' of Walter the Steward. 'Twere just *wyrd* that a man killed 'im for another reason.'

'What Walkelin says is true, my lord. *Wyrd* can do that, and no point in worryin' over it.'

'Yes, you are right, both of you. The problem I see is that removing the death of Old Cuthbert does not give us a new view of things. There are no more people we need to speak with, and thus far there seems little to make any one person more likely than the others. Every time something pointed at a man, something else countered it.'

'What if we goes, just for a bit, on gut feelin', my lord? Just to see if it gives us any new idea. Of all those we spoke

to, once or more, who would you discount completely?'
Catchpoll thought it might help to gather in mind all those
they had interviewed.

'The Widow Potter and her sons; the tailor; the
thatcher – in fact everyone except Hubert the Mason,
reluctantly, Oswald Mealtere and, even more reluctantly,
Wulfram Meduwyrhta.'

'I thinks the same, my lord, 'cept I cannot see the mead
maker as the killer.' Walkelin was sifting the information in
his head. 'You could say 'e possesses more reason than others,
what with Mærwynn as well as bein' cheated. Added to that,
I cannot forget 'e lied about 'is lost strap end, though we
now knows the design is common in Evesham and so even if
Wulfram owned one and lost it, there can be no proof it is the
same one I found. 'Tis another little thing.'

'Aye, but the coppersmith put a strap end on a new belt for
Oswald Mealtere within the last week.' Catchpoll reminded
them. 'We did not prove that was afore the steward died, and
the man shows temper easily.'

'Agreed. Let us therefore look first at every little thing
we have discovered about him and speak with him again.'
Bradecote's head had cleared of thoughts of his lord, and he
could focus again.

Alnoth was not a man who rushed things. His life was
itinerant, and based around market days and fairs, where
his 'minding' of stalls provided an income, and there were
more folk about to be charitable. Since he also stayed when
he could within the security of religious houses, pilgrims
often also proved to be in a giving frame of mind. Whilst
he would otherwise have spent the morning in the Evesham

marketplace, he did not begrudge waiting for the lord Sheriff's Underserjeant, and he felt that Walkelin would return as soon as he could. He sat upon the grass, in the sunshine, leaning against the south side of the trunk of an apple tree that had been planted by brethren now long inhabitants of the monks' churchyard, and which had a gentle dent in the trunk that formed a comfortable place to lie back and relax. The bees, already at work, hummed what became a low lullaby, and Alnoth slept, lightly.

Brother Petrus was glad that Chapter had not been a long affair this morning and he could get to his bees. Last evening he had sat by the 'sick' skep and listened, and felt melancholy. Fanciful as it seemed, he felt the buzzing of the bees was a bidding of farewell. It was intuitive, but not, as Brother Justus had rather spitefully suggested, 'superstitious nonsense'.

The abbey hives faced west and sat upon the shelf in several doorless 'cupboards', designed to keep out the winter wet and the heat of summer noontide. Brother Petrus had got the carpenter to incorporate timber from the orchard trees that had grown too old and unproductive, at least where he could, because he thought it would encourage the bees to collect nectar from the apples, cherries and pears more particularly. Even as he drew near to his 'village of bees', Brother Petrus could sense a difference. The hive that had worried him was silent. He sighed. He would find new bees, for whenever Wulfram Meduwyrhta learnt of a bees' nest in the locality where he could get wild honey, he always passed on the information to the Benedictine. With his abbot's permission, Brother Petrus could leave the enclave and the skep, fully cleaned and freshened, could be used to lure in new occupants, but it was midsummer already, and a new hive would need any honey it made to help it overwinter, so he would get no more honey than lay within it now. He opened the twine-hinged door in the side of the skep. It was deserted.

He stepped back, opened his arms and looked heavenwards, offering up thanks for the bees and hives that remained, then clasped his hands, closed his eyes, and began intoning prayers for the bees that had departed, wishing them well. His voice was a soft monotone that blended with the gentle buzzing around the other hives. Bees and beekeeper were in harmony. So lost was he in his prayers that he did not hear the soft footfall upon the grass behind him.

Oswald Mealtere did not think about bees unless he was swatting a buzzing insect from about his head. He did not like the idea of being stung. He had lain in his bed before falling asleep, and tried to work out how Walter the Steward could have hidden his stolen silver in one of the hives without that happening to him. He decided the only way would be for him to have had the aid of the beekeeper, and that since he had threatened townsmen to get what he wanted, he must have found out something he could use against the monk if he did not comply. He wondered if bees would be too sleepy to sting at night, but it felt too great a risk. His only option was to go to the hives when the bee monk was present, and he could not see the hives from his holding. He decided the best option would be to cross Wulfram Meduwyrhta's land just below the bridge, where the two tracks diverged, since he would be less likely to be seen. He could then enter the orchards and keep watch from behind a tree. He assumed the beekeeper tended his hives daily, and hoped he would not waste too much of his day.

On rising, he told his son his first tasks and said that he was going to speak with the lord Undersheriff. He thought this a clever ploy, since, if they came to pester him again, his family could say that he was in fact seeking them and must have missed them at the abbey. He did not go as far as thinking what he would say was the 'information' he had been seeking to pass on.

He was delayed at the first by Mistress Meduwyrhta, bearing a basket, walking up the track to the bridge to go to the market, and until she had disappeared from view he lingered outside the *mealthus,* slowly raking the ash from the previous day's fire, and readying the wood for the next burning. Then he strode purposefully up towards the bridge and, at the last minute, diverted to the right. With a small smile he shut the sluice that the mead maker must have opened that morning, and jumped, with a grunt, across the slowly draining channel. He then headed towards the abbey enclave wall. When he could see the bee hives in their shelter he stopped. There was no sign of the beekeeper, and Oswald felt vaguely annoyed, as though he ought to have been there to save him time. Then he realised that the Benedictine would not tend his bees until after Chapter. He hoped there was not much abbey business to be discussed, and felt fortune favoured him when a figure, veiled, hatted, and garbed in linen, came into view. He watched as the man turned and, rather to his surprise, lifted his arms in a welcoming gesture, like a priest at the Mass, and then clasped his hands together and began what looked like prayer.

Oswald was not sure how long the praying might last, so did not advance tree by tree, taking cover, but approached directly, with his steps almost silent over the grass, which had been cropped short by the small flock of sheep that roamed the orchard and provided milk and cheese for the brethren. This morning they were grazing close by the river, and so could not give away his presence. As he drew close, Oswald noticed that the monk was standing before a hive with its door open and no sign of any bees coming out of it. That was how the steward hid his silver! The elation at this thought precluded Oswald wondering how the beekeeper had concealed a lower yield of honey.

'So, Brother, have you taken the treasure within?'

Brother Petrus jumped in surprise, and turned.

'Oh! I am sorry. I did not hear you. No, though however much is there will be a blessing to the abbey.'

'But much of it does not belong to the abbey.' Oswald was annoyed at the monk's presumption of ownership.

'How could that be?' Brother Petrus looked perplexed. Why did this man, whom he vaguely recognised as the maltster from beyond Wulfram Meduwyrhta's in the abbey demesne, think the honeycombs belonged to anyone but the monks?

'Suffice to say, my own unwilling contributions lie within, so I will take them.' Oswald pushed the monk aside, and reached, just a little cautiously, into the hive. His hands could feel nothing but the sticky, honey-filled combs. He withdrew them, rubbing the stickiness onto his cotte, and stared angrily at the Benedictine. 'Lying is a sin, Brother. Where have you put it? In another hive?' He grabbed Brother Petrus by his thin shoulders and shook him. 'Where is it?' His voice grew loud and aggressive. He could not see the monk's expression very clearly through the thin veil over his face, but had he been able to do so he would only have seen great confusion and some fear.

'I do not know what you mean. The bees were still there yesterday, and I have not removed the honey.' The beekeeper's voice was uncertain and plaintive.

'Honey? What care I for honey? Where is the silver, monk?'

'Silver? Are you mind-addled?' Brother Petrus now thought this must be the case, and wondered how he might calm the madman. 'Let me take you to Brother Augustine, our infirmarer. He can help you as I cannot.' He put a hand on Oswald's arm, and it was thrust away.

'I will take it,' Oswald shouted, and pushed the monk hard in the chest so that he fell backwards to lie on the grass. Brother Petrus, slightly stunned by both the fall and the very fact that he had been attacked, sat up slowly.

'No more will I be cheated, no more, do you 'ear. No more.' Oswald's temper, never well leashed, broke loose, suffusing him with the red mist of anger that consumed him. He waved his fists at the Benedictine, even as the monk began to both edge away and get up, and then, seeing the old censer lying in the grass, took it up and swung it in a great arc.

Alnoth was more than half asleep in the sunshine, though it would soon be too hot to bask in the direct rays. The sound of a shout brought him to full consciousness, and he opened his eyes, blinking in the brightness, and pushed himself up, back against the tree trunk, until he stood. He turned, for the cry had come from towards the abbey. He saw one man standing over another, and then recognised the garb of the abbey beekeeper. The standing man did not look as though he was about to offer assistance, and then he saw the monk sit up and raise his arm protectively, as if to ward off a blow. Alnoth had no fist to clench, but indignation filled him. Violence towards a monk was unthinkable, surely. He began to run towards the abbey hives. The angry man was shouting and gesticulating, and then, as Brother Petrus tried to get up, grabbed the old censer that provided smoke for calming the bees, and swung it round at the beekeeper's head. Brother Petrus fell, insensible, and Alnoth feared he would not reach him before the angry man hurt him further, though he was not sure what he could do beyond cannon straight into the man and knock him down.

Then something happened that Alnoth had not expected.

The bees in the hive adjacent to the empty one became agitated. Their colony seemed to be under attack from some large, loud animal. They reacted as they would to a bear and swarmed out to defend it. In a matter of moments Oswald was surrounded by angry bees, and was flailing his arms about his head, roaring in pain, which incensed them the more. He tried to run, but the swirling swarm kept with him, each bee intent upon defending the hive with its life. Alnoth, now as close as he dared, could see no way of rescuing the man, and feared also for the beekeeper, lying upon the ground. The bees, however, saw no threat from the inert heap that was Brother Petrus, and ignored him. Oswald's cries diminished, not least because bees flew in and stung inside his mouth. He dropped to the ground, moaning and writhing. Alnoth lay prostrate upon the grass, praying for the tormented man in his agony, for the beekeeper and himself. Then there was no more human sound, not even a groan, and the bee-fury abated to a concerted buzzing. It was this that Brother Petrus heard as consciousness returned. The bees sounded angry, and for a moment he could not think why. He moved, cautiously, aware of the blood upon his face, which stuck his veil to his cheek, and aware that his bees were dangerous if afraid. He raised himself, turning so that he could sit up, and a sound between a sigh and a whimper left his lips. He saw Oswald's body, so covered by the swarm that he looked a man of bees. Tears came to the Benedictines eyes, not just for the man, but for all the bees that would have given up their lives to save their hive. Then he became aware of Alnoth, on the edge of his vision.

'Stay where you are, I beg,' he called, in a singing voice. His bees heard him chant psalms to them, so he thought the sound would not increase their fear and wrath. Alnoth obeyed, willingly.

The lord Sheriff's trio gave up their horses to be taken back to the stable, and then all three went to the little door that led from the enclave into the orchards, with the intention that Walkelin conduct the search of the anchoress's old home, with Alnoth, and his superiors would go to speak again with Oswald Mealtere. When they stepped from the claustral into the pastoral they had no expectation of anything more than seeing Alnoth awaiting them among the fruit trees.

'Holy Virgin,' whispered Walkelin, crossing himself. Three figures were upon the parched grass, two prostrate and one sat, head bowed, and body bent forward. All three were very still, as though frozen, but upon one body there was movement, a strange ripple as thousands of tiny creatures moved in concert.

Bradecote was about to stride forward, but Catchpoll, put an arm before him to hold him back.

'Not yet, my lord. Saw somethin' like this many years past, when a lad disturbed a bees' nest just beyond the butts, outside the Worcester walls. A bee sting or two is not more 'n painful for most, though once or twice a single sting has led to a death, but if a whole swarm attacks 'tis more stings than could be counted and – whoever lies there be dead, or be beyond savin', and the bees is not yet calmed.'

'And the sitting man looks to be "Brother Bee",' added Walkelin. 'If any can calm them it will be 'im.'

So they watched for what seemed a very long time, as Brother Petrus slowly crawled away from where the bee-covered body lay, dragging the old censer, and filled it with a little dry grass for kindling, and some twigs from beneath an apple tree. It would not give thick smoke, but it was a start. It looked, from a distance, that he was summoning the smoke, and once it was more than a curling wisp, he began to swing it, very gently, and advance towards the swarming bees, chanting softly in Latin. The movement on the body slowed, or so they imagined, but then the monk stopped and simply knelt upon the ground and waited, gently swinging the censer.

'What is he waiting for?' whispered Bradecote, lowering his voice by instinct.

'I suppose the bees will go back to their hive when the threat is over, and if they feels sleepy. What was said to me, when the lad died, was the bees must 'ave thought some animal was come to destroy the nest and defended it. Most like 'twas the same thing 'ere.'

Inaction was frustrating, but there was nothing else they could do but watch and wait. Eventually a few bees left the corpse, and once the vanguard had led the way, the other bees followed. Alnoth dared to raise his head when the beekeeper stopped chanting.

Walkelin gave a sigh of relief, not having known whether Alnoth was the victim.

'So who did they attack?' Bradecote wondered, stepping forward, but without haste. With the only bees remaining on the body being dead or dying, the man's face could be seen, though it was red and swollen almost beyond recognition.

'I believe it is the maltster,' Brother Petrus lifted the veil from over his face, revealing a visage where blood and tears had mingled. 'I do not understand why, but he had it in his mind that one of the hives was full of silver. He was not drunk, not by the smell of him, but clearly his mind was disordered, poor man.' He sighed and shook his head.

'I wonder why he thought that,' mused Bradecote. 'Brother, you have had no sign of interference in your hives? I imagine not, if the result of such a thing would be what we see before us.'

By now, it had dawned upon the beekeeper that these were the three shrieval officers staying in the guest hall.

'None, my lord. I think the hive I found empty this morning has been ailing some time, and when a hive is "sick" and the number of bees within it becomes too low to carry on, those that are left just leave. Nobody could have hidden anything inside a hive without – this.'

'Yes, I understand. Walkelin, go and find something to cover the body, and an abbey servant. If we carry the body to his family rather than use a cart or barrow, we can avoid any idea of another murder panicking the townsfolk.'

'Yes, my lord, but I will aid Alnoth first.' Walkelin could see Alnoth was now kneeling. He went over to him and took him by the upper arms, so that he could be steady as he stood.

'I must ask you to await me a little longer, Alnoth. Meet me at Mother Placida's in a while?'

'I will be glad to go there and pray, after this.'

'Did you see what 'appened?'

'I did, Underserjeant. I were asleep in the sun, against an apple's trunk, and 'eard shoutin'. When I looked, I saw a man wavin' 'is arms about and Brother Petrus on the ground, and when 'e tried to get up, the man swung that censer bowl at 'im and knocked the poor Brother senseless. Then the bees came out o' the skep there, to defend their keeper, and attacked the man, all over 'im they was, and the cries awful to listen to as 'e suffered. Then 'e lay still, and Brother Petrus told me to lie quiet until the bees was calm.'

'You did not hear what had made Oswald Mealtere strike Brother Petrus?'

'No, Underserjeant. I were sun-sleepin' then. 'Twas 'im?'

'Aye. Now go and sun-sleep by the anchoress's cell and I will come to you.'

'Assuredly, I will try, but I fears bad dreams.' Alnoth sighed and turned down the gentle slope towards the dilapidated dwelling, and Walkelin went off at the run to find another pair of hands and a blanket.

Oswald was not so light a man that his body was easy to bear when four men each held a corner of a rough blanket, and in crossing the mead maker's channel, the abbey groom slipped so that they nearly dropped the body in the mud, though thankfully it was only the man's feet that got damp, which led to some muttering.

The maltster's wife was hoeing the weeds from the vegetable plot when she heard, not the footfall, but the muttering and heavy breathing, and looked up. She wore a wide-brimmed, loosely woven straw hat over her coif, and it hid some of her face. Bradecote was looking carefully at her, and saw the way she stopped, as if holding her breath, and stood motionless. She made no exclamation of distress, or even surprise, but just stared at them for several moments, and then lay down the hoe, dusted her hands on her skirts, and walked slowly towards the house, which was clearly where they would go. She arrived almost at the same time and opened the door without a word to let them pass in before her. Catchpoll gave silent thanks for the calm reception. Bringing the news of a death, and a body as proof of that reality, was often met with outpourings of grief and heartbreak. Whilst inured to it, and accepting it as part of his position, Catchpoll did not enjoy being the bringer of such news, especially when it also might mean casting the rest of the household into poverty or destitution. What neither he nor his companions had expected was the reaction of Siward Mealtere. The old man had been seated upon a chair, though it was little more than a stool with a pair of arms so that he might push himself up to stand, and staring into space. He did not move until he registered more than his daughter-in-law entering, and then he turned. His milky eyes could not make out much, but there were a group of men, and they did not greet him. He sensed, rather than saw, something calamitous, and pushed himself upright to come towards them, leaning forward so that he might see the quicker. When he saw them lower a body, he let out an anguished howl, like a wounded animal.

'My son!'

Bradecote wondered if his eyesight was better than had

been thought, since it could have been his grandson who had come to harm. Then he realised that if it had been the lad, Mistress Mealtere would have been inconsolable, a mother's love being a thing that was always total, whilst wives did not always grieve for husbands, and even gave quiet thanks for release. From what he had seen of this household, Oswald's wife was in the latter category.

'My son!' the old man repeated, and stumbled forward to reach down towards the body. 'Who did this?'

'No man. A swarm of bees attacked him when he threatened their hive.' Bradecote spoke calmly, but a little louder so that his words would be clear to the old man.

'The fault is mine! God punishes me!' Siward began to tear at his hair.

'That cannot be so.'

'It is, I tells you. All my fault. I dared to think none would ever know, but God sees all and punished me worse than the fires of Damnation!'

'What has He seen?' Catchpoll sensed more than a strange outpouring of grief, though it was not uncommon for folk to put blame upon themselves when a loved-one died, as though there was a need to feel even more crushed.

'I did it.'

'Yes, but what?' Catchpoll wanted confession.

'I killed 'er, put my 'ands about 'er white throat and took the life from 'er, when she said she would not come away with me.'

Bradecote's mind was racing to catch up, but Walkelin's natural filing system meant he came up with the answer in a trice.

'Old Cuthbert's wife.'

'O'course. Never good enough for 'er, the useless bastard. I loved 'er, afore I wed the wife, and she me, but 'e "persuaded" 'er that it were better to wed 'im, and she fell for it. Could not get 'er from my mind and 'eart, though, and after she lost a babe she came to me for – comfort. When she came and told me to my face it were over, I could not bear 'er to be Cuthbert's and not mine. And though God proved 'is innocence, I 'olds that the Almighty also left 'im hand-crippled so 'e would suffer for bein' a weak 'usband. So long ago, and now look! My son! My Oswald!'

'And he never knew of this?'

'You think I would tell my son of it? Would any man? No, course not, and 'e were but a little 'un when it all 'appened.' The old man had tears running down his cheeks.

'Could Walter the Steward have found out?' Bradecote was now able to take the next step. If the steward had discovered the truth he would, knowing his character, have used it against the maltster.

'None but God knew.'

'My lord.' It was Mistress Mealtere who spoke up, calmly, without emotion. 'When you came 'ere the yesterday, you was still interested in whoever killed Master Walter the Steward. Well, I can tell you the night 'e were killed, my 'usband went out, when Father 'ere were asleep, but afore full dark, and came back a while later. 'E groaned when 'e got into bed but said nothin' to me. In the morn, I saw 'is clothes was dusty and bloody and there were a rent in the sleeve of 'is oldest cotte. Said 'e fell over in the dark, 'e did, but I saw 'is ribs when 'e dressed, and they was black and blue in different places, like a man 'ad punched 'im. Doubt you can tell now, if them bees stings 'as made the body all red, but the left side should be darker.'

It was Walkelin who knelt by the body, pulling up the cotte carefully, since there were a few dead, or nearly dead, bees tangled in the fabric. The skin was inflamed all over, but there were clearly patches of bruising, still dark and discoloured.

'Just tryin' to foul 'is name! Never a good wife, always sulky.' Siward Mealtere, roused from his misery to point a bony finger at his daughter-in-law.

'Nothin' did I ever 'ave to smile about, other than our Ernebald, but then my son does not take after 'is father nor oldfather neither, and 'as a sweet nature.'

'Did you play Oswald false, then?' The old man challenged her.

'Never. A dutiful wife always, but never was there love. Why would there be with a man as found fault, and carped and berated, and took 'is belt to me when we was younger.'

'Oswald wore a new belt when we saw 'im, mistress. When did 'e begin to wear it?' Walkelin asked the question.

'Day after the killin'. Had it ready, mind, for the old one showed wear, but the end 'ad gone and it were near torn in two, so the new one came out.'

'Thank you.' Walkelin looked at his superiors and did not need to ask whether they felt they had discovered who had killed Walter the Steward. Whether it was self-defence or not would never be known, but it all fitted.

'Walter the Steward was keeping back rent due each Quarter to the abbey, and, if he treated him as he did others, quite possibly making Oswald pay more than the rent sum as well, by using some threat or unfulfilled promise. We may never know which. It was most likely the steward who demanded the meeting by the well pit, since it was just before the paying day at midsummer, and perhaps asked for even more. Whatever the reason, a fight ensued, a brawling fight, and it seems beyond doubt that Oswald hit him with a stone and cast his body into the pit. Had it come before the Justices in Eyre, it might have been adjudged a killing emendable, and silver due to the steward's widow, or else a hanging offence. This morning Oswald took it into his head that the stolen silver was in a beehive, and that led to his death. We cannot know why he—'

'I told 'im last eventide, my lord. I 'eard Wulfram Meduwyrhta's little girl, Win, tell 'er mother you 'ad asked Mærwynn if there were anywhere the silver could be in the steward's 'ouse, and then somethin' about bees, but the two was not connected. I-I did not make that clear, since Oswald would not like to know I was friends with next door. Better it sounded over'eard. Does it make it my fault?' A note of doubt entered the woman's voice.

'No, mistress. Oswald came to his own conclusions and was driven by a desire to get the silver. At least we now understand a little why he attacked Brother Petrus.'

'Oh, the poor man!' Mistress Mealtere was not feeling sorry for her husband, but the Benedictine.

'I am sure the priest will tell you that you are not to blame for others' sins.' Bradecote saw no reason why the woman should blame herself, since she could not have guessed what her husband would do with the information.

Siward, who had been attending enough to be outraged at his daughter-in-law's 'disloyalty', sniffed, and straightened a little.

'So, you will be takin' me.' It was not a question, and he did not seem in any way concerned by the thought, but it posed one, as far as Bradecote was concerned. The man had admitted a killing, one for which he had seen a man he knew to be innocent risk the noose, undergo ordeal, and suffer thereafter to his life's end. It was also true that a death was owing for Cuthbert's strangled wife. Yet the trouble lay in presenting the case before the Justices with the confession of an old man who looked so nigh to the grave as one finger-push would send him into it and be glad to be there. Distant kin, like Ansculf, might be found for the wife, but it would be unlikely any could speak accurately of what happened perhaps nearly forty years past. He looked at Catchpoll, whose face was grim. The serjeant shook his head, slowly. Bradecote then looked at Walkelin, which surprised the underserjeant, who did not think his view would even be considered. He bit his lip, frowned, and then also shook his head.

'No, old man, we will not, and the most important reason is that a quick end, for you, would be the easy one. This way you know your guilt, and how a harsher judgement than any the Justices could bring upon you has come down. Life is harder than death for you, and you are condemned to carry on living a while longer.' Bradecote heard Mistress Mealtere give a small sigh and looked to her. 'You are not his gaoler, mistress, but I would also say you are not his servant. You and your son run the malthouse as you see fit, and look to the future. Let your peace with your neighbours be seen, and – live.'

It was a licence to step from subservience, and she nodded.

'I will, my lord. Ernebald and I can manage.'

'Then we are done here.' Bradecote acknowledged her obeisance, and the three sheriff's men left her to tell her son and arrange a funeral.

Chapter Sixteen

'My lord, why did you ask my view?' Walkelin could not hold back the question, as they headed to cross over the channel and meet with Alnoth.

'Because I value it. You have earned the right to give it, for yours is a head that keeps what we learn as if a scribe had written us a list.'

'And now you thinks like a serjeant,' added Catchpoll. 'Three heads can make things a mess, or can make things clearer. Our heads is different, but between us, well, we seems to find the answers.' He looked at Bradecote.

'I agree. Just do not tell the lord Sheriff.'

'Oh no, my lord.' Walkelin looked horrified at even the thought of doing so.

'And now we do not have Siward before us, I would ask whether you came to the same answer as me on this with the same reasoning?'

'You was right, my lord. The man will suffer more alive than facing a hangin'.' Walkelin thought his 'sentence' to life the harder option.

'And the Justices in Eyre would not be best pleased to 'ave us bring a man before 'em for a death so long past, where we can give the man's confession but little beyond that. They faces enough put in front of 'em to keep 'em busy, and would not care for it. So, for both reasons, it were the best justice.'

'Good. It feels wrong to decide to ignore the Law, but—'

'We is not ignorin' it, my lord, but applyin' it proper. Sometimes the Law can be blind, and that works well. Other times it can be plain unjust. Siward faces a painful slide to the grave, and will face God's judgement thereafter. Whatever we says, 'e will blame 'imself for 'is son's death, and that broke 'im.'

'Yes. So now we hope that Alnoth the Handless has given us the missing silver to set before Abbot Reginald, since not only will he be the happier, but I am sure those who receive what Walter the Steward extracted from them by threats will be more interested in that than the death of Oswald Mealtere.'

'No, my lord, I doubts that. "Death by bees" will give tongues work for weeks and be remembered for years.' Catchpoll's experience of people was right, and Bradecote acknowledged it.

They reached the anchoress's crumbling cell, and found Alnoth, not asleep but very awake, a little out of the sun's glare, for it was now mid-morning, and there was enough heat for a man to feel it pass through his clothes and be uncomfortable on his skin. Seeing the lord Undersheriff and Serjeant Catchpoll with Walkelin, he scrambled to his feet as swiftly as he could and bowed low. What life had taught Alnoth was that everyone thought themselves more important than an itinerant who made a few pennies from watching over stalls and otherwise lived upon Christian charity, and they liked that superiority acknowledged. Underserjeant Wakelin, somehow, never let that show, and Alnoth liked him the more for it.

'I see you made the wise choice and chose not to let the sun dry you like a hay stalk. It is Alnoth, yes?' Bradecote greeted him in a friendly manner, taking him aback so much that for a moment Alnoth could not speak and just nodded. Then he found his voice.

'Indeed, my lord.' He thought that answer could not be construed as either curt or forward.

'So, you think that the inside of the chamber has been "visited" in recent times, long after the good anchoress's death.'

'I do, my lord, but I may yet be wrong.' Alnoth sounded cautious.

'We shall see. Open the door, Walkelin.'

Walkelin stepped forward and Alnoth reminded him in an urgent whisper to offer a prayer for Mother Placida when they entered. Walkelin nodded. The door opened outwards, as befitted a cell, and did so a little creakily, but was not difficult to open. Walkelin stepped slightly to the side so that all three shrieval officers could see within. At first it was just gloom, mottled by little patches of light where the holes in the roof let the prying sky peep in. Then their eyes adjusted from the sunshine, and the ghosts of the anchoress's simple life could be discerned. To one side there were fragments of coarse linen, the last remnants of the thin palliasse upon which she had slept and which had provided nesting material for generations of mice since her demise. Upon the south-facing wall was a wooden cross that had been carefully placed to catch the best light from the narrow window opening high on the opposite wall. There were cobwebs, many dust-bedecked, and the sound of scurrying mouse feet was the only sign of life. The dirt floor had once been hard packed and perhaps rush-strewn, though Mother Placida might have eschewed anything beyond bare earth. There were mouse droppings on the hearthstone, which had not felt a fire's heat in years, and a little detritus that had accrued as the structure above it had 'watered' it with a rain of thatch fragments as the roof fell into disrepair, but not as much as would be expected when one looked up at the gaps.

'God grant peace and rest to she who lived her life of prayer here,' murmured Walkelin, and crossed himself. His companions added an 'Amen', and Alnoth, stood outside, breathed a sigh of relief and added his own.

Inside, Walkelin got down on his knees, not for further prayer, but to look along the edges of the hearthstone.

'There be some dust and dirt in the cracks, but they still shows clear.'

'And if you wanted to lift it, you would use this.' Catchpoll, quite happy to let Walkelin's younger eyes and knees save his own, had noticed a short metal bar left upright against the door jamb on the hinge side. Anyone glancing in would not see it. He picked it up. 'I doubts the holy woman used this as a fire poker. Too heavy.'

'Then let us see if it achieves what we think it was used for.' Bradecote was confident that this crumbling cell had been used as a hiding place, but was the silver still there?

Catchpoll leant to press the bar into a hearth edge, noting as he did so a small flake had been chipped from very close to the place he set the bar to get under the hearthstone. He pushed down and felt the bar catch beneath the stone, then levered it slowly up until Walkelin could get his fingers under it and pull upwards. The sigh they both gave was not from their exertions.

Beneath the hearthstone a small hollow had been scooped from the earth, and nestled into it lay a cloth bag, not yet quite full, but certainly well filled, with things that were hard enough to give bulges in the fabric. Catchpoll reached in to take it up, since Walkelin was holding up the hearthstone. He gave a small grunt as he lifted it, at first with one hand, but then supporting it with the other. He handed it to Bradecote.

'If that holds less than my full year's wage twice over, I will ride Walkelin's idle horse back to Worcester.'

Bradecote loosed the string that held the bag closed and looked within.

'All silver, right enough. I would prefer to see it counted at the abbey rather than scrabble in the earth here.'

'And she would not like it, my lord.' Alnoth, curious, now stood in the doorway. 'Wealth meant nothin' to Mother Placida. Would be lackin' respect to count it 'ere.' Speaking on the anchoress's behalf gave him a more confident tone.

'I agree. We will go to Abbot Reginald with it, and you come too, Alnoth, for without you, this, which belongs to the abbey and to Evesham, would still be lost.' Bradecote felt a weight as great as that of the silver lifted from him. Whatever William de Beauchamp felt, Evesham and Abbot Reginald would account their visit a success.

'Oh, I am not so—' Alnoth's confidence fell away.

'Come with us, friend.' Walkelin, dusting off his knees, smiled at Alnoth, and the smile achieved more than any verbal request.

'If you wishes it, my lord.' The words were for the lord Undersheriff but he was looking at Walkelin.

Abbot Reginald was not a venal man, but he gazed with pleasure upon the silver pennies as the abbey treasurer piled them upon the counting cloth. Not only would the abbey coffers, emptying by the day as the building work continued, be replenished with lost funds, but the townsfolk, who had been forced to pay the abbey steward on top of their rents, would be recompensed, and Abbot Reginald knew that would do much to mend any rift in trust between abbey and town.

'This is indeed a matter for some rejoicing.' He smiled at Bradecote, and then looked at Alnoth, standing as far back in the chamber as he could without the stonework hurting his back.

'You have shown great honesty, though it is no surprise to those in this House who see you often, Alnoth. Not only that, but you have shown us the way of humility and charity of spirit. I know that you travel from place to place, but we would be happy if you chose to remain in Evesham. It seems to me that God has guided you to be here at this time and perhaps shown you a way forward also. According to our Rule, to work is to pray, but it seems to me that the Almighty, in crafting you as you are, calls you to pray as your work.'

'My lord Abbot, I possess no learnin', no Latin beyond the prayers we learns at the Offices. I am not fit for the tonsure.' Alnoth coloured.

'But God hears prayers spoken and thought, in whatever tongue. If you would care to remain with us, we offer you shelter, food and a welcome at the Offices.'

'Brother Almoner shows me great kindness, but if'n I stayed, there would be one fewer place for another, more deservin'.'

'Again, you think not of self but others,' Abbot Reginald smiled, 'which is an example we should all follow. I would be happy to restore Mother Placida's cell as a dwelling for you. What has happened inclines me to think that it would be right for her memory to be kept with us, and from what has been said, you feel a connection to her.'

'My lord Abbot, I could not live as she did, so enclosed. My life has ever been out in the open, in God's good air. I am not called to be in the dark.'

'And I do not ask it of you. Live a life of prayer within our demesne, eat as simply as you choose, attend the Offices as you feel called to do. We are none of us saints, Alnoth, but I believe you are an example to us. Think upon it.'

'I will pray upon it, Father.' The change in appellation, Abbot Reginald felt, boded well.

'Good. Now I will have further consultation with the lord Sheriff's officers about the . . . other matters.' Abbot Reginald nodded a dismissal, and Alnoth went to the abbey church to seek divine guidance. The abbot looked at Bradecote. 'Make all plain to me, if you would.'

Bradecote set out the reasons for the belief that Oswald Mealtere killed Walter the Steward, being careful to say that it might have been an act of the moment, and defending himself, and that the killer of Old Cuthbert was in the lord Sheriff's charge and being taken to Worcester to face the Justices in Eyre upon their next visit.

'There is one other death that is "solved", but it is not one we would publish to all Evesham, Father.' He explained the confession of Siward Mealtere, and why they were not also taking him to Worcester. The abbot nodded, frowning.

'I think you are right. That Siward feels his son has been taken because of his own sin is so great a burden upon him it will crush him. I hope he seeks confession before his priest, and lives what is left to him in penance. There is no reason to pronounce his guilt before the town, but I would have you make public what you have told me concerning the other deaths. Let us go into the marketplace and I will confirm that those "debts" falsely incurred, are paid, and that any who have been discovered to have suffered loss from paying Walter the Steward other than their due rents, will be paid back. I will also give something to the young widow, for what you have told me of him makes me feel it would be unfair to do otherwise.'

Bradecote, Catchpoll and Walkelin all felt that the one person who might resent these acts would be the new steward, but said nothing.

With a novice ringing a bell before them to call the attention of the crowd, the representatives of Law and Church declared what had been discovered and decided, and if not all Evesham heard it from their lips, they soon knew of it from their neighbours.

Abbot Reginald gave the lord Sheriff's men his blessing as they departed, even if a blessing for William de Beauchamp might stick in his throat, and a little after noon the trio left Evesham. Since they had concluded their investigation quicker than they, or the lord Sheriff, had expected, Bradecote decided it would be better to ride to the castle at Elmley, and reveal the outcome to William de Beauchamp there. They could also take up Ansculf to Worcester without the lord Sheriff having to do so, unless he wished to be in Worcester in the June town-stench, which was doubtful.

They entered into the castle bailey mid-afternoon, having taken the time to cross at the Hampton ferry and tell Kenelm what had happened since he had been attacked, for which he gave thanks and free passage across the sluggish Avon. They were hot, dusty and tired when they arrived, even though the journey had been but a few miles. Bradecote hoped that William de Beauchamp had been able to cool down, in every sense, upon his own arrival, and also hoped that the fact that the man who killed Walter the Steward would not be presented before the Justices in Eyre would not reignite his ire. When he had woken he had thought his tenure as Undersheriff was about to end, but now, though he still risked being in William de Beauchamp's disfavour for some time, which would not be pleasant, that fear was gone. All he wanted to do was deliver the prisoner to Worcester and return to Christina and the children.

They left their horses with the grooms, and went directly to the hall, but found the lord Sheriff was still in his private chamber, which meant the trio had to wait. What occurred to all of them as time dragged on, was that the length of that wait was controlled by the lord Sheriff. Almost certainly, this was showing his continued displeasure.

When he did choose to receive them, he did not look delighted.

'You have it all sorted out, then.' It was not question, and nor was it praise. He might almost have added 'at last' in a voice of weary acceptance.

'Yes, my lord. The killer of Walter the Steward was Oswald Mealtere, though whether the killing would be judged as murder, or an emendable killing that occurred during a fight in which Oswald was the smaller and on the defensive, is unsure.'

'No matter. That is for the Justices to decide.'

'My lord, they cannot sit in judgement on Oswald Mealtere, for he is dead.' Bradecote kept his eyes firmly on those of his superior and kept any hint of apology from his voice.

'How so?' De Beauchamp scowled. 'Did he resist being

taken?'

'No, my lord. He was attacked by a swarm of bees.' Bradecote was not surprised that William de Beauchamp's eyebrows flew up in disbelief. 'I should add that this was not mere mischance, for he sought the hoard of silver stolen from the abbey and its tenants, and had attacked the monk who tends the hives and then attempted to break into a hive, believing the silver to lie within.'

'Was he mad or foolish?'

'Perhaps a mix of both, my lord. The bees, naturally enough, defended their home, and so many stung him that he died within a short time. His widow gave us the information that proved beyond all doubt it was he who killed Walter the Steward.'

'And the silver was not in a hive, I assume?' De Beauchamp was always interested in silver, even if not coming to him.

'No, my lord, but it is discovered, and has been returned to Abbot Reginald, who will see that those to whom silver is due will receive it. He is relieved that all is now understood, and reparations can be made.'

'Hmm.' William de Beauchamp took no pleasure at all in the relief felt by the Abbot of Evesham.

'And we still has Ansculf to set before the Justices for the killing of the old man, Cuthbert.' Catchpoll felt that their hard work was not really appreciated.

'No. He is dead also.' William de Beauchamp's voice was expressionless.

'My lord?' Catchpoll looked taken aback.

'How did he die, my lord?' Bradecote tried not to sound accusatory, but an unpleasant thought had occurred to him.

'The fool tried to escape, and I had no alternative but to get an archer to put an arrow through him. It is not the outcome we wanted, but a death was owing and that debt is paid.' De Beauchamp shrugged. What was done could not be undone.

'Indeed, my lord.' Bradecote did not take his eyes from his superior. Had it truly been a case where there was no alternative, or was it 'convenient' that the man had not stood trial before the Justices, and perhaps made too much of the fact that he saw himself as doing the bidding of his lord? The Justices would have seen him hanged, regardless, but mutterings might have arisen and reached King Stephen concerning how William de Beauchamp ran his shrievalty.

De Beauchamp's eyes did not so much as flicker. He could see what was going through his undersheriff's mind, and he did not care. If Bradecote had doubts, so be it. The man was far too inclined to see things in a way that verged, in de Beauchamp's eyes, on the monastic and moral. Being but a vassal lord, he had no concept of the realities of power, and especially those involved in keeping power. His actions over the last few days proved that. He had run counter to his overlord's wishes by involving himself in the actions of Bengeworth Castle, risking his future as undersheriff, and for what? 'For the Law', he would say, or 'what is right'. William de Beauchamp told himself that he could not afford such a moral stance and looked down upon those that did. He had come close to dismissing him, but two – no three – things held him back. The first was that Ansculf, the idiot, had gone too far and committed murder, murder without any semblance of a reason. That could not be condoned. The second was that Bradecote, pox on him, was the best undersheriff de Beauchamp had ever had and he could be trusted not to betray his lord, even if he stood up against him. The third reason was Serjeant Catchpoll, who was standing in an attitude of casual observer, but whose eyes held a glint that de Beauchamp might take as indication that Catchpoll knew just what was in the heads of both his superiors and would 'advise' both to step back from anything irreversible.

Catchpoll knew both men well enough to judge their strengths and weaknesses, and found himself somewhere between the two of them in the current situation. He stood with the lord Bradecote on the Law being greater than any man, but he also realised that the lord Sheriff was part of things way above Catchpoll's knowledge and understanding, and, since Ansculf would have hanged anyway, the fact that he had not reached trial was not vitally important, and justice had been done; a life had paid the blood debt. He did not think the lord Sheriff had done more than lords tended to do, which was give out aims and instructions and leave others to work out how to implement them. Sometimes such things led to 'misunderstandings'. Ansculf had been a nasty piece of work who implemented his instructions in a way that caused his own downfall. In Catchpoll's eyes, William de Beauchamp's fault had been putting the man into a position of power by making him the garrison serjeant at Bengeworth, but there was nothing that could change the past, so everybody ought to just get on with facing the next day's challenges.

Walkelin, meanwhile, was absorbing what he could from it all. Not so long ago he would have not even dared to listen, but now he too had some insight into those who directed his life, and, very privately, made judgements. He was sorry for Old Cuthbert, who had been failed by the Law twice, since he had died without the man who killed his wife being brought to account, and the man who had killed him did not have sufficient respect for, or fear of, the Law. In Walkelin's view, the lord Bradecote had been in the right in all he had done. He did not get as far as the thought that the lord Sheriff had been in the wrong, for that was too dangerous a step for a mere underserjeant.

There was a silence in the chamber, like a long breath that ended with a sigh that was Bradecote's emotionless request to know whether the lord Sheriff required him further. It was a phrase that might have two meanings, and William de Beauchamp could choose which he would take.

'There is nothing more to be done here. Go home and oversee your acres.' De Beauchamp left a little pause, just as a reminder that his decision could go either way, and then relented, though without a smile. 'I will send one of these two to fetch you next time there is need of you.' He waved a hand vaguely towards Catchpoll and Walkelin.

'As you command, my lord.'

'As I command, Bradecote. Life is always the easier when you keep that in the forefront of your mind.'

Easier in the short term, yes, thought Bradecote, bowing, but not necessarily on the conscience.

When they emerged into the sun's glare in the bailey, Walkelin went to fetch their mounts. Catchpoll looked thoughtfully at Bradecote.

'There's times, my lord, when the right can be wrong, the wrong can be right, and everything gets in a tangle. You just has to let things settle, like the dust.'

'Do you think he made sure Ansculf did not get to speak before the Justices, Catchpoll?'

'I think the lord Sheriff did not say the prisoner should be close-bound or close-watched, my lord, so if the man decided to try 'is luck and run for it, well, it were Ansculf's decision. Once fleein', it would be likely an archer would make a kill, not wing the man. Let us say 'tis easier for the lord Sheriff that Ansculf, his man, will not stand before the Justices, but if Ansculf had not run for it, 'e would be at a rope's end soon enough.'

'Do you agree with it?' Bradecote was at least relieved that Catchpoll thought events had developed in much the same way that he had. It showed he was not just being excessively suspicious.

'I does not need to agree, my lord. I am the lord Sheriff's Serjeant and I does what the lord Sheriff's Serjeant needs to do, best I can, in whatever circumstances.'

'In spite of the lord Sheriff?' Bradecote's face eased for the first time since they had entered the castle.

'That would be tellin', my lord.' Catchpoll's eyes said the rest. 'Do not go back to your lady and keep all this in your mind, my lord, and make more of it than you should. The lord Sheriff 'as never been the saintly sort, but then the saintly sort would make poor sheriffs. We is all sinners, and best we leave the judgement of a man's soul to God, and sticks to just keepin' the peace as best we can.'

'The voice of wisdom, Catchpoll?'

'The voice of long experience, my lord.'

'Indeed, Serjeant.' There was the smallest hint of a smile from both men.

Once mounted, the three men rode out of the castle gate and headed down the hill to the Pershore road, each thinking of home and hearth, leaving murder behind and with the cheerful sound of the skylarks and the yellowhammers on the hint of a welcome breeze.

Author's Note

While this is a work of fiction, many of the details relating to real historical characters and events are true. There had been rivalry between the Abbots of Evesham and Sheriffs of Worcestershire since the time of Urse d'Abitôt, the first post-Conquest sheriff, and Bengeworth was a focal point of that antagonism since both claimed the land. William de Beauchamp had a wooden castle erected there in the early years of The Anarchy, ostensibly to protect the bridge over the Avon, but the *Chronicon Abbatiae de Evesham*, written by the monks, recorded many depredations of abbey property by the garrison, and states that during the abbacy of Abbot Reginald's successor, William de Andeville, a particularly bold raid involved the demolition of the abbey cemetery wall and plundering of the enclave. Abbot William promptly excommunicated William de Beauchamp, and the abbot's forces took the castle, razing it to the ground. The site was then turned into a cemetery.

Reginald Foliot's lineage and family connections are genuine, though whether that added to William de Beauchamp's animosity is purely my conjecture.

The stewardship of Evesham Abbey was an inherited post for several centuries after Abbot Walter installed one of his kinsmen as steward, and at one time in the early twelfth century there were two anchoresses living within the abbey demesne.

Recent archaeological excavations in Evesham have unearthed the little stone bridge over the water course that ran towards the Hampton ferry, and two channels off it, with indications of buildings that were not just domestic, though these actual remains could be later and producing almost anything. However, they gave me a plausible location for the maltster and mead maker.

SARAH HAWKSWOOD describes herself as a 'wordsmith' who is only really happy when writing. She read Modern History at Oxford and first published a non-fiction book on the Royal Marines in the First World War before moving on to medieval mysteries set in Worcestershire.

@bradecote
bradecoteandcatchpoll.com